love and prayers, Kara

a novel

KAREN DE GREGORIO

ISBN: 979-8-218-24741-6
Library of Congress Control Number: 2023913901

This is a work of fiction. Names, characters, places, organizations, and incidents either are products of the author's imagination or are used fictitiously. Any resemblance to actual events, places, organizations, living or dead, are entirely coincidental.

Book design:
Y42K Publishing Services
https://www.y42k.com/publishing-services/

Sold Souvenirs Press, Sherman Oaks, California, 91403

http://karendegregorio.com/

For my friends, past and present, in Perú

It is part of probability that many improbable things will happen.

-Agathon, 445--401 BC

Contents

Prologue:
Gasping for Air

As we pulled away from the bus station I began to cry. I feared the unknown but, still, I had chosen this. I closed my eyes and rested my heavy head in my hands.

Am I up for this? I wondered.

Many of my fellow passengers had left the town I was going to, deep in the mountains, to start a new life on the coast only to end up in the shanty towns not far from where I had spent the last two years. The buses were jam-packed; standing-room-only didn't deter passengers, many heading home for Carnaval celebrations. They kept piling on with urgency. I almost vomited when more and more smelly bodies pressed up against one another, and me, overcrowding the bus. Not only people came for the ride—chickens, hens, dogs joined us while crates and boxes filled to the brim with food blocked the aisle. Luggage and everything imaginable got carried on; any excess baggage was tied to the roof. I wasn't sure why I had chosen to be with those people.

The first time I had traveled into the mountains I had been in a private vehicle. It was comfortable, there was ample space for each passenger, and we stopped when Mother Nature called.

This trip, in contrast, was grueling. Under my breath, so that Sister Tricia wouldn't hear me, I whispered to myself: "I should have returned to the States when I had the chance." I was annoyed by everything and everyone—the bus, and the people all seemed so dirty and irrational. I judged it all. *Didn't people bathe? Why would anyone bring animals on a passenger bus? Didn't they know that packing a vehicle this tightly was dangerous?*

Several hours from the coast, it started pouring. I would learn that when it rains in the Andean mountains, it rains hard—*llueve a cántaros*, as the locals say—the kind of rain that bruises the body if you're caught out in it without protection. During the rainy season, December to early March, it would rain nonstop. And this was February. As we climbed, unpaved dirt roads turned to mud, then into muddy rivers, ponds and even lakes, and eventually became impossible to pass. Bridges were flooded, disintegrated, and fell into bodies of water that had been roads.

To cross from one bank to the other, all bus passengers had to get out and the suitcases tied to the roof had to be taken down to lighten the load. Only then could the bus pass. As the bus moved through the river, I watched it tilt to one side, nearly tipping over. *That would be a disaster. It would never find its way right-side-up.* I was on edge as I watched the fiasco. After a considerable amount of hard work and patience, the bus made its way through the washed-out path. Thank goodness for the passengers' willingness to trudge through grassy riverbanks to meet the bus on the other side.

*

My parents had taken it poorly when I announced that I was extending my stay in Peru. When I told them I was thinking about moving to the mountains and living with the nuns of Our Lady of Angels, they flipped out. Regardless of our poor communication, I still heard parental voices in my head, strong societal and familial expectations tugging at my insides. The old self who had arrived in Peru in the summer of 1985 thought I ought to return to the United States sooner rather than later, please my parents, find a nice man to marry and start a family in the suburbs. Another Kara considered moving to the mountains. As for joining the convent, I hadn't made any final decisions about entering the flock, but I was curious to see the work the Sisters were doing in their parish. Several months earlier, I had visited an orphanage run by the Sisters of Our Lady of Angels. The orphanage provided a home to many of Peru's abandoned children, and it had moved me.

Even though I had already been living in Perú for more than two years, this bus trip put me at the very edge of my comfort zone. Unsettled. If only I had known then what I learned in the mountains, and know thirty-five years later, I might have enjoyed the ride more. But, nothing in my twenty-three-year-old brain made much sense. Being raised in a comfortable, privileged lifestyle, and attending college in the United States hadn't prepared me for twists and turns and bumps in the road. You might have thought that surviving my college roommate's grim diagnosis would have toughened me up, but it didn't—it made me insecure. Nor had my teaching stint at Colegio Ignacio Loyola, a Jesuit school in Takana prepared me for the adventure. That day on the bus, I did my best to consider the positive aspects of the events unfolding, the lessons to glean. I didn't admit to Sister Tricia how much I was struggling. I kept my thoughts and emotions to myself and made as little eye contact as possible. The ride felt endless. I was nauseous, feeling the change in altitude, and I had to squeeze my legs together so as not to pee in my pants.

When we got on the bus in Takana, I had deduced from the attire my fellow passengers wore that many were from the shanty towns on the outskirts of town. Most likely these squatters, who once lived in the mountains, now lived in La Victoria. Now I wondered how the conditions compared to what I would see in the mountains. As the bus left the coast behind and climbed higher into the Andes, the air got thinner and breathing became more difficult. I gasped for air. The anticipation of landing in a new place made me nervous. What and who did my fellow passengers leave behind, and what would I find when I got to the mountains.

My first introduction to Andean culture had come on a trip to Cusco and the ancient ruins of Machu Picchu. I traveled there during a school break from Colegio Ignatius Loyola with my colleague Mercedes and her boyfriend, César. We stayed in a cheap hostel in Aguas Calientes and bused to the citadel. We bumped into some American tourists who told us that a four-star hotel with stunning views was under construction at the top of the ruins. We didn't have money for that kind of thing. Hiking among the ruins at Machu Picchu and boarding a launch to the Island of the Sun on Lake Titicaca whet my appetite and planted excitement for future adventures in the

Andes mountains. Our tourist trip was merely a tease; there was so much more to learn than what was written in *Fodor's* or *Rough Guide*. Even though my Peruvian companions had never been to Cusco either, they laughed at me when I flipped through the pages of the tour books. They did, however, encourage me to continue reading *Los rios profundos* by José María Arguedas, required reading for Ignacio Loyola students. It took effort to read a book in Spanish, but I was determined to finish it. Every page shone a new light on Peru's complex culture.

Now as we proceeded on to the small town of Chuqiyapu, the bus started screaming and then the motor petered out. We were in the middle of nowhere but the snow-covered mountains I could see far in the distance helped ground me. Repairing the bus might take hours, Sister Tricia told me. Some passengers chose to wait but others retrieved their luggage and started walking. As there was no town in sight, Sister Tricia and I weren't sure what to do, but we decided to follow the lead of several locals and began walking in search of help.

Sister Tricia was in her mid-thirties and dressed in street clothes. Her longish blonde hair peeped out from under her cap, unlike the nuns I had seen when I was a kid whose hair was hidden beneath a veil. There was little to distinguish me from this nun as we walked on the mountain road. We also had more in common than not; we both understood what it felt like to be outsiders, strangers in a foreign country. We walked for over an hour, getting pounded by the heavy rain. I had left my protective wear back on the bus and wore only jeans and a tee shirt. Sister hadn't prepared either, but it didn't seem to faze her.

Water dripping off the rim of my hat blurred my vision. Then, through the thick fog, I spotted a truck in the road, the headlights moving in our direction. We flagged it down. Sister Tricia and I as well as several other passengers from the broken-down bus climbed into the back of the truck. Passengers already on the truck adjusted themselves to make room for new bodies. Not an inch of space was spared in the truck packed with people, animals, and produce. I landed on cases of beer that would later be enjoyed at celebrations. The truck filled with locals headed up the mountain to dance *los Huaynos* and *Carnavales* in Chuqiyapu, Sister said. I was pressed up against a middle-aged *serrano*. Normally this proximity would have made me uncomfortable, however, the local man's warmth felt good next to my cold wet body. The truck smelled like a mixture of manure and alcohol, but it was oddly satisfying. I had to hold myself onto the back of the truck so as not to fall. My hands froze as the brutal, cold mountain rain hit my unprotected skin. When we hit a bump on the rough, uneven road, we were all thrown around. Almost ten hours after leaving the bus station for the Andes, I raised my head to look toward the front of the truck. Through the bodies that obstructed my view, I caught a glimpse of a small colorful banner with a gold fringe hanging on the rearview mirror just to the right of the driver. The banner read: *Dios Guia mi Viaje.* As I considered its message, God Guides my Trip, the tightness in my shoulders released. I felt more at ease. It was *a sign from God,* or *the universe,* I thought. I knew everything would be all

love and prayers, Kara

right and I held on a bit longer. Soon the small Andean town of Chuqiyapu was in sight. I hoped to find the peace I was searching for in *la sierra*, the mountains.

love and prayers. Kara

Chapter 1
My Buried Heart

I wasn't one hundred percent sure why I was going to Perú after my college graduation in 1985 but I felt excited to embark on a new experience that few of my classmates would have considered. My parents were even more uncertain but because speaking about our emotions almost never happened in my family, I could not provide a satisfying explanation for them. *Maybe I needed more support. Maybe I needed to bawl in their arms.* But that wasn't how we dealt with difficult feelings. My parents didn't pursue further questions to understand my motives for traveling to Peru. Or perhaps they didn't know how to express themselves. Their main concern seemed to be my safety and financial well-being. They also questioned why I would want to work at a Jesuit school.

Although I had been raised and initiated into the Catholic Church by the sacraments, my parents had a very casual relationship with the Church. Whatever devotion my parents may have had was certainly not one they modeled — they only attended Mass on important holidays like Christmas and Easter. When we reached the age of thirteen, my brothers and I were granted permission to decide for ourselves whether we wanted to continue attending Mass and catechism classes. Despite my parent's erratic attendance, I continued to go to Mass. I had a fascination with the rituals, and I loved singing hymns. I often wondered why I couldn't assist the priest at the altar like the boys could. In catechism class, we were told that altar boys, or altar servers, were children and teenagers who followed the example of Jesus by serving humanity and even sacrificing themselves for God. *And I can't do that?* Not in the Catholic Church anyway. When I asked, I was told that the work of the altar was truly a "man's job" and that girls were not suitable for such a role.

From a young age, I had had what I would call a personal relationship with God. I believed that if I got on my knees in prayer each night before bed, some good would come of it. And good things did: I attributed many of my childhood successes to the grand mystery. It wasn't clear who I was speaking to, but at the time that didn't matter — believing made me happy.

My family, extended family, and teachers in grade and high school all assumed I would get married and have children soon after graduating high school. When I went to university and then announced I was going to Peru, Mom and Dad tried to talk me out of it and flung questions at me: *Why would you want to volunteer? Why with the Jesuits? How will you pay off your college loans? Is that any way to use the bachelor's degree you just earned? Why would you turn down your dream job at a museum in the States in exchange for a volunteer job in a poor country? What about Tom? Aren't you going to marry?*

No one imagined what was coming: I turned down two marriage proposals and a job offer from the Isabella Gardner

Museum before boarding a plane destined for Peru. I couldn't bear to remain in Boston. I was on a mission to erase my past. One proposal was from my high school sweetheart, James, who was still waiting for me to return to the neighborhood where we grew up. James never went to college; he had his own construction company in Worcester, Massachusetts. If I had married James, my world would have narrowed considerably, I thought. The other proposal came from my on-and-off-again college boyfriend, Tom, who declared his love only when I announced I was going to Peru. Tom took all kinds of measures to dissuade me from going, highlighting information from misinformed reporters about the dangers of South American countries and how foreigners were at risk for all kinds of deadly diseases. These warnings were not completely unwarranted, but I ignored them. I politely declined Tom's offer. I intuited that Tom and I weren't a great match and anyway, my roommate, Julie, didn't get along with him. That mattered a lot to me at the time. She and I fantasized about what it might be like to be married to best friends—"That way, we'd see a lot of each other." Seeking a husband was what *we were supposed to do*. The problem was, it wasn't the right time for me. And life had other plans for Julie.

Instead of doing what I was supposed to do, I decided to join the International Jesuit Volunteer Corps where I would work on Peace Corps-type projects in the under-developed South American country of Perú. Along with two other Benton University graduates, I was assigned to teach in a private all-boys school founded in the 1960s and run by Father Ignatius Brown, a Californian Jesuit who had relocated to Perú .

17

I supposed I was destined to be surrounded by men. Being the only girl in the family, I had learned to hold my own with my five brothers who ganged up on me and played practical jokes all the time while we were growing up. I remember the time they dug a deep hole at the beach and convinced me to lay in it as they proceeded to bury me alive under a mound of sand. They said it was an experiment "to see if it could be done." I don't think my life was ever in danger since I was only under for ten to fifteen minutes, but I'll never forget how it felt to be under the ground hearing the boys talking about me as if I wasn't there. That was one of the many ways I developed a strong character. I have been told I am stubborn and tough as nails.

Besides stubbornness, there was also a certain amount of romance, adventure and altruism wrapped up in my decision to go overseas. Working with the Jesuits or the Catholic Church in general was questionable to my parents. But I didn't see (or chose not to see) the obstacles ahead. Maybe the spark that propelled me forward was a form of grace.

*

When I left for South America, I knew little of the history, lifestyle, social norms or economic situation in Perú, and I was oblivious to any real danger that loomed ahead of me. I had grown up in the suburbs of Boston and, before attending a private university, I had gone to public schools. My family was fortunate to enjoy the benefits of a middle-class American lifestyle. While my folks often disappointed us with the news that they couldn't afford the trendiest fashions or footwear, nonetheless, they provided my brothers and me with a great education and we had everything we needed. I had no experience with, nor had ever seen, real poverty before I volunteered to work in a poor country I knew nothing about. Brave? Stupid? Perhaps a bit of both.

In fact, the closest I came to experiencing poverty was through books and social studies class. Mr. Monroe, my eighth-grade Social Studies teacher, opened my eyes to other countries and cultures, as well as my own. In Mr. Monroe's class, we learned the sad history of the United States and its Indigenous people. I wept after reading Bury My Heart at Wounded Knee, the brutal account of the destruction of the American Indians during the second half of the nineteenth century. I stood in front of all my peers in tears while summarizing a chapter of the book. At that time, being highly sensitive was not a popular trait. The world was not yet ready to embrace the quiet, softer, gentler side of people. Extroverted classmates, those who took up a lot of airtime, were often rewarded for their participation more than the rest of us. My classmates didn't understand my sensitivity and my tears meant I acquired the nickname "Niagara Falls," a name that stuck until the end of junior high. But other people saw that trait differently. Within weeks of the start of Social Studies class, Mr. Monroe knew I was deeply empathetic towards people from different backgrounds and cultures. He saw how I would get emotional each time we discussed the realities of those who suffered from any form of poverty or lack of access to opportunities. When classmates laughed at me or called me Niagara Falls, Mr. Monroe would say, "Just ignore them, Kara. It's wonderful that you feel so strongly for people you've never met." It was hard to ignore them, but Mr. Monroe always had my back. He was one of the rare teachers I would remember with fondness.

But I was not only sensitive—I was also naïve. Not only was this the first time I would be leaving the United States but there was genuine danger in moving to South America at that time. When I accepted the job offer, I thought I was set, at least in the short term, but I had a lot to learn. The sheer act of going to Latin America in the 1980s was risky, and perhaps even somewhat prohibitive for many young women. I headed to Perú during one of the most challenging periods in its history. But even Tom and my parents didn't know that Perú posed many dangers because of its political climate and the threats of the terrorist group *Sendero Luminoso,* the Shining Path. I had heard of *Sendero Luminoso,* the Shining Path, but I had done little investigation about Peru's political climate and the terrorist group before leaving. The topic never came up at my interview with Father Ignatius. Much of what was ahead of me I simply accepted sight unseen. In those days there was no online research, comments or reviews weighing into my decision to accept the volunteer opportunity; it required a level of trust in the Jesuit priest who was soon to be my new boss. The move also required a degree of trust in myself.

All I knew of the country were bits about Peruvian pre-Columbian ruins and artifacts that piqued my cultural curiosity and love of art history. I hoped my geography studies in school (I had memorized all the capital cities, gross national products, imports, and exports of all South American countries) would be of some use, but when I landed in the country, I faced a rude awakening: these memorized facts were useless accessories layered onto my naïvete.

I would soon learn the truth about my new home. In the 1980s Perú had been suffering from a triple crisis for at least a decade: economic chaos, drugs, and civil war. Tensions were further escalated by strikes, poverty, unemployment, food shortages, and civil unrest. I arrived amidst an internal conflict that had begun in June 1980. Brother Andrew who ran the Augustinian monastery would tell me more about the principal foe and enemy of the government in the escalating civil war, the Maoist guerrilla army of an estimated two to five thousand youths called *Sendero Luminoso*, the Shining Path. He told me the situation was more complicated than he was able to explain but the movement had begun at the University of Ayacucho in the 1960s, led by philosophy students seeking to fill a moral and intellectual void that traditional value systems failed to satisfy. Because the country's political parties were so corrupt, people became vulnerable to almost anyone who promised a new approach. *Senderistas* sought to demolish what was then the state, saying they would replace it with a Maoist-communist utopia. Instead, they spread chaos and terror.

Fortunately for me and the other Benton University volunteers, most of *Sendero Luminoso* activity and efforts centered in the province of Huancayo, to the east of Lima, the capital city where we landed. Although there were reports of *Senderista* activity in the capital city, we saw only mild disturbances compared to what was taking place in rural areas in other parts of the country. Puno, an Aymara city that sits on the shores of Lake Titicaca, was one such rural area that did not

21

fare well. Puno was closer to Takana, the town where I knew I would soon be living. Learning this gave me some trepidation. Cities like Puno were easy targets for the *Senderistas* — Indigenous populations were and would always be especially vulnerable to the violence and exploitation of militant groups. Their poor population, with families living in homes without electricity, and a lack of medical and educational opportunities, suffered by the hand of the *Senderistas.* Violence and weapons instilled fear, innocent people were murdered, and women were abused and raped by soldiers.

News of Perú on the front pages of newspapers back home would frighten my family, Tom, and anyone who knew I had moved to South America. Alarming headlines in *The New York Times* would land on my parents' kitchen table every morning after the paperboy dropped the newspaper on their doorstep. In December 1985 my parents would come across headlines such as: "Officials Slain in Perú "; "Perú 's Capital Blacked Out" and "Hundreds More Found Dead at the Hand of The Shining Path'." These watered their already-planted fears. In the letters I wrote home from Lima, I would deliberately omit any news about how the city would experience blackouts for chunks of time during the day and evenings. Some of the blackouts were provoked by terrorists, while others were due to lack of resources. My letters never mentioned the horrors being committed during the Civil War either. Why would they? I was careful to curate all my correspondence to the States. And as a young American, I was shielded from much of the truth.

*

I had met Father Ignatius Brown during my senior year of college. On a recruitment trip to Benton University, Father Ignatius said he was "looking for a few good men" to work at his all-boys Jesuit school in a small city in southern Peru. I was one of three graduating students chosen from a group of twenty altruistic young adult volunteers, the only female in the group. During our interview, Father Ignatius asked about my family. I suppose having been raised among boys had appeal and added points to my candidacy for the teaching position. He showed particular interest in my father and where he had grown up. I was very nervous and wondered why Father Ignatius asked questions about my father, but it turned out to be a good place to start because it put both of us at ease.

"What does your father do for a living?" Father Ignatius asked.

"My dad is a journalist."

"Is that so? My Dad was also a journalist; he wrote for the *San Francisco Chronicle* for twenty years."

There was an unusual amount of silence between questions. It made me wonder whether Father had much experience talking with women. In the silence, I fidgeted in my chair and buttoned and unbuttoned my blazer.

"As you know," he finally said, "I have a Jesuit school in Perú. I really came here to Benton University to recruit young *men* to teach, but... perhaps, I will make an exception for you. What interests you about working in my school?"

"Obviously, living in Perú would be amazing," I said. "And....the other Jesuit schools recruiting are in English-speaking countries. I would like to learn another language while teaching."

"Would you be interested in teaching English?"

I told him I would. "My degree is in art history so I would also like to teach art if there is a need."

"We'll see about that. We don't offer art classes in high school...but perhaps you could change that."

I smiled.

"You strike me as a very strong young woman. I have a good feeling about this. I would like to offer you a job at my school in Takana," he said. "Keep in mind...you won't be earning a lot. You'll receive a small stipend to cover some living expenses."

I told him I understood, that I would have to give it some thought, but that it sounded like an amazing opportunity. He said he would write up a contract detailing the position.

The Jesuit was a Hollywood-like handsome, tall, fit man. I was mesmerized by Father Ignatius's good looks and charm. Perhaps my attraction to him prevented me from asking more questions before accepting his offer. He didn't fit any of the models I'd seen for a priest. Still in midlife, he said that he started each day with some yoga; he stood on his head for an impressive ten to fifteen minutes. He had started the practice, he said, when he was in the army.

At the age of eighteen, he had been drafted and positioned for combat during World War II. Like so many men, he carried scars on his body, and on his soul. In 1945, he had witnessed the death of a close buddy on the battlefield. Father Ignatius credited the devastation caused to Japanese citizens, and the part he had played in it, for his spiritual conversion. He said it became clear during the military service that he had to devote the rest of his life to helping people rather than hating them. This tremendous change of heart led to his decision to enter the Society of Jesus and to devote his life to God. Soon after his ordination, he was assigned to a small town in Peru. Father Ignatius's story was compelling. *How does an American soldier become a Peruvian priest?* His story of redemption and renewal catapulted me into the start of my own transformation in Perú.

love and prayers, Kara

Chapter 2
¿Cómo se dice?

In mid-August 1985, I arrived at Jorge Chavez Airport in Lima for the first time. Any confidence I'd had in the States went out the door as soon as I opened my mouth in a foreign country. It became apparent that despite being a young adult in body, my communication ability was that of a four-year-old child. I had optimistically hoped that my three-week summer crash course in Spanish would be sufficient preparation for entry into the Spanish-speaking country but I was mistaken. My limited Spanish was of no use even at *la aduana*, the airport customs desk, where the agent spoke a few Spanish words that I couldn't understand. I became frustrated and resorted to sign language before the agent waved me and my companions along. Before I knew it, we were faced with a massive wall of people.

Months before, arrangements had been made by the Jesuit International Corp for the other Benton graduates and I to stay at an Augustinian monastery near Lima for six to nine months, and then in the South American summer we would study Spanish with a native speaker in a nearby private language school. The monastery was owned by the Augustinian Religious Order and was run and very well-maintained, by an American brother, Andrew, who was originally from Bethlehem, Pennsylvania.

Brother Andrew was to pick us up outside the airport. The only description we had been given was that he was a Caucasian man with a long gray beard. We entered what felt like total chaos—crowds of brown-skinned people yelling out names and grabbing luggage. We plowed our way through the crowds, dragging our luggage into the unknown, accidentally crashing into people and saying, *perdón, perdón,* the only Spanish we could utter. Last names written on signs were flashed before new arrivals as we stepped outside the airport into the heat.

There was no sign of Brother Andrew but suddenly a taxi driver grabbed our bags, and placed them in the trunk of his car without checking to whom they belonged; there was little we could say so we followed the luggage. I recalled that Brother Andrew had sent me the monastery's address and I had written it on a piece of paper I now pulled out of my knapsack. I handed the address to the taxi driver as we climbed into the back seat. He didn't say anything. Just before the taxi pulled away, we heard a voice shouting our names, "Kara! John! Paul!" A short white man with shoulder-length gray hair and a long white beard approached the vehicle, banged on the car window, and insisted the driver halt.

It was Brother Andrew coming to our rescue. "What were you thinking?" he said when we got out of the taxi.

"When we didn't see you, we figured we would get ourselves to the monastery," I said.

"How were you planning to do that in a city—not to mention a country—you've never been to before?"

I showed him the address scribbled on the scrap of paper.

Laughing, Brother Andrew said, "That wouldn't get you anywhere but to the post office."

"But it says the number of the house, *casilla*!"

"*Casilla* is the word for a post office box," Brother Andrew said.

Brother Andrew was with his chauffeur, Augusto, a handsome Afro-Peruvian man who had learned the required few English phrases to greet the American guest: "Hello, how do you do? My name is Augusto...Fine, thank you very much." Augusto took our luggage and transferred it to his car.

On the drive from the airport to the monastery, the contrast between rich and poor neighborhoods was striking. Just beyond the airport, I noticed a lot of what seemed to be temporary tin and straw huts, and heaps of garbage lining the roads. Coming from the suburbs of the United States, I wondered if an explosion or a hurricane or tornado had leveled the outskirts of the city. I searched for something recognizable as a house—I was used to three-story wooden structures with glass windows lining a front porch overlooking a manicured green lawn. I saw more dirt and sand than anything else. *Where are the houses.*

Then we moved into a different neighborhood with much more luxurious houses. The driver pulled up the driveway to one of them, my new residence, the Augustinian monastery. Up on the hill, on the other side of the wall that surrounded the houses, were millions of dwellings without roofs, water, or plumbing.

*

There was excitement in being in a new country, but not being able to speak the native language and connect with others made my loneliness and isolation more intense. The loneliness sparked thoughts of where I'd been only months earlier. I remember when my college roommate first noticed something was wrong: her hearing had started to fail, then her vision blurred. Julie's big brown eyes were no longer vibrant, no longer functioning properly. I am ashamed to admit, now, that I used to say, "I would die to have her gorgeous eyes." *Forgive me, Julie.* She was a head-turner, for sure. She got way more dates than me, too. Yes, I envied her stunning beauty. What a waste of time that was. Within months those beautiful eyes were rolling uncontrollably into her head. All her hair fell out. Her body and face puffed up from drugs. She could no longer walk. I asked myself, then, what I would do if Julie didn't survive. All answers fell short.

*

August 30, 1985
Dear Mom and Dad,
I am settling into my temporary life at the monastery in Lima. The house is clean and safe. Brother Andrew is a wonderful host and sees to it that we are well fed. I still have some peanut butter left from the jar I packed in my luggage. It's been a godsend.
Being in a monastery is strange, but at least it keeps us, for good or bad, protected from the outside world with its noise and chaos. As

a young American woman, it is probably the best way to gradually adjust to living in Perú . Our main daily focus now is learning Spanish so staying here helps facilitate that. I sleep well and study a lot. The classes are hard. I get a headache after hours of hearing the teacher rattle off drills, but I will learn some Spanish. I hope to make friends when I am more confident and able to say more in Spanish. Right now, it's only English-speaking foreigners (mostly religious) I chat with. It has become apparent how desperately one needs to hear one's mother tongue. Without it, one can feel very lonely.

As you know from our brief phone call last week, communication will be a challenge. My two-year commitment may feel like an eternity now, but I will write as often as I can. Remember that mail is very slow here so we may have infrequent correspondence. What I write in a letter here today may no longer be true when you get it weeks later in your mailbox.

Love, Kara

*

Nothing was easy about my arrival and the first few months in South America. I had dropped into a new world and the adjustment was, well, crazy hard. Even writing home felt difficult. But I loved the house staff. They were more interesting than the clergy and much more fun to hang out with. I preferred the kitchen to the dining room, and I ate there often, against Brother Andrew's wishes, his groans never deterring me. I spent hours in the kitchen, sometimes eating, or helping the cooks chop vegetables, or simply chatting.

I enjoyed Augusto's company most of all. He brought normalcy and tenderness to the place. If it hadn't been for him, I might not have endured living in the monastery. He was born

Augusto Benicio Sanchéz on the 3rd of August. He told me that his mother had chosen the name, Augusto, to commemorate the birth of her first son on the blessed day in August. Some evenings when I couldn't sleep, I would go down to the kitchen to fetch myself a peanut butter sandwich (Peanut butter was a comfort food from the States that was hard to find in Peru) and would hear guitar rhythms and a gorgeous voice seeping out of the small back room off the kitchen where Augusto slept. When I heard the guitar start to play, I would prepare and eat my sandwich at a snail's pace just so I could hear him sing.

Every weekday morning at eight, Augusto drove me and the other volunteers to language class. Most religious orders funneled soon-to-be missionaries and volunteers into a school in Cochabamba, Bolivia, but staying in Lima at the monastery cut costs tremendously. It also made a lot more sense since we would be living and working in Perú for the next two years. We just needed someone at the monastery to transport us to our classes on Monday through Friday. Thanks to the generosity of Augusto Benicio Sánchez, the monastery's personal chauffeur, our plans fell into place. At first most of the rides were silent. John, Paul, and I were groggy from just waking up from a night's sleep and even if we wanted to engage, we weren't yet able to maintain much in the way of conversation with Augusto who knew about as much English as we knew Spanish. Yet, the rides were pleasant, and he went out of his way to make them so.

One hot and humid evening, Augusto caught me rummaging around in the kitchen pantry late at night.

"*Oye*, what's going on?" Augusto asked.

"I couldn't sleep," I said. "Hey, the other night I heard you playing the guitar. Can you play for me now?"

"You were spying on me?" Augusto said.

"*Jaajaa. No exactamente*...Not exactly. I come down to the kitchen a lot. A few times I have heard you playing and singing. You have a beautiful voice."

"*Gracias*! Do you sing?" Augusto asked.

"I do. I used to sing in the college choir," I responded.

With that he went to his room to retrieve his guitar. From then on, we met almost every night in the kitchen after everyone in the house was asleep. He often serenaded me with Afro-Peruvian rhythms, and blues music called *Landó*. He taught me a *cumbia* called "Una calle nos separa." I sang and he accompanied me on the guitar. Learning the lyrics challenged me to use new vocabulary in Spanish. I didn't have words for certain feelings, yet, and music provided a way to express them. We got into the habit of singing and rehearsing songs late into the night simply for the fun of it.

Months into our rendezvous, word got around that we were up to something. Instead of scolding us, Brother Andrew summoned us to perform for guests in the main sitting room. Not only did music soothe our souls, but it also became a great method to improve my Spanish fluency. As part of my language acquisition, I began adding Spanish music into a daily routine; I soon sang along with the Spanish radio stations and looked up words from the lyrics I didn't understand. My Spanish vocabulary grew exponentially.

Augusto was a handsome young man, maybe five years older than me. I was very attracted to him, and there was chemistry between us but neither of us acted upon it. Instead we poured all our repressed passion into the music. Of course, the other household staff witnessed the spark between us, but it was clear that nothing would ever happen between monastery walls. He was my one true friend in the monastery and the sound of our music broke the silence of the monastery and replaced silent prayer with tangible celebration. It brought a skip back into my step and a smile to my face. My language classes might be intense, but Augusto and I shared the language of music.

*

During the months in Lima, language errors and barriers presented themselves regularly and so having a good sense of humor helped a great deal. It was essential not to take myself too seriously. Eventually, I did start to laugh along with new acquaintances, but I still knew that proficiency in Spanish would be essential to defend myself from misunderstanding. It was difficult to build trust among strangers, including men, until I could communicate better in Spanish.

I found this out the hard way. Back at Benton University, I had met a Peruvian man through a mutual friend. Carlos had promised he would call me when he returned to Lima for a vacation and said he would take me out on the town. I was all in—I thought it would be great to see Lima through the eyes of a local. Even better, he was familiar with my home country and spoke pretty good English. When Carlos arrived and came to the monastery to pick me up for dinner, Brother Andrew insisted on meeting my date. He had already demonstrated a sense of protectiveness toward the new volunteers, and especially me. He wasn't happy about releasing a young woman into the big city with a strange man. To me, his sentiment was sweet but somewhat stifling: I had been cooped up for weeks and couldn't wait to get away from the monastery for an evening. I might not have been ready for marriage but I wasn't ready for the contemplative life of a monk either.

As introductions were made in the main corridor of the monastery, Carlos turned to me and asked me if I was ready and hungry. I replied in Spanish, "*Sí, estoy lista y tengo hombre,*" I said, delighted to show off the Spanish I knew. When everyone started laughing, I realized I had made a big error in language. At first, I was in the dark, but Brother Andrew explained to me that I had said, "Yes, I have a man," not "I am hungry." In this case, one little letter in Spanish made a big difference. While Carlos thought the error was cute, I was quick to make it clear that I hadn't meant to say that—romance was the last thing on my mind as I had too much to learn and absorb about Peru and myself. Anyway, I had no sexual attraction whatsoever for Carlos. For one thing, I was six inches taller than him, with no heels

Several weeks after my initial outing with Carlos, I accepted an invitation to join his family at their ranch on the outskirts of the city in San Ramon. I was excited to see another Peruvian landscape, to get away from the city noise and pollution, and to learn more about different lifestyles. It occurred to Brother Andrew that Carlos might have attached another meaning to my acceptance of the invitation, but I made light of it. As we arrived, I saw dark-skinned workers harvesting coffee in the fields and smaller huts perched on a hill not far from the family's gorgeous ranch house which was surrounded by eucalyptus trees.

My Spanish was still minimal, and Carlos made no effort to explain all that was being said during our three-days' stay. It seemed to me that he liked being in control. My interactions with his family were cold and distant. Except for meals around the table twice a day, when no words were exchanged and eye contact was barely made, we didn't visit with his relatives at all. During much of our stay, I felt as if I were just a tourist Carlos had brought along. *But, aren't we college friends?* I wondered. Although the hills that surrounded the ranch were lovely and framed each evening's sunset beautifully, there were few memorable moments to record in my journal. I spent a lot of time on my own and in silence.

I slept alone in a guest room on the second floor of the ranch house. Carlos had told me the rooms on the second floor were a bit warmer than those below. It had a nice view of the mountains and a private bathroom and I was comfortable there. Late on my final evening, after everyone had turned in for the night and I was nearly asleep, I heard a rattle at my door. It disturbed me but I thought it was the wind until the bedroom door opened. Before I could see who it was, Carlos jumped into my bed. I asked him to leave. He covered my mouth with his hand, drew a finger from the other hand to his lips, and said, "*Shhhh...*" He started touching me in places I didn't wish to be touched and continued to grope me until I started to cry and managed to shout "No!" He then stopped and left without saying a word. *Lucky for me, the word "no" is the same in English and Spanish*, I thought.

36

In the morning, I felt nauseous. My stomach was cramping, and I had diarrhea, in part from experimenting with new foods in a new country, and in part due to the emotional upset from the experience of the previous night. I felt vulnerable, fearing for my safety. How would I fare in Peru? I feared for my safety and questioned who I could trust. I passed on breakfast and we returned to Lima in silence.

When Carlos dropped me off at the monastery, Brother Andrew was there. As I began to climb the stairs leading to my room, he said, "Kara, how was your trip?"

"I don't want to talk about it now," I said, storming to the top of the staircase. Brother Andrew had good instincts and had been right about Carlos. I hadn't heeded his warnings.

love and prayers, Kara

Chapter 3
El Progreso

I don't believe in inhuman hatred,
And I don't think man is an enemy.
I believe that with your hand and with my hand,
Against the wicked and against their punishments,
We will fill the homeland with gifts
Golden and flavored like wheat.

–from "I Call You" by Pablo Neruda

I turned twenty-two while living in the monastery. It felt strange not going to parties and meeting people my own age. I didn't have close friendships with the other two volunteers and as they had one another and the privilege of being male on their side, they didn't have too much need for my company.

Mostly John, Paul and I rubbed shoulders in the house with men and women who had chosen a religious life; priests, brothers and nuns often came to the monastery to recharge from stressful work. The clergy came from wealthy countries from many parts of the world, the United States, Sweden,

Germany, France, Spain, Australia, and Canada among them. Their missions ministered to poor communities and their days were long and exhausting. By contrast, the monastery was clean, spacious, quiet, and offered amenities that the houses in their community did not. Indoor plumbing was especially welcomed by those living without it in the *pueblos jóvenes*. Except for toilet paper (as rough as sandpaper) and the cold showers, the monastery accommodations were quite comfortable.

All guests ate meals in a formal dining room at a long old European dining set that seated twelve people. It was like being at the Last Supper.

The monastery had several maids and a cook as well as Augusto, the chauffeur, working for them. These were all Peruvian locals seeking to improve the lives of their families.

Little effort was required from the guests: our rooms and bedding were cleaned for us, and we didn't even need to clean our own plates after dinner. The house staff did everything. Initially, I had a problem with this arrangement because I had been raised to help in the kitchen, cook, set the table, and wash my own dishes. (It had been a different story for my brothers. While they had to take out the garbage, they didn't have what one might call the same domestic responsibilities.) When I first arrived at the Augustinian monastery, I had a difficult time breaking old habits, and I often cleaned my own plate. Brother Andrew had to explain to me that this was the way things were done in Peru. I accepted many new customs, while remaining unsettled with the fact that the workers in the house were eating in the kitchen as the guests sat in the dining room for meals.

Growing up, my family didn't have nannies, cooks, chauffeur, or any kind of helper at all. I'd wanted to believe that if we had had helpers, they would have eaten meals at the same table with us.

The house staff were the only native Spanish speakers in the monastery. It was curious to learn that English was the common language used among guests. This didn't enhance the Americans' exposure, practice or learning of Spanish, but it allowed us to absorb details about the country, the life and work of a missionary and the reality of the poverty in Peru.

But although I was often lonely, the monastery was a refuge for me in those early days, offering a slow and gradual ease into a country so completely different from my own.

*

As the only female, I had to share my room with temporary female visitors. The women, mostly older than me, were often family of the monks, nuns passing through Lima en route to other Peruvian towns, or nuns needing retreat.

Rooming with the Swedish nun, Sister Karin, for several weeks was delightful. She was a very kind woman; honestly the most loving, patient, and considerate person I'd met. For example, when she saw that I was having a particularly tough day, she would place cookies, just out of the oven, on the nightstand next to my bed with a note saying, "Bless you, dear. Have a beautiful day." She did this the day after I returned from my trip to San Ramón with Carlos. I thought about confiding in her, but then decided not to. I didn't think nuns were the most well-informed resource for such things. I wondered if it was even appropriate to talk to a nun about encounters with men.

Was there some kind of Catholic rule against it? I wasn't comfortable broaching the subject, but Sister intuited, all on her own, that I was not okay. On the few occasions we both found ourselves laying our head on the pillow at the same hour, we chatted about our lives. I was curious about why a woman would devote her life to a convent.

One day I asked her, "Have you ever regretted your decision not to marry and have children?"

Sister Karin said, "For me, marriage would have been a jail. No, I am content with my work here in Peru. Serving this community brings me joy. Of course, we are all called in different ways." She paused. "What about you, Kara? Have you had thoughts of joining a religious order?"

"Me? No, that's not a life for me. At least, I don't think it is," I said.

*

When Sister Karin's retreat was over and it was time for her to return to her parish in *el pueblo jóven, El Progreso*, she invited John, Paul, and me to join her for a weekend. John immediately accepted the invitation, but I was indecisive at first. Sister told us that the house we would be staying in at *el pueblo jóven* had no running water, and sporadic electricity. This concerned me.

"It is not as bad as you think, Kara. It's only new to you. That's all. You'll be fine. Trust in the Lord," Sister Karin said.

"Where will we sleep?" I asked. "Where will I go to the bathroom?"

"You will be fine on a mattress on the floor, Kara. There is an outhouse not far from our parish house. I will show you," she said.

John chimed in that he would love to go, and then I heard myself saying, "I will …. join you as well."

The next day, when a taxi dropped us off at Sister Karin's parish, I had to dodge garbage and human waste in the road beside their house. The smell was strong, and I held my breath. Sister Karin caught me squeezing my nose and pouting.

"What's the matter, Kara?"

"I didn't know that people lived like this," I said.

"Well, they do," Sister Karin said calmly. "And we are here to help, not to judge."

She told me that Augusto had been raised in *el Progreso*, and that his family, parents, grandparents, and sister still lived there. His job at the monastery was "a promising way out of poverty, and a godsend for his parents and extended family," she said. He had never mentioned where he was from, and it didn't matter to me. At least I didn't *think* it mattered…until I arrived in *El Progreso* and my initial reaction indicated otherwise. When I learned that Augusto grew up there, I wanted to learn more.

Each morning and evening began and ended with a Mass at the parish church, attended by many *El Progreso* residents. A large percentage of parishioners had recently arrived from *la sierra*, the mountains. I could tell which ones were from the mountains because of the way they dressed, from the weathered skin on their faces, hands and feet, and the way the women carried their babies on their backs with colorful woven wool blankets. They spoke a language I couldn't understand.

During the Mass, the Spanish-speaking population shared prayers. Families begged God to protect their sick ones and pleaded for mercy for their hungry children. With the same intention, women offered gratitude for having found shelter in Lima. Many offered thanks for "all that the Lord has done for us."

At the end of the first day in *El Progreso,* I pondered the challenges these families faced as they tried to provide for their children. I thought about Augusto Benicio and his family. Before I laid my head down on the pillow, I checked that there were no bugs in or beneath the pillowcase. I felt uneasy but tired enough to allow my bones to sink into the mattress. But I had so much on my mind. *How can it be that children were starving? What is being done to change this? Are prayers enough? How can I help?* I was distressed and fought to find comfort. Within minutes, I began to pray. I asked God for guidance and gave thanks for my own good fortune. When calm came over me, the sleeping arrangements no longer occupied my mind, and I fell asleep.

My introduction to poverty was through the lens of Sister Karin who, like so many other nuns offered moral and financial assistance to those most in need. *Las Madrecitas,* as the locals called them, also spread the gospel of Christ and offered communities the belief that following the Church's teachings would raise them above their circumstances. Their conviction in the Church's teaching spread to many. I couldn't deny the nuns and priests did extraordinary work and provided aid, and I envied the way they showed compassion towards everyone, even strangers. I was impressed by that strength of character. I also had a healthy skepticism in the institution known as the Catholic Church.

In her mission, I watched Sister Karin pour her loving heart out in the young town without hesitation. According to her, there were many *pueblos jóvenes* scattered around the outskirts of Lima. *El Progreso* was one of the poorest communities in all Perú . She said that the population of Lima was approximately five million and growing. Of this population, nearly thirty-five percent lived in squatter settlements. These young towns had been built by families who had recently come from other parts of the country in search of work and schools for their children in the capital city. They traveled long distances on rough terrain and in challenging conditions only to be met with little hope. They lived in makeshift homes made of tin, cardboard, straw and other found materials or objects while attempting to build a future for themselves. In time, families would build homes with adobe and gradually add walls as their budget permitted. There was no water nearby; if a settlement was lucky, trucks came in once a week to fill up cans for each squatter. The lack of sanitation meant that it was commonplace to find numerous illnesses and diseases, such as hepatitis, typhoid fever, and tuberculosis, in *los pueblos jóvenes*.

But on my first day with Sister Karin, what struck me were the hundreds of scrawny dogs scattered about the streets scrounging around for scraps of food to survive. I felt outrage and sadness at the same time.

*

Families living in *los pueblos jóvenes* demonstrated their generosity to volunteers and to the clergy by inviting us to their homes for a midday meal. The day after our arrival, after venturing out to meet some families, we stopped at the

Cardenas family house for lunch. Though they offered us a warm welcome, upon entering their small makeshift homes, I felt cramped. Where would I sit? There didn't appear to be any furniture in the home. A short plump woman emptied and turned over a produce box for me to sit on. "*Siéntese, siéntese.*" The hosts politely served me a plate filled to the brim with a large portion of meat, boiled corn, and three large potatoes. Fixated on the dirt floor and the flies swarming into the sauce covering the potatoes on my plate, I felt afraid to eat the food. But how could I refuse to eat a meal offered from the heart? The invitation was joyful — the hostess was happy to have me, John, and Sister Karin in her home. I didn't quite know what to do: my selfish, judgmental self said I ought to decline the food. I could say I wasn't hungry, but thank you, *señora*. A generous, gracious part of myself said I had no choice but to indulge in the meal. I took the fork, said, *muchas gracias*, and placed some food in my mouth. The hostess smiled. Others around me didn't share my hesitation — they jumped into the situation without resisting the reality that lay before them. I wasn't yet able to do that.

The food didn't sit well: I was on the toilet most of the night with diarrhea, and intestinal pain followed me through the rest of the week. However, I did learn a lesson about the true meaning of generosity that day. I considered that my physical discomfort was a small price to pay in exchange for honoring the family's generosity of spirit, and kindness.

On our last evening in *el Progreso*, just before sunset, I walked with Father Joe, the parish priest, to the top of the hillside to gaze down upon the settlement. Father Joe wanted me, the young American, to see how far it extended along the outskirts of the capital city. He wanted to educate me "about the magnitude of poverty in these parts," and in Perú in general. There were thousands of shacks in *El Progreso* and the immensity of poverty overwhelmed me, tearing my insides apart in a way that is difficult to explain. My body went limp. I wanted to leave. But we didn't — we stayed until the descending sun made its way to and then below the horizon, painting the sky. But then the colors of the sunset bled into the red orange emanating from burning bundles of trash. My nostrils filled with the smell of burning garbage. I had never smelled that before. In the darkness, I heard the music of dogs barking and babies crying. I was perplexed. I stood on the bank above the development, mindful of the fact that I had never been to a place like this, and *if I could help it*, I thought, *I would rather not return*. Here on the hilltop, now miles from home, I did everything I could to keep from crying. But it didn't work; my muffled sobs joined the choir from down below.

I had felt this agony before. I recalled the day the doctors said the tumor in Julie's brainstem was inoperable. She embarked on chemo that was supposed to help, but I could see that she was losing her physical capabilities at a rapid rate, and there was not a darn thing that I, or anyone for that matter, could do about it. During yet another chemotherapy appointment, Julie and I sat for hours with other patients in the lounge adjacent to the treatment room waiting our turn. Then the nurses called us, and Julie was hooked up to a chemo drip. She dozed off. Then awoke and dozed again. My eyes wandered around the room and met those of strangers of all ages. It was upsetting to see sick children in the ward, and yet, they brought the greatest joy. I searched for an affirmation in the room, a connection with a stranger who might understand my fear of pain, death and of being alone. I hoped the older bald gentleman gazing out the window, despite his age, would beat the odds.

Chapter 4
What Lies Beneath

Days after celebrating the New Year, John, Paul, and I were traveling north of Lima. Our language school was closed for the summer. Soon we would be traveling in the opposite direction to our new home in Takana. Brother Andrew had conveniently arranged a personal driver—Augusto couldn't join us as the monastery couldn't spare him for two weeks—and we headed up the coastline in a pick-up truck.

This trip marked the beginning of my obedience to the Catholic Church. While we would earn a stipend once school began, for now we had little money of our own and were therefore at the mercy of the Jesuits for food, transportation, and lodging. As soon as we departed for Chiclayo, it became obvious that the priests' generosity would have its trade-off. We had to always honor our hosts; disobedience was frowned upon. My male companions had a bit more leeway than I, and unfortunately, this drove a wedge between what was already a distance between us. If I chose to venture out, and explore northern cities on my own, I would have to organize an excursion myself and pay for it out of my pocket. I had some *soles* for personal needs, but without my own money, I had little freedom.

All that was in sight on the road were miles and miles of white, hot desert sand framing the coastal zone of Northern Peru, set between the Pacific Ocean and *Cordillera de los Andes*. We spent many challenging hours in transit. Everywhere we went, I became conscious of the fact that I was the only female traveling in the group; there were no rest stops, toilets or toilet paper found anywhere along our route. The lack of sanitary facilities made the trip uncomfortable, especially because I was menstruating. I hadn't anticipated the conditions and I hadn't packed sanitary napkins or tampons for our short trip. This was a big deal for me—there were deeper inequities to contend with in the country, of course, but discomfort and annoyances grew large in my young, spoiled mind. It was common to see men urinating wherever was convenient, but women had to squat and therefore tried to choose more discreet locations when possible. My tight blue jeans were an impediment when squatting behind rocks or an occasional shrub, if one could be found. It became apparent why the Peruvian women's long skirt was a purposeful choice.

The weather, dust and dirt, and the scarcity of water were further annoyances. There was poor hygiene and there were limited sewage facilities, and no one was complaining other than the young American woman. The deeper we traveled into other regions of the country, the more economic and societal challenges became visible. But their plight wasn't my primary concern—I was simply uncomfortable and annoyed, and no one around me seemed to care. To be honest, I still had a hard time mustering empathy for Peruvian folks living in poor conditions. Compassion and acceptance would come later in other villages and towns.

After over twelve hours on the road with only one brief stop, we young volunteers arrived at the Jesuit parish in Chiclayo, tired, sweaty, and famished from a long journey. Father Dan, a very pleasant American Jesuit and a friend of Brother Andrew's, met us at the main door of the rectory.

"Bring your bags along. You must be exhausted and in need of a wash." he said to John and Paul, and then he turned to me. "If you would be so kind to wait here, I'll be back to see about a room for you over at the Sisters' quarters."

"Fine," I said. "That will be nice."

Two hours later when John and Paul came down the stairs all sparkling clean and refreshed, I realized my wait was not fine at all.

"What were you doing all this time?" I asked.

"We showered, and I took a nap," Paul said.

When Father Dan rejoined us, he suggested we follow him to town to do some sightseeing. There was no mention of where I would be staying. I left my bags in the vestibule of the church rectory as I was instructed to do. I was exhausted and needed a shower, but I said nothing and followed Father Dan out the door. I felt perturbed but didn't show it. (Even though I couldn't believe the priest behaved in that way, it seemed to me that complaining wouldn't change anything.)

After a brief tour of Chiclayo main plaza and dinner at a local restaurant, we returned to the rectory. It was almost eight o'clock in the evening when Sister Constanza, a neighbor and nun, came to the rectory to meet us. She showed me to the Sisters' residence about a block away.

The accommodation was sparse but comfortable. Sister Constanza was a kind soft-spoken forty-something Peruvian woman. She wore a white habit that hung just above her shins with a large wooden cross supported by a long leather rope on top. A white turtleneck was visible under her habit while her head was covered in a white veil. Since it was hot and humid in Chiclayo—I wore a light cotton sleeveless dress and perspiration dripped off me—it seemed odd that she was covered up.

Sister Constanza invited me to join all the resident Sisters for morning prayer at the break of dawn, "if interested," she said. "And we celebrate daily Mass immediately after." I wondered if my attendance at the prayer meeting was the price of a night's lodging, but I concluded I was free to decline the invitation. My curiosity lay elsewhere, not in the Catholic parish: I had other plans.

As an art history student, I had long dreamed about seeing the ancient ruins at Lambayeque Valley. Buried beneath the long stretches of Perú's dry coastal desert lie thousands of years of history, cultures and civilizations and the passing of lives who have come and gone. I had read that the Moche culture had flourished in northern Perú from about 100 AD to 800 AD, while Chimú lived there from 900 to 1400 AD. Life and death were revealed in every archeological dig from north to south, and east to west of the capital city, Lima. I wondered: *what might these ancient civilizations existing long before the Incas on Peru's North Coast teach me?* I knew that new buildings were being constructed on top of the country's past, that we drove and walked on the graves of Peruvian history not knowing yet what we would find.

My interest in archaeology was not new, but after everything with Julie, it intensified. I recalled a day in the hospital when Julie woke from a brief nap. She had squeezed my hand and whispered, "It's okay—you will not be alone." *Had she read my mind?* Julie's words frightened me to the core. I panicked. I knew the severity of what we were dealing with; the prognosis was grim, and Julie likely would die. *She is lying,* I thought. *If she dies, I will be alone.* I excused myself, went to the restroom, and bawled so much that I began to hyperventilate. Once I was able to compose and calm myself, I returned to the treatment room to find Julie's parents had arrived. I left the hospital thinking I would see her again.

I had read that I would find *las huacas,* pyramid-like mounds of sand, on Perú's northern coast. and perhaps stumble on artifacts in burial sites that had been found beneath them. I had high hopes of visiting the Brüning Museum in the Lambayeque Valley which, as I saw on a map, was only seven miles from the city of Chiclayo. I had learned at Benton about German-born archeologist Walter Alva, founder of the Brüning Museum. It seemed it would be a shame to be so close to the museum and not to try to meet Señor Alva. I knew he was a man of small stature who had spent his whole life recording findings from past civilizations. Each *huaca* held the promise of a revelation, one that might answer questions about how people lived and died. I needed a personal revelation, too.

Would I get to see Perú's archeological sites, Sipán, or the pre-Colombian city of Chan Chan near Trujillo? There wouldn't be a better time than now because I would be moving to the southernmost tip of the country when I started my job in Takana. I had some crazy notion that somehow I would be comforted by exploring these burial sites, that there I would find the answer to my nagging question: *where do we go when we die.*

While I suppose I didn't technically have to ask anyone for permission to come and go as I pleased, from the moment I became affiliated with the Catholic Church in Perú, I felt like I should obey its rules. It wasn't clear to me if I was imposing this obligation on myself or whether it was imposed on me by the Church that had mastered the art of instilling guilt into its followers.

I will plan an early morning escape from the convent, I thought. The idea seemed brave and perhaps a bit prohibitive, and that excited me. On our second day in Chiclayo, I struggled out of bed, barely awake, and prepared a day bag for my excursion. I wrote a brief note to my hostess and, before leaving, put it on the kitchen table. I didn't want them to worry when they realized that I was gone.

Dear Sister Constanza,
I have decided to take a day trip to Lambayeque Valley to visit the Brüning Museum. It is an opportunity I do not want to miss. I will be back for dinner.
Regards, Kara

It felt exhilarating to break free, at least temporarily, from the grip of the Church. I was happy to be on my own walking to what seemed like every corner of Chiclayo. I looked up at the sky. It was very blue that day and it looked beautiful against the beige sand below. I didn't find street signage or marked bus stops—there were no routes posted or maps available anywhere to guide me in the right direction. Instead I asked directions from random strangers, in my bad Spanish laden with an American accent. They were of little help, only responding with awkward stares. Other strangers approached me with requests and shoved pieces of paper with ads of some sort on them into my face. I didn't understand much of what they were saying but it was clear they were selling gadgets. I felt bewildered and frustrated by the locals' behavior but I never felt unsafe.

But being out in public made me self-conscious about my height. It wasn't uncommon at home to see other tall women but at five foot eleven, I towered over most folks in Chiclayo.

Finally I admitted to myself that I was lost and that my brave escapade was over. I concluded that I wouldn't make it to Lambayeque Valley that day and thought it best to find my way back to the parish. I used the few Spanish words I had in my vocabulary in asking for directions.

"*Dónde está la iglesia?*"

My question stopped a woman on the sidewalk in her tracks. She smiled, and her face lit up. Every town had at least one church and every townsperson knew where it was. She pointed in the direction of the church. "*Allí cerquita.*"

55

As determined as I was to get to the Bruning Museum and the burial sites, it didn't happen. I returned, defeated, to the nearest Catholic Church in town, the Jesuit parish. No matter how hard I tried to break away from the Church, a magnet seemed to pull me towards it—like a handsome man, the Church both attracted and disappointed me. But I needed to put my trust in something so for the time being I placed it in the Catholic Church.

I was back where I had started from. It felt like I had been gone forever but I had left only an hour before, Father Dan had started his daily six o'clock morning Mass soon after my early morning departure and it was still being celebrated when I returned. As was customary, Sister Constanza was in attendance, on her knees in the pew. I tiptoed into the back of the church. Instead of taking a seat, I hesitated and remained standing.

It would take years of digging before I could understand and come to terms with my relationship with the Catholic Church.

Chapter 5
La Maestra

Educators are only helpers for men and women to seek the truth in the depth of their consciousness.

Every corner of my new home was sprinkled with angel dust left by four Marian Sisters who had lived in the space for years before I moved in to teach at Colegio Ignacio Loyola in Takana. The large apartment sat near the main entrance of the campus grounds of the school. I would live there alone; the other two Benton University volunteers would share a small cottage beside the school's farm that provided fresh produce every day for student lunches. My three-room apartment was more than adequate, and I thought, as soon as I moved in, far too big for one person. The idea of living alone gave me a queasy feeling in my stomach. Growing up, I always had my own bedroom, but this was different. I was alone in a foreign country, alone on the campus of an all-boys school, alone in the desert.

Takana sat just above the Chilean border in the middle of the world's longest, driest, desert valley. Takana's bus station was located outside the city center and near the contraband markets that smuggled untaxed goods over the Chilean border as part of the Peruvian underground economy. It was not the safest part of town for foreigners. The Jesuit school was not far from the market.

The first day I stepped off the bus from Lima in early February 1986, Takana was in the midst of a heatwave. I thought: *Is it my destiny to live in this place for two years?* Even beyond the heat, my initiation was brutal. The very moment I disembarked from the bus, I was grabbed and shoved to the ground by a beggar—presumably the thief could spot an oblivious white foreigner from miles away. Perhaps to him, I exuded wealth although I had only a few coins in my pocket and the money I would earn in the coming months was only small stipend of 125 soles a month, the equivalent of around thirty dollars. The assault left me with a few bad bruises. It would be more difficult to understand how I would bear the intense solitude and isolation.

When I first arrived, the Jesuits suggested I work in the elementary school as an English teacher, but I persisted in asking to teach art to the older students. Despite Father Ignatius's excitement in bringing me on as one of the American volunteers in his school, it was clear that the presence of a young female in his all-boys school was disconcerting for him at times. I tried to remain patient, remembering that he had never had sisters and had been a military man since the age of eighteen before joining the Society of Jesus. He had gone from one boys club to another.

"Few women teach the older boys," Father Ignatius said. "We feel it is important that these boys have strong male role models." He paused. "I am not sure we ought to make an exception now."

"Female teachers present issues that we would like to avoid altogether," another Jesuit priest added.

"I am willing to give it a try," I said. "I'd like to teach art classes."

In the twenty-five years of the school's existence, they had only hired one woman to teach in the high school, my colleague, Mercedes. It was true that few women applied for a position but also that the Jesuits didn't seek female role models for their school. One of them suggested the boys might give a young American female teacher a difficult time, that the small age gap between seventeen and eighteen year old students and a twenty-two-year-old teacher would send hormones flying. While there was no mention of a cultural barrier, I suspected that was also a concern.

Mercedes, the first female teacher, was full of stories to tell about her experience teaching mathematics to boys in the upper school at Colegio Ignacio Loyola.

"One day during my first year teaching, the boys brought mirrors to class and placed them in such a way that they could look up my skirt. I'm not sure how I didn't notice but they got a glimpse of my underwear before I was aware of it!"

"Oh my gosh. Is that what I should expect from a class of adolescent boys?" I asked.

"Perhaps," she said. "But we can't put up with that behavior. You'll need to be tough."

"You must have thicker skin than I do…"

"You'll grow thick skin, too, Kara," she said. "You'll have to."

A few factors worked in her favor: she didn't have the obvious language and cultural barriers I did. She was also engaged, and soon to be married, to a fellow faculty member, César. The boys didn't dare harass Mercedes knowing that Cesar was always in earshot. But Mercedes had gained the respect of her students, and I believed I would as well. She believed in me as well: despite her honesty about the challenges, she didn't discourage me from joining the team.

On the surface, Colegio Ignacio Loyola was an extraordinary place, something like an oasis bursting forth in the desert. The building and campus rivaled any American private school campus, except there was no large swimming pool since such a luxury would seem shameful and unjustifiable in a desert town. The school was well equipped with fully stocked classrooms, a library, a science laboratory, playing fields, and two chapels for weekly worship.

Unlike most schools in Perú, Father Ignatius's school admitted boys from all over the city of Takana — wealthy and poor, light-skinned, and dark students sat shoulder to shoulder, poised for daily lessons. Father Ignatius insisted that the school provide scholarships to boys not able to pay for their schooling.

My first day of teaching was March 7, 1986. It was still March the day my students played a practical joke that deeply upset me. I had given them a homework assignment to sketch "something from nature" in a notebook and bring it to class. The next day as I walked around the classroom to check each student's homework, the first boy opened a page in his biology notebook and showed me a drawing (not one of his own) of the female reproductive organs. As I moved from one desk to the next, I saw that each student had the same drawing. The prank had been well planned: all the boys would present a drawing of the uterus, ovaries, fallopian tubes, and vagina at the moment *la maestra* Kara checked their homework. Tears came to my eyes. Embarrassed, disgusted and insulted, I stepped outside the classroom to collect myself. Perhaps the assignment should have been more specific to avoid such adolescent interpretation. The students weren't wrong — their drawings were "something from nature." I blamed myself for the debacle.

Cesar, Mercedes' fiancé, happened to also be the boys' classroom advisor. When he saw me crying outside the classroom, he approached me. "What's going on, Kara? Are you okay? Can I help in some way?"

Barely able to speak, I conveyed what happened and asked for advice.

When he offered to talk to the boys, I quickly agreed. I welcomed the support because I didn't know how to proceed on my own. The classroom was filled with laughter but when the advisor entered, the room fell into dead silence.

"Sit down and be quiet!! What kind of behavior is this? You ought to be ashamed of yourselves. *¿Qué son...animales?*"

The students bowed their heads in shame as their advisor continued. "What a lack of respect. Would you treat your mother in this way? your sister? your grandmother? You owe Miss Kara an apology."

The students must have held this teacher in high regard for they were silenced, at least for the day. I hoped for an apology from my students, but one never came. I suppose some of the boys were simply embarrassed. As for me, I could barely continue my lessons for the weeks that followed, let alone discuss what happened. We all had a lot of growing up to do over the next few weeks, months, and years.

At Colegio Ignacio Loyola, the boys were always respectful in the presence of their male mentors, but when left alone with their young female American teacher, there were countless shenanigans. They treated me badly. The Jesuits didn't always help—instead they would defend the boys at all costs. I grew disappointed in Father Ignatius who, despite my insistence that he speak to the boys, never acted. He had warned me, but that was no excuse. He just didn't seem to *get it*.

"They're just boys—they don't know any better. You know, you are an attractive young woman. You are quite a temptation for a young man," Father Ignatius said.

"It's *my* fault that they act that way?"

"I am not saying that, but you understand….it does contribute to the challenge we face."

"That's ridiculous," I said.

"We do the best we can," Father said.

In my eyes, the school *didn't* do the best they could but I was at a loss for how to respond and, for the most part, I felt paralyzed. This went on for months. I felt livid, but I rarely showed it. Guilt still plagued me and I wasn't willing to risk losing my job. *What is the real issue? Is it because I'm almost the same age as the boys? Is it because I'm American? Am I an anomaly to the boys? Have they seen fantasized images of American women* from movies? 'Boys will be boys,' but shouldn't they be held accountable for their perverse behavior.*

To "avoid any issues," the faculty and the Jesuits told me I should probably not wear any clothing that revealed my figure and that I should avoid awkward encounters with the boys. I followed the rules. I wasn't a provocative dresser to begin with but, in the prime of my youth, I found myself doing everything possible to cover my body. I wore long skirts that concealed my long, slender legs, and loose-fitting tops that carefully disguised my breasts. I learned to conceal my body and hide my sexuality. But resentment and disappointment built up inside me. It wasn't okay.

For me, the silver lining of teaching in Colegio Ignacio Loyola was the opportunity to create a program to open the world of art to young men. I was eager to share what I had studied at Benton University. I had assumed that Peruvian high schoolers would already know about the masterpieces of the world of art. Who hadn't seen Michelangelo's *Pieta*, or the Pantheon in Rome? Who hadn't heard of the Impressionists, or Jackson Pollock, Georgia O'Keeffe, and Andy Warhol? To my surprise, these names and images were not part of my students' vocabulary and there had been no art curriculum at Colegio Ignatius Loyola. *What a pity they know little of these artists.*

I was brimming with enthusiasm about the subject and worked hard to make art history fun by complementing lectures with hands-on assignments and projects. I set up still-life models for them to draw; I taught linear perspective and showed them how to create three-dimensional space; I encouraged the boys to observe nature and to draw the natural world around them. In one drawing class, I laid a leafless tree branch on a table for them to draw on draft paper and encouraged them to explore possibilities in their drawings. "Rather than copy the object with exact precision," I said, "try to interpret it. Perhaps recreate what you observe."

One student, Miguel Angel, took me at my word. At sixteen years of age, he had an original way of thinking that caught my attention and helped me to see differently. When he left the white page empty on the day I brought the branch to class, I asked him why he hadn't draw anything. He replied quite genuinely, "This is the branch — can't you see it?" Miguel Angel was a quiet, sensitive teen, and an exemplary art student. Other boys were too afraid to take a risk like that but most of the boys loved putting new knowledge on paper by sketching, making forms, calculating distances, and creating spaces. Teaching art perspective was a metaphor for my new life; now living and working in a culture different from my own, my perspective of the world would be forever shifted.

All the boys in Colegio Ignacio Loyola were required to read Los Rios profundos by José María Arguedas before graduating from secundaria. I wasn't aware that it was a requirement when I first came upon the novel one day in an art class. One of my students, Vicente, was much more interested in reading the book than doing the drawing assignment. Annoyed, I confiscated the paperback. I later read the back cover and concluded that my actions had been insensitive. I hadn't read a Spanish book in its entirety yet and the book's summary piqued my interest. It made sense that the student was more engaged in the book than in my class — the main character, Ernesto, is a fourteen-year-old boy who has lived in Spanish and Indian cultures. Raised by Indian servants, Ernesto tells of the events of his adolescent years in a Catholic boarding school for boys in the Andean city of Abancay. Like my student Vicente, Ernesto is diligently trying to find his cultural and personal place in the world. I started reading the book for myself and I was soon hooked. Despite having a difficult time with the language, I did my best to read a few pages a day. The novel tackled themes that surrounded me, whether I fully understood them or not: biculturalism, bilingualism, Catholicism, and the oppression and exploitation of indigenous cultures. Los Rios profundos or Deep Rivers changed my perspective of Perú as did Vicente. I, too, was trying to find my place in the world.

Not all the boys were disrespectful. There were moments of delight when students offered me their chair, the last one in a crowded cafeteria, or when a parent thanked Miss Kara for all she had taught their son. But those moments seemed far and few between. I had to hold tightly to the belief that in some small way I would make a difference in the lives of my students. And, I had to convince myself, and perhaps my family too, of my reason for being in Takana.

April 1986
Dear Mom and Dad,
It's been a while since I arrived at my job at Colegio Ignacio Loyola in Takana, and lots has happened. First, I am fine, so please don't worry. Father Ignatius treats me well and is always looking out for me (although, I wish he didn't treat me as though I am fragile). He

often invites me and the other volunteers to the beach on weekends for the day. The Jesuits have a small house there. I think we are becoming his surrogate children. I like to go as often as possible because it helps me clear my head after a long week of teaching. The day trips are perfect for walking and collecting shells.

My teaching job is nothing like I thought it would be, but then again, nothing here has been. For one, I thought I would have more materials to work with, or at least a budget to order some. But here it is limited and even more so for the arts. It's cool to introduce the boys to a piece of art they have never seen before! But, to do so, I had to photograph color plates from old art history books I found on the shelves in the school's library and have them made into slides. It was a lot of work. Hopefully, the boys appreciated it....but I am not so sure they did.

I hope this note finds you well. Let's plan a phone call soon. I know the line's connection has been terrible in the past, but we can keep trying.

Love, Kara

As my first year of teaching was coming to an end, I volunteered to chaperone the annual senior class trip. Perhaps it was a silly idea after all I had gone through with the students, but I was a bit stubborn—all I needed was for someone to say *you shouldn't* to make me fight harder. Somehow I thought that I might have the power to change these boys. Also, I wanted to go to the beach.

"It is rare," Father Ignatius said, "to have a female chaperone on a class camping trip."

"There's always a first time. It will be fun," I said.

I tried to convince myself it would go well but not even Mercedes had ventured to chaperone the seniors on their annual camping trip. It would be thirty-five teenage boys, two priests and me. It will be fine. I am lucky to have two very nice, considerate, young priests as the other chaperones. Plus, I will get my own tent. As we loaded the school bus to head to Viña del Mar, several students rushed over and offered to carry my backpack and tent. I waved them off.

As soon as we pulled away from the school gate and headed towards the campsite on the beach, the bus filled with loud noise and adolescent energy. Long before a view of the ocean came into in sight, I began to wonder if I had made a huge mistake by insisting I chaperone the boys. Why did I insist on breaking a long-held tradition? Perhaps the boys didn't want their brotherhood invaded or threatened by Maestra Kara. Or perhaps they were thrilled with my presence. I wasn't sure. It had, after all, been a challenging year in the classroom. What was I thinking.

The school bus was crowded with no empty seats. Many boys volunteered to sit next to me but one senior boy pushed ahead of the rest, sitting beside me on the shared seat. Halfway through the journey, he fell asleep and his head made contact with my shoulder. This seemed harmless and innocent so I did not disturb him. Then, I felt the boy's hand creep between my legs. Wondering if he was asleep or awake, I grabbed his hand and removed it from my crotch. This startled him, woke him, and elicited a peculiar giggle from him. Hearing this chuckle made me feel sick to my stomach. Had he really been asleep? Have I been violated? Should I confront him? I don't dare look his way to see if he has a boner. In disbelief, I became paralyzed. I sat motionless and said nothing, telling myself I didn't want to make a scene in front of everyone on a moving bus. Is this my fault? I never should have come on the trip.

Once we arrived at the campsite, everyone quickly engaged in the business of pitching their tents. I pitched mine too, although it took a lot longer than usual because my hands were still shaky as I hammered the pegs into the shifting sand. Afterwards, I approached Father Sam, one of the other chaperones, explained what had happened on the bus, and asked him if he could talk to the boy. He was somewhat noncommittal when we first spoke. When I asked him a second time, he said he would talk to Alejandro privately when we returned to Colegio Ignacio Loyola. He didn't want to "make a fuss during the trip," he said. I felt uneasy about being alone in my tent that night, not because I minded being alone (I had become accustomed to that), but because I thought a boy might try to enter. The incident with Carlos in San Ramon still lingered in my mind. Then I felt ridiculous and terrible for thinking such a thing. These Christian boys wouldn't think of it. Would they?

The following morning, I pressed the issue with Father Sam.

"Did you speak to Alejandro yet?" I asked.

"I told you I would speak to him when we get back to Takana… Are you sure he had his hand there?"

"Of course I am sure. It's not something one makes up!"

"Had you fallen asleep as well?"

"No. I was wide awake," I said.

"Perhaps he was having a dream," he said, "I am sure he didn't mean anything by it."

Back at Colegio Ignacio Loyola nothing was done for days, Father Sam never spoke to Alejandro or the administration as he had said he would.

At first, I remained silent. Then, one day, I found the courage to speak with Father Ignatius. I explained in detail what had happened and how it had made me feel. His response was like Father Sam's — he said nothing. It wasn't my nature to get outwardly angry but this provoked a different response from me. I no longer believed that these types of incidents were my fault. The facts were clear: I didn't deserve what happened.

"It saddens me that you are not able to see this situation from my point of view…. And that you feel no need to address it with the student. Don't you see how wrong this is? This is wrong, and I deserve better than this. "

Father Ignatius was noticeably uncomfortable but he didn't respond.

I felt lighter after defending myself to the priest, but I also disappointed with him. Experiencing sexual harassment and, worse, keeping it quiet was exhausting. I also felt ashamed of myself for not putting an end to it. The weight of these incidents affected my sleep, my daily performance, and my confidence. Gender roles were clearly defined both in the Catholic Church and in everyday life in Latin America. Opportunities for men far outweighed those for women. How could I have known that being a volunteer in Perú would present more difficulties for me than for my male companions? It was hard to stop dwelling on what seemed to me Colegio Ignacio Loyola's inability to deal with boys' raging hormones and misbehavior. I was tired of being cautioned about my inappropriate dress and being falsely accused of making gestures toward the boys. I didn't get the support from Father Ignatius I had hoped for, but then again, priests and the Catholic Church were notorious for treating women as second-class citizens. They couldn't own up to any wrongdoing.

At least I had said my peace. There was some satisfaction in that.

I soon aligned with my female colleagues, friends, and the nuns from the local parish, hoping that they might offer some insight. Two women in particular — my colleague, Mercedes, and Rina, the mother of one of my students — were reassuring and offered encouragement. But they cautioned me not to get my hopes too high and said, "Things won't change any time soon." Their ability to accept things as they were — especially sexual harassment — troubled me as much as the harassment itself. It appeared, at least for the time being, they were right: things weren't about to change.

Chapter 6
Moments of Solitude

Once a week, I redirected my attention and energy from the students at the Jesuit school to patients at *el Hospital de Santa Teresa*. They came from all over the city of Takana and surrounding villages. I loved it and especially working with Marian Sister Sarah. Once I had felt settled in Takana, I had begun accompanying the Marian Sisters in their work outside of school hours, but I especially enjoyed visiting the sick with Sister Sarah. In fact, I couldn't wait for the school day to end on Tuesdays because it meant that I would join in her ministry of visiting. All Catholic nuns and priests performed Extreme Unction, the Roman Catholic sacrament of anointing the sick and dying, and Sister Sarah was no exception.

Each Tuesday at three in the afternoon, Sister and I entered Hospital de Santa Teresa. We visited the infants and children in the pediatric ward, many of whom had been abandoned and forgotten. The appalling conditions were eye-opening: infants and toddlers were neglected, lying in sheets drenched in urine that hadn't been changed in days while ventilation was poor in the rooms and staff was minimal. I thought, this is no place for children to live. Several babies had been left there for months. Those who had the misfortune of living in the hospital learned to crawl, stand, and walk in their cribs. I hadn't heard of children growing up in a crib during the first years of their life. Then I met Soledad.

I smelled urine and perspiration as I approached the crib where the fragile, bruised baby lay. Her big, dark brown almond-shaped eyes, framed in eyelashes like daddy's long-legs spider legs, peered up at me, reminding me of Julie's eyes. They lit up her face. Despite her apparent injuries, she offered a brilliant smile to the world. I reached out to touch her, hoping a connection might help her recognize that she was not alone, and might convince me I wasn't either. She flinched when my fingers met her soft, cinnamon-skinned arms. *Soledad Esperanza Mamani* had been born into the world ten months before at the start of 1986, just about the same time I arrived in Takana for the first time.

Soledad had suffered at the hand of an abuser before I started to visit Hospital de Santa Teresa. The worst of her bodily injuries had healed when we met, but she still cried a lot. The nurses told Sister Sarah and me that it had taken months for her to adjust to being handled or held. The little girl was destined to live a life of solitude: her given name, Soledad, meaning loneliness, expressed as much. I managed to roll her tiny, delicate body to one side so I could change her bed sheets. Sitting in the corner of the crib was a cotton blanket dotted with yellow ducks. It was insufficient to warm her from the cold, damp building during the winter months but it was something. When I gently stroked her petal-soft skin, Soledad would show some interest and then abruptly retreat away from me. I hoped one day she would allow me to cradle her in my arms. She's precious, I thought.

Within days of being in Soledad's presence, motherly instincts I didn't know I had began to kick in. Could I adopt her? I had never considered such a thing before but I began asking questions. Still, an inquiry about such an undertaking was one thing, but taking actual steps to make it happen was another matter. It would be more uncharted territory for me. All I knew for certain was that the child triggered a desire in me I had not known before. I wanted Soledad to be loved and cared for and to have a home, not a temporary holding place. I wished this for all children and for myself: a clean place to rest one's head, a mother's breast offering comfort and providing nourishment, a gentle embrace, and a lullaby before falling asleep. A sense of belonging somewhere on earth.

One Tuesday, I planned to visit Tomás, a toddler I had sung to the week before, but when I went in search of him he was nowhere to be found. The nurse on duty said he had not recovered from meningitis. Now a new boy was occupying his bed. I thought about how this disease wasn't killing anyone in my country. Nor was tuberculosis, hepatitis, or malnutrition. But in Perú it was different.

Despite the conditions, I loved visiting the hospital and would continue to volunteer for over two years. I changed bedsheets, played games, read stories, and sang to the kids. Sister Sarah and I even knitted sweaters and booties before and during our visits; they provided much-needed warmth in drafty rooms. Despite the fact that I didn't have any medical training, I felt my presence was useful. Sister Sarah assured me that "It's not the body alone that needs tending to—the heart also needs attention." I was only beginning to understand what those words meant.

The Marian Sisters in Takana were involved in all kinds of outreach in the poorest neighborhoods on the outskirts of town. They served the same parish as Father Ignatius and assisted at his Sunday Mass in a small chapel across the street from Colegio Ignacio Loyola. The Sisters also played an active part in the lives of many Takaños, providing meals for sick and elderly people in their homes and visiting prisoners in the local jail. As far as I could tell, the Sisters were happy with their lives. Sister Sarah told me that the Marian Order had women serving in 365 countries around the world.

"What kind of work do they do?" I asked.

"All Marian missionaries focus on fighting poverty, providing healthcare, building communities, and advancing peace and social justice. The Marian Mission has built orphanages, hospitals, and primary and secondary schools," Sister Sarah said.

"Do lay people work in these missions?"

"Absolutely! An important part of our mission is recruiting strong devout lay people, like you, to do His work," Sister Sarah said.

I paused before I spoke words I had never said aloud before. "Sometimes I think about whether I could be a nun. I'm not sure yet—I might want to get married and have children someday."

"Kara, you know you need not be a nun to carry out God's work. There are many ways to express God's love."

"Is there an orphanage run by the Marian Order in Peru?" I asked.

"As a matter of fact, there is one not far from here in La Joya. Would you like to go one day, Kara? I can go with you."

"I would really like that," I said.

Sister Sarah was an inspiring woman who seemed to be made of steel. In time she became a loyal and trustworthy friend. However, I knew little of her personal life—she was somewhat of an enigma. Nuns were trained to conceal fears, doubts, and sadness, and I supposed that included their personal histories as well. It was as if the life Sarah had lived before taking vows had vanished. I only knew that she had grown up with a single dad in Pensacola, Florida, where she attended Pensacola State College for just over a year before becoming a nun. She had been only eighteen when she entered the convent. She shared no details beyond those, and never mentioned her mother. From my perspective, Sister Sarah was ageless and tireless. She was a tiny person, barely five feet tall, with endless amounts of energy.

The two of us were a sight for sore eyes entering the pediatric ward. The children chuckled every time we arrived; me, a tall white woman, and Sister Sarah, a short stocky nun. We were like the image of Don Quixote and Sancho Panza to them. She was twenty years my senior but far more energetic and enthusiastic. Perhaps it had something to do with her devotion to others. She was selfless and it seemed she had never learned the words *no* or *never*—and that the community knew it. She remembered the names of every baby ever born in the Ignatius Loyola parish as well as those in Juliaca, the Aymara town where she had served before transferring to Takana. She knew every family in Takana regardless of their wealth, status, or attendance at Mass. I think she rather liked being called *Madrecita* by those she befriended. I wondered if she knew how to take care of her own needs and her health. I mean: what price does one pay for always being available to everyone, all the time?

Sister Sarah and I made a brief trip to Juliaca on the shores of Lake Titicaca in the province of Puno for the occasion of her godchild's baptism. She was the godmother of many Peruvian children but the Amparu family held a singular place in Sister's heart — she couldn't miss the baptism of their youngest child's firstborn.

The country was still in chaos and travel was dangerous so I probably should have stayed home but I offered to accompany Sister Sarah because I didn't know any better at the time. The trip from Takana to Juliaca was demanding because none of the roads were asphalted. Because of the unrest in the country with *Sendero Luminoso's* violent tactics, there were many road blockades. The checkpoints were guarded by soldiers with rifles in hand. It was routine to ask foreigners to disembark from their vehicle and show documentation. They asked to see our passports, and soldiers frisked us. I hated when the men touched me in inappropriate places, but it bothered me even more when they touched my dear friend who was an older nun. It could have been worse but still we felt violated.

Every time we stopped it was the same drill.

"*Americana?*"

"Sí."

"De los Estados Unidos?"

"Sí."

"*Religiosa?*"

"*Sí,*" I would reply.

Sister Sarah's advice had been, "Do what they say." Being a single American woman would have been suspicious, she said. Had I not posed as a nun, who knows how they would have reacted.

I deeply admired Sister Sarah's ability to surrender control of life and its circumstances. She placed her love, faith, and trust completely in God and His divine plan. No one was excluded from the plan — not the poor, the sick, not even cruel people or criminals. They were all God's children as far as Sister Sarah was concerned. I was trying to wrap my mind around how anyone could be so non-judgmental, so compassionate. When I asked if she ever felt lonely, she was quick to respond, "That's preposterous — there's no time to feel lonely." Then I asked her, "Do you ever sleep?" She responded, "I sleep enough. It's overrated, you know."

*

I started my second year of teaching better prepared for the unexpected. Long periods of adjustment and difficult ups and downs were behind me. I still thought a lot about my best friend but I was coping better. Takana was beginning to feel a bit like home. My work with the Sisters contributed greatly to helping me find a purpose in life, and spending time with babies and toddlers made me happy. My Spanish had improved considerably and I was adapting to the norms in the country, the desert environment and climate. I had found some girlfriends, too—outings with Mercedes and Rina filled my weekends, and I celebrated the major holidays in their homes.

Meanwhile, at the hospital, as Sister Sarah suggested I would, I found joy in tending to the souls of little ones. When Soledad Mamani Esperanza and I had first met months earlier, she had already been in the hospital for just under a year. The entire time she had been in hospital, no one had visited Soledad since the day her birth mother had dropped her there. One nurse said, "Frankly, I hope the mom doesn't come back for her—she is not fit to be a mother and she might kill her." There were no child services available to protect the child who had arrived with a concussion, broken bones, and bruises.

On Tuesday, July 4, 1987—I remember the day well because it was Independence Day in the United States—I arrived, as usual, at the hospital around three o'clock to find Soledad's crib empty. This was highly unusual since she never left it. The nurse told me that Soledad's birth mother had come for her. Because of the mother's history with the child, everyone on duty hesitated to release the child into the custody of the mother, but because Soledad was her flesh and blood, they could not stop her. Her disappearance came as a real blow to me. So much progress had been made—she had begun to let me hold her in my arms. While no one in the hospital could confirm Soledad's whereabouts, when I heard that she had been seen leaving with her birth mother, I felt a certain heaviness in my chest, the kind that signals an inevitable dire outcome.

love and prayers, Kara

Seven days after Soledad's disappearance from the hospital, I read in the newspaper that a child who met the description of my Soledad had been found dead in the river that cut through town. A witness came forward and said, "The mother was yelling at the child on the bank of the river while the mother was doing laundry." The news report said the toddler had accidentally fallen in the water and drowned, but the child had apparently suffered a beating and contusions to her head indicated that it had been hit against a hard surface, perhaps a rock. When the victim was identified as a fifteen-month-old female, Soledad Mamani Esperanza, daughter of Elisa Esperanza Diaz, resident of La Victoria, in the city of Takana, my worst suspicion was confirmed.

Within hours of the news, Sister Sarah knocked on the kitchen door to the apartment. As soon as she saw me and my agony, Sister Sarah grabbed me in her arms and said, "My dear, Kara, how you loved the child." Then, after a long pause, she whispered, "It is in pain that God is revealed."

I stopped eating for weeks. The death of Soledad was painful, and it triggered another huge loss I had suffered not long before.

Two months after my last hospital visit with Julie, I was vacationing on Nantucket Island when a friend from Benton called my hotel and left a message for me to call as soon as possible. I knew what that meant. When we spoke, she said, "I just received a call from Boston...Julie...she died this morning." It was four o'clock in the afternoon on a foggy Tuesday in July. I had never lost anyone so close to me. Both of my grandfathers had died when I was a toddler so I had no memory or experience of death.

Julie died. It was gut wrenching and scary.

Soledad died.

In search of relief from the sorrow that engulfed me, I poured my heart onto the pages of my journal and wrote the beginning of a poem in honor of Soledad.

Para Soledad

In moments of solitude, I think of her
Soledad was her name.
She had big brown eyes
Like mine.
A sweet and alluring bundle
Like a cinnamon bun stuffed
With pain and joy.

Mi Soledad
I wanted to take You home.

In moments of solitude
I think of You as you floated down a small river
that snaked down
from the Andes
in an unattended
laundry basket.

My beautiful angel
Mi Bella Soledad
Beautiful solitude haunts me.

With the news of Soledad's death, I decided I hated hospitals, and so it would be some time before I was willing to return to see the children. All her life Sister Sarah had been on a mission to prevent the death of children. She understood the sad reality that I would eventually learn: many children in Perú died from circumstances not common to families in the United States. Sister Sarah's dedication to all children so inspired me that eventually after several months had passed, I returned to the pediatric ward in Hospital de Santa Teresa. "There will always be another child to sing to....to love," Sister Sarah said.

To my surprise, a deep sadness led me to a greater awareness of love. I hadn't believed I would heal from Julie's passing and didn't imagine I would attach myself to another human, let alone a Peruvian child, and love her so deeply. Now this was a second loss. While the pain inflicted from Soledad's death was different from that of the loss of my best friend, it was just as sharp. Death became my most demanding teacher, and I, its student. After Soledad's death I would eventually focus my attention on a little boy who shared a surname with Soledad. I thought it odd, but Sister said it was one of the most common surnames of all the people from *la sierra*. Thousands of mountain families had the surname Mamani.

"I suppose on some level all people are from the same family," I said.

81

love and prayers. Kara

"Yes, my dear, I think you're right," she said.
Sister Sarah loved all of God's people without exception.

Chapter 7
Calling

"Faith is an act, not a series of idle remarks.
Hope is an undertaking bathed in light, not a pious sentiment.
Charity is an event, not a devotional little prayer".

-Carlos Carretto

Once I had been in the country for two years, it had become clear why we were asked to make a two-year or more commitment to our volunteer placement in Perú. It took a whole year to adapt and feel comfortable with the language, food, and culture. Only two years in, feeling settled and being fluent in Spanish, was I able, if at all, to make a true contribution in the country.

During those two years, I had spent a lot more time with the Marian missionaries than I had imagined I would. The American religious order maintained a residence in a neighborhood about a five-minute walk from my apartment. The nuns spoke English and it was nice to have a respite to give my brain a rest from immersion in Spanish. Within months of moving to Takana, the Marian Sisters were like family and became role models to me. Their work would soon open a doorway for me into a whole new world, one I had a glimpse of when I visited El Progreso in Lima and northern Perú.

During those first two years, letters were a godsend. Much like my journaling, my letters in response to family and friends at home captured details of my new life in Perú that might have otherwise been lost. (Although, I must admit that I could have written home more.) I wrote letters to Julie, but she never responded, at least not in a way I was able to grasp. Tom continued to write, and we would talk on the phone now and then but with each new day in Peru, our relationship became a thing of the past. Something was brewing in my heart, and it wasn't a pang for Tom.

June 1987

Dear Tom,

How are you doing? I have been thinking a lot since we last talked and I want to share some thoughts with you and respond to your last letter.

Yesterday, Sister Sarah accompanied me, as she had promised she would, to the small town of La Joya. La Joya is northwest of Takana, about an hour and a half bus ride. We stayed at an orphanage run by Sisters from Our Lady of the Angels order. Five nuns live at the orphanage with twenty eight Peruvian children in an old colonial mansion transformed into a convent and home for orphans. The children living in the household range from infants to teenagers. According to the Sisters, in Perú, fifty percent of the population is under the age of fourteen and are homeless. Imagine that! The children at the orphanage arrived for many reasons: some were orphaned due to deaths in the family and others were abandoned by parents due to a variety of harsh life circumstances, or because they suffer mental illness or have physical disabilities. Perú has few services for children in these conditions. The Sisters haven't explained all the reasons and I didn't ask. They shared one story about a family who left their disabled child locked in a bedroom for years because they were ashamed of him. Some families fear the stigma placed on them bearing such a child and their shame prevents them from seeking help. Some families can't afford wheelchairs or special equipment needed. Often the Catholic Church and donations from countries abroad step in to assist. But it's not enough for everyone in need.

The orphanage provides a safe, loving home for the children. Several of the children in the orphanage will be adopted into a family, but the majority will not. It makes my desire to adopt a child even stronger. At the convent, it feels like one big happy family with several mothers caring for children, and brothers and sisters, not through bloodline, but siblings nonetheless, helping one another. The older children have household chores, cook, and help the Sisters with childcare. It's inspiring. My heart is bursting open unlike I have ever experienced before. I wonder if you can see why I am drawn to work at a place like this. I have witnessed a new definition of family.

In your last letter when you mentioned my work with the nuns, your reaction upset me. You said, "Do me a favor — before you go and enter the convent, at least come back to the States, and give me a chance." It upset me because you never asked me about my life and work here, the Peruvians, the children, my friendship with the Sisters…. Rather than seek to understand, your response was selfish. And you jumped to conclusions. As I shared with you on the phone, I am excited about my work outside of the Jesuit school, maybe more. I am learning tons alongside the Marian Sisters. You know how challenging it has been at times working with the boys at the Jesuit school, and while it's improved some, it's an uphill battle. The Sisters have shown me support, respect, and love. On days I wanted to quit, they encouraged me to carry on. I would hope for the same from you.

My experiences here in Perú have been extraordinary and life-changing. I fear you can't begin to understand this, and maybe I shouldn't expect you to. What are you afraid of, Tom? There is no guarantee that you and I would be together regardless of my decision to join a convent or not. Please, don't take my decision personally. The last thing I want to do is hurt you. I care for you, and I always will. However, what I know for sure, and as hard as it may be to hear, is that I am not going to cut my time in Perú short to be with you. And, for now, I think it best you don't come to visit me.

Love, Kara

*

The first thing I noticed as I approached the plump sixteen-month-old was the size of his head, and his large bulging eyes, one with a cloudy bluish film obstructing his vision. *He is large for a toddler*, I thought. The child attempted to move in my direction, but his body was encased from his armpits down to his ankles in a plaster cast that made it impossible for him to move much more than his hands and fingers and toes. Instead his eyes followed my every step around the crib. One would think that this horrible restriction of the body would be unbearable for a child nearing the "terrible twos", a stage when the child bounces between reliance on their parents and a burgeoning desire for independence, and it most likely was, but *Rodrigo Quispe Mamani* grinned at me rather than screamed. He hadn't yet learned to walk. Confined to a hospital crib like many of the abandoned children, he hadn't received the proper encouragement and coaching a child needs to take first steps. There were no parents to teach him, and few nurses who therefore had to attend to the most urgent and essential care. As a result of this neglect, I was told that Rodrigo had recently been confined to the body cast to correct bone structure defects. Once the cast was removed, rehabilitation would begin. I wondered how he would learn to walk after the removal of the cast. It wasn't clear to me who would help rehabilitate Rodrigo.

Sister Sarah informed me that Rodrigo's mother had been admitted to a mental health facility and that it appeared there was no hope for her discharge. No one was able to clarify what the mother's condition was exactly, and as I had seen before, explanations regarding the circumstances under which Rodrigo had been left in the hospital were at best vague and bizarre. Even though I had no first-hand experience, it seemed to me that most mothers would go to any lengths to care for a child they had brought into the world. *Under what conditions or circumstances might a mother abandon a child?* One nurse explained to me that, "In some cases, a poor woman who already has many children, and doesn't have a husband and means to care for them, can't bear a new pregnancy. If the mother couldn't provide for the child, then, perhaps she would willingly give him up." I was certain it wasn't as simple as that, but there was truth in the nurse's explanation. Unwanted pregnancies were due to many factors: lack of contraception, belief systems, abuse (some in the wife's own household), and rape. None of this would be discussed when I talked about

Rodrigo and the other abandoned children with Sister Sarah. Abortion was illegal in Perú, opposed to by the Catholic Church. I was confused and dumbfounded but I wouldn't press the issue. I didn't fully understand the circumstances of Rodrigo's abandonment, not did I know anything except through hearsay about the mother so I could not judge. From what I could glean from my limited experience, caring for many children while also juggling impossible poverty would be a difficult accomplishment for any woman in any part of the world. My concern for all women was whether they were able to make their own choices. Clearly, in Perú, they could not. My concern for all children was that they find a safe home, a place where they might thrive and grow into adulthood.

Rodrigo also had issues with his vision.

"His eyes seem swollen and he doesn't seem to have vision in one of them," I said.

"He has glaucoma in both eyes," Sister Sarah said. "He has lost his vision in the left eye."

"I didn't know kids could get glaucoma."

"We see it a lot here," Sister said.

"Can we get him some help?"

"Kara, my dear, Rodrigo has even bigger problems than his eyesight....when his cast is removed, we'll have to encourage him to stand and teach him to walk."

I was afraid to open my heart to another abandoned child but, it became clear that I no longer had control of it. It would have been more painful to keep my heart closed. The ache from Soledad's death could only be soothed by passing love onto

Rodrigo. He became my new focus, my new adopted child. Weeks later, I helped Rodrigo take his first steps. It was magical.

*

I had heard Father Ignatius's transformative story, from soldier to priest. I honestly wasn't sure what it meant to be "called" but I wanted to understand. *Did one choose to become a nun, priest, or monk? How would being a nun differ from being a priest? How would I know if I were called.*

I wasn't sure what appealed to me about religious life but I was certain about a few other matters. I knew that after fulfilling a two-year teaching contract at Colegio Ignacio Loyola, I no longer wanted to work there, but, I also knew I didn't want to return to the United States either. There was so much more to learn about Perú, the Catholic Church and myself. Secondly, it had become clear to me that after two years living alone and working with boys and men, I longed to live in community and in the company of women.

I had loved living with Julie. Julie and I had met during a freshman social gathering, and we hit it off. We shared freshman year growing pains, threw ourselves into our respective studies, dated several college boys, and became roommates our junior year. Like many college girls we spoke of marriage and having children: Julie wanted to have lots of kids while I was ambivalent. But we had never discussed other life options.

Now I wondered what her opinion would be about the possibility of me joining a convent. We had conversations about marriage, family, religion, faith, and even the Catholic Church, but never about becoming a nun. Both raised Catholic, we

89

agreed that regardless of the group one belonged to, all worship the same God. We were also both aware of some of the Church's shortcomings. We were very open to exploring different religions. In fact, despite our Catholic upbringings, we had visited various places of worship: Baptist churches, Buddhist temples, and Islamic mosques. We had even attended our resident assistant's Campus Crusade for Christ meetings held in our dormitory (although we went to those meetings to remain in the RA's good graces rather than to follow their club doctrines). We were both spiritual seekers — it was one of the reasons we were drawn to each other. At the end of our junior year, we had been happy and our lives at the university seemed to be falling into place until one day it all changed and suddenly Julie had been in the hospital battling for her life.

That was when all we had learned about religion and faith would be tested. When Julie came home from a doctor's appointment and told me the doctor had expressed concern and scheduled a CT scan as soon as possible, we understood our need to call upon a power larger and stronger than ourselves. We had bowed our heads and prayed as we had been taught for a positive outcome. When the scans revealed Julie had a brain tumor, our foundation and all we knew cracked. I'll never forget when she said, "Something is wrong with my brain." We were devastated. The news was too hard to face alone. We had to put our faith and trust in something.

I was still looking for exactly where to place my trust for the future.

It was around the time of contemplating pursuing a religious life that I met the Sisters of Our Lady of the Angels who occasionally visited the Marian Sisters in Takana. As we spent some time together, we really hit it off. I especially liked Sister Flora, the Mother Superior, and the feeling was mutual. Sister Flora and the congregation invited me to join their parish in a town nestled in the mountains. There I could observe the work they were doing with the Aymara people. The idea piqued my curiosity and, as my teaching job was winding down, it sounded like a good option. *An adventure in the Andes mountains – who wouldn't say yes to that.*

Growing up in my family, we were exposed to Roman Catholicism from the day of our baptism but the nuns in my hometown parish never impressed me much. Let's just say that I felt sorry for them. Those nuns hid their bodies and hair under long, loosely fitted habits. I used to wonder what color and length of hair was under their ugly bonnet-like head covering. The nuns I knew weren't adventurous; they rarely traveled far from home, and lived near the Church in my suburban town. I knew a few girls from The Immaculate Academy. They didn't inspire me either – they were closed-minded and few of them dated boys. The Immaculate girls told me stories about the nuns who taught at their school. "They don't seem very happy, and some of them are cruel," they said. One of the girls told me had been put in a broom closet as a punishment for speaking out of turn in class.

My First Communion led to some confusion about the institution of marriage. I remember the white dress, and veil from the ceremony. It was like I was a mini-bride. I was a sucker for a new pretty dress and I loved that I got to carry a bouquet of freshly picked flowers. As a young girl, I was told that some

91

nuns were bitter because they had never married or had children. After my First Communion, I wondered: did they marry God? Did I want to marry the Church? Or a man? It never occurred to me, then, that not all women needed to be married or to have children to find happiness or a strong sense of self. Nor should they have to.

James was my serious older boyfriend throughout all four years of high school. When I was seventeen years old, this young man whom I had dated since eighth-grade proposed marriage so during my junior and senior years of high school, I wore his engagement ring. But my true feeling about marriage was that it honestly didn't appeal to me at all. I felt guilty because I was lying to James and myself. *Shouldn't every girl be delighted about the prospect of getting married? What's wrong with me?* My intuition about my future was strong, though not clairvoyant — I never imagined that I would go to Perú or that I would consider being a nun — but I intuited that my path would be different. I broke off the engagement with James and went to Benton University.

In Peru, meeting the Marian Sisters and the Sisters of Our Lady of the Angels, I began to ask what it meant to give one's life to God and the Church. Unlike the nuns I had met in my childhood, these women were kind, smart and resourceful, missionaries who had left their native country, and learned languages so they could serve others. Opting out of marriage and raising children, they dedicated their time, energy, and compassion to a population of people far from family, language, and their own culture. As I was learning for myself, this was not an easy endeavor, but it was deeply gratifying.

They lived in a community of like-minded women, creating a family committed to one another and to all God's people.

Two main aspects of their lifestyle stood out for me: the nuns' service to the poor and marginal communities, and their willingness to forego having their own families for the good of a larger human family. What sacrifice. Never in the States had I met or seen nuns like these Sisters. These nuns were cool. They wore street clothes — Sister Sarah even wore dungarees! Unlike the Jesuits who lived in a large house in the center of town and were cared for by women who cooked and cleaned for them, the nuns lived in a simple, bare-bones house in the same neighborhood as the people they served and took care of themselves. The Sisters worked in *los pueblos jóvenes* of Takana alongside the poor communities on the outskirts of the city. They didn't have personal cars like the Jesuits; they used the bus like most locals. They imitated the life of Christ by living simply, praying daily, and reaching out to those people most in need in the community and those who were alone in prisons and hospitals. They learned to speak Spanish (and some Aymara and Quechua) well enough to communicate and understand the people. They cooked meals for one another. They did their own laundry.

It all seemed admirable to me.

*

On my second Christmas in Perú, away from home and family, rather than wallow in self-pity (I couldn't be back in the States and no one was coming to visit me.) or indulge in feelings of loneliness, I decided I would follow the Marian Sisters' example and reach out to others. *Being alone does not need to feel lonely,* I thought. To my knowledge, poverty had meant a lack of money, food, shelter, material goods, but the Sisters had taught and showed me that a lack of love, connection, and faith in something greater than oneself is a great deficiency as well. Nowhere is this poverty better exemplified than in the life of a prison inmate. Is there any other population more deprived of human connection, forgiveness and hope than prisoners? I had visited the local prison before and had met prisoners locked up and removed from the world, from society, loved ones, for months, years, a lifetime. But being imprisoned, on a major holiday—I could think of no greater poverty.

I contacted an officer at the local prison and arranged a Christmas Day visit. When I showed up that afternoon at the main entrance, I was greeted by two grumpy, overweight, tall men holding rifles. Other guards just inside the door were well-equipped with holsters and guns that signaled they were in charge. I carried freshly baked bread, brightly decorated cupcakes and gifts wrapped in festive paper. This was all confiscated—it was a policy regulation that no food from outside was allowed onto the premises. It hadn't occurred to me that I couldn't bring baked goods to the prisoners on Christmas Day. I managed to convince the officers to let me hang on to several gifts, although it wasn't until after unwrapping each one, inspecting the toys and stuffed animals that the guards allowed them to pass with their approval. "For the children's sake," it was understood. After all, it was Christmas.

The women's prison had several new inmates and children since I had visited, so the already-cramped quarters were even more full than usual. Additional bunk beds had been added to one cell. I anticipated encountering disgruntled, self-pitying individuals, especially given that it was a holiday, but that couldn't have been further from the truth. After a few awkward introductions, the women welcomed me in and were eager to share life stories and some details of the crimes and misdemeanors that had landed them behind bars. Most of the prisoners were waiting for a trial, although in most cases that would never come. The new inmates were eager to talk and perhaps, even more, to be heard. The adult conversation was mostly banter, but I could tell that it was cathartic in some way. The youngest children—those living temporarily in a cell with their mothers—were occupied with the new toys that had passed through security, toys that indirectly gave their mothers a break.

The most common prisoner offense among the women I visited was drug possession. One woman said, "We have to provide for the family at all costs." Feeding their children was the reason they had gotten involved with drugs in the first place. "Dealing with drugs was quick money," they said but they were paying a high price for this source of income. Where were their husbands, or the fathers of their kids? I wondered.

I had not met Maria Luisa, the youngest of the prisoners, on my previous visits. She was an outspoken twenty-one-year-old woman, noticeably different in appearance from the other inmates. She was lighter skinned than the other women and wore denim jeans, not a *pollera* skirt. She proudly introduced herself and said she had been affiliated with the revolutionary terrorist group *Sendero Luminoso*. Until that introduction, I had forgotten that the country continued to endure civil war and terrorist attacks. She said that she had been interrogated in Lima while boarding a bus to Takana and had been detained upon arrival here. Maria Luisa couldn't believe she had been arrested.

"I did nothing wrong. My association with the group never once caused any harm to anyone. I had nothing to do with any violence whatsoever. I promise you that," she said.

Even though Maria Luisa reassured all of us that she had nothing to do with any violent acts committed by *Sendero Luminoso*, I still felt uneasy in her presence. So much terror and violence continued to rain down on the Peruvian people. The mere mention of the name Shining Path and, even more, a person affiliated with the group sent chills through my body. Frankly, I was amazed the other inmates weren't beside themselves, sharing a living space with an ally of the terrorist group that murdered their people. She continued to reiterate that she had simply been in the wrong place at the wrong time, that her only crime was loving someone.

"*Me enamoré de un miembro de Sendero Luminoso*. I fell in love with a member of the Shining Path. Is falling in love a crime?" She swore that if not for her love affair with this man, whose name she could not mention, she never would have gotten hooked up with any terrorist activity.

I needed a moment to digest what I had just heard. *Is that what love is?* I thought. The romantic love I knew in college, the one that sent us blindly off to chase men we hoped would make us happy — was that love? My mind began to wander, straying to that place and time, days when Julie and I ran through the quad at Benton University along with so many other twenty-somethings, streaking, naked and free to go wherever we wanted, free to have sex, *to make love*. When I remembered that Julie was no longer alive, that she died at the same age Maria Luisa was now, I was jolted back to the present day, to the small jail in Takana, Perú where I sat between mothers and their children, women incarcerated for crimes not yet proven. An alleged terrorist. Alleged *narco-traficantes*. They were innocent until proven guilty, but not free.

What is love? Falling in love wasn't a crime, but blind love could lead to bad consequences. I was growing more and more curious about a different kind of love, one that had nothing to do with my feelings for an attractive man, one that also embraced a larger circle.

As I left the women's prison, I heard myself saying *Feliz Navidad*, Merry Christmas. The words sounded trivial, meaningless, but what else could I say? I took a moment to watch the children playing with the toys I had brought. I wished I had brought books instead of toys. Books illustrated with beautiful, bright colored landscapes they could not see from the prison. Books about connection, love, hope and freedom. I also wished the kids could have indulged in the foods I had baked and decorated for them. Leaving the building I saw that the food had already been devoured by the guards. Visiting the inmates allowed me to redirect my loneliness. It became clear to me that mine paled in comparison to theirs. I wanted to think that we had all enjoyed one another's company.

The short taxi ride back to my apartment was quiet. The taxi driver said nothing but I saw him glance at the rearview mirror with curious eyes—who was this young American woman traveling alone on Christmas Day from a prison to a private Catholic school some three miles from the center of town? I avoided eye contact, got lost in my thoughts and wanted to keep it that way. I considered what I was missing back home at the annual Grey Family reunion in New York City. The family on my Dad's side had childhood roots in the Big Apple, so, for years, we'd been celebrating the holidays there. Maybe the family was gathered at the dinner table with a stuffed turkey or a honey-baked ham? My favorite part of the season was the six-foot tree that Dad and my brother Henry picked out every year. It was always decked out with an eclectic mix of ornaments, some handmade, some passed down for generations, some representing superheroes. I missed the walks along Fifth Avenue, the ornate holiday window displays at Macy's and Saks Fifth Avenue. I thought of the Salvation Army volunteers on every corner ringing bells, drawing attention to their buckets collecting charity for those most in need. I recalled how, many times, I had passed by without contributing a dime to their cause. I was ashamed of that now. I reminisced about visits to the Metropolitan Museum of Art to see the hand-crafted Napolitano nativity surrounding the museum's tree and hearing the Gregorian Chants that echoed in the room. I loved that gallery. As a kid, I would close my eyes and be transported from the museum to a medieval monastery. I was in awe of how one could leave the hustle and bustle of the grand metropolis that is New York City and within minutes be in such a divine, holy place. For an instant, I felt a similar magic in the back of the taxi.

That Christmas, as I spent the afternoon sitting in a tiny, dingy, damp prison cell in Takana, I was light years away from our typical family celebration. I missed my family and yet, I was content. Holidays are meant to be festive, but this day had been stripped of Christmas lights and carols. What would remain without the candies, cookies and chocolate treats, without the gifts under the decorated tree, without the glitter, the six-course meal with wine, without the cake and champagne for dessert? *Amor*, love, family. People who show up for one another. *La familia*, a family, gathered around the table, for a meal. Women who do what is necessary to feed their children; love and resilience that keeps them together as a family.

I spent Christmas Day in a jail cell, and I was grateful for it. My perspective had been changing ever since arriving in Perú and that day, I experienced an *ah-ha* moment on the ride from the prison to my apartment in Takana. I knew I would no longer be the same woman. It reminded me of the inner stirring I felt when I first saw *El Progreso* and when I met abandoned children in the hospital. It was an uncontrollable heart shift towards others. Faith in something greater than myself took center stage. Love, God, Life Force, call it what you may, is found among the least of our brothers and sisters. It is found in pain and loss. It found me that day. Perhaps this was the transformation from soldier to priest that Father Ignatius experienced. A bolt of lightning struck me. I was not a hundred percent sure what a calling was, but I was certain, on Christmas Day 1987 that I had undergone an epiphany.

From the backseat of the taxi, I said aloud, "Could I devote my life to God? Am I called to be a nun?"

The taxi driver, although unable to understand English, heard my voice coming from the back of his car and he glanced in my direction. This time our eyes met in the rearview mirror.

"*Buenas noches, Señorita. Feliz Navidad*, Merry Christmas."

He left me at the gate of Colegio Ignacio Loyola, waited patiently until my key unlocked it, and seeing that I was home safely, pulled away.

If a calling of this nature meant I could no longer have sex, marry, or have my own children, I couldn't be certain how I'd respond to the call. I both feared and admired the vows of celibacy, obedience, and poverty. I wasn't ready to surrender fully but I would explore further. *One step at a time,* I told myself.

January 1987

Dear Tom,

Happy New Year! I hope your Christmas was wonderful. Although I couldn't travel home for the holiday, it was nice all the same. I have some big news: I've decided to go with the Sisters of Our Lady of the Angels to their parish in Chuqiyapu. I want to learn more about religious life, and this is one way to do it. I don't know if I am meant to be a nun or not, but what I do know is that I want to do God's will. I am attracted to a missionary's way of life. I am still not in the mountains but will be soon. I am thinking about how I might be of service to the people and parish there.

When I accepted the invitation to live with the nuns, I made it clear that I am still uncertain about taking vows. We will see what transpires. "I am open to exploring my options," I said. Mostly, I look forward to seeing the mountains, and the Aymara way of life. The Sisters don't need to know all I am thinking at this point. I still must sort some stuff out and make decisions. What seems to be the big concern with me becoming a nun, anyway? What if I chose it? Or, if it chose me? Would that life choice be so awful? Would my family disown me?

Another young American woman will be volunteering with me in Chuqiyapu. Her name is Ellie. She is from Chicago, is twenty-four years old, and she doesn't speak any Spanish. Ugh! No Spanish? Every time I speak, read, or write in English, I lose ground in Spanish. Now, I am concerned about speaking too much English with the gringa. Ha-ha. I forget that I too am una Gringa. It's become easier to think in Spanish and not switch back and forth. I have even had dreams in Spanish! I remember thinking how nice it would be to really share the Peruvian experience through the language, therefore understanding their lives better. Well, I am almost there! Now, I will be around a volunteer that doesn't speak Spanish. Geez. Anyway, many of the locals in Chuqiyapu speak Aymara, not Spanish. Yet another challenge to conquer.

I am confident with my decision to go to Chuqiyapu. I am happy! I hope you are happy for me too. The opportunity I had to share my talents at Colegio Ignacio Loyola was nice, but now onto something new, and perhaps an opportunity to share and learn even more. I look forward to seeing another part of Perú and working with women (for a change). I like being here; I am not ready to go back to the United States.

Love, Kara

P.S. My next letter will have a new return address: % Parroquia Santo Domingo, Chuqiyapu, Takana, Perú

love and prayers, Kara

Chapter 8
Real Adventure Begins Here

Sister Flora sent her assistant, Sister Tricia, to pick me up in the Sisters' new-to-them but used 1977 Jeep Renegade. My first impressions of Sister Tricia were that she was young, cool, and very beautiful for a nun. She was also a Canadian and had lived in the United States for several years. We left Takana on a Saturday morning for the Santo Domingo parish in Chuqiyapu.

I had been in Chuqiyapu for a brief visit once before moving there. The Andean town was about six to seven hours by car from Takana on mostly unpaved dirt roads. Excitement was building as we took a leisurely trip over the *altiplano*, the high plains, through towns that all looked the same. I knew the views ahead as we got into the mountains would not disappoint.

One reason I was glad to stay longer in Perú was that it was a huge country with rich and spectacular geography to explore. The country was divided into three bands of diverse landscape: the desert coast, the Andes mountain range, and the dense jungle. Each area provided its unique topography, language, and culture.

The landscape gradually changed from flat desert sand to grassy mountain soil dotted with cattle, llamas, and alpacas on either side of the road. As we drove closer toward our destination the landscape became more beautiful and desolate. Snow-capped mountains and volcanoes in the far-off distance suggested hours and miles of terrain to cover before we reached the Andean town. Around me were years of history and culture impossible to fathom.

We stopped the Jeep, sat in *paja*, straw-like grass on the side of the road, and dug into a small cooler holding our lunch and water. From our view, we noticed oil dripping from underneath the jeep. Sister Tricia stood and lifted the hood of the vehicle to check the engine. Whatever the issue, she couldn't detect it. Farther down the road, the Jeep made a cranky sound and stopped cold. Sister Tricia put the jeep in neutral and we pushed it to the side of the road. We started walking to Barata, the nearest town, to find help.

On the road ahead, we met two Andean women. The women carried bundles of grass tied firmly to their backs in a handwoven wool blanket. We asked them if they could watch our vehicle while we continued ahead in search of assistance. Sister Tricia offered a few *soles* in exchange for the favor. With a smile and nod the women agreed. It was clear that Spanish was not their first language. Quechua? Aymara? I couldn't tell. It didn't matter; I knew that all women understand one another on some level regardless of their mother tongue.

"What are these women doing out here in the middle of nowhere?" I asked. "I wonder how far the closest town might be?"

"Welcome to the *altiplano*, Kara!" Sister Tricia said, "We'll soon find out."

When we arrived in Barata, we went to the post office to leave word with the Sisters in Chuqiyapu that we had been delayed. But there was no phone line at the post office. Sister Tricia suggested we call on the only priest in the town of Barata. All the religious orders and missionaries knew of one another in Southern Perú. "The local priest can pass a message on to the parish in Chuqiyapu," she said. She was confident he would come to our rescue, as well.

Father Rosas was an eighty-seven-year-old Peruvian priest who had lived alone for forty years in a small parish in Barata. No religious community presided over the parish so he was therefore required to fulfill his religious duties as the sole manager of the parish church and healer of souls. He suggested we call *el cuartel*, the army barracks, for help. "One was certain to find a mechanic at the camp," Father Rosas said.

We called and were told that *el jefe*, the boss, was not available. Instead of taking no for an answer, Sister Tricia and I went directly to *el cuartel* thinking that our presence might get them to respond and work faster. We knew being young, attractive females would carry some weight and, given our circumstances, we were not shy about using our assets. At the same time, we were aware that this might make us vulnerable as military men in the poorest Andean towns were notorious for violent atrocities and abuse towards women. Our status — a Canadian nun and an American volunteer — shielded us from immediate danger. Our white complexions also afforded us protection not granted to darker skinned Indigenous women.

We met with success at the *el cuartel* military encampment. The soldiers agreed to retrieve the abandoned Jeep from the open road and bring it to town for inspection and repair. I noticed that the baby-faced soldiers approaching us were no older than my former students, their machine guns almost seeming too heavy for their scrawny arms to support. Still, they generated fear. They had been indoctrinated well. They stared at us, asked us to turn around and grazed our buttocks with the barrel of their guns. I pondered, *should we have been so friendly*? I grew progressively more nervous, fearing the soldiers might sexually assault us. Who knew what orders these boys were following. At gunpoint, we were told to get in the back of an army truck where two other armed soldiers were already seated and waiting. They too had rifles. The boy soldiers pointed the rifles at our heads for the duration of the trip back to our Jeep and said nothing. When I tried to speak, the weapons clicked to a ready position.

The ride to retrieve the Jeep lasted a long fifteen minutes. During this time, I managed to build up a sweat that would stain the armpits of my shirt. The army truck parked itself beside the stranded Jeep in the middle of nowhere. The two Andean women we had asked to watch the vehicle were still watching over it. I was surprised the ladies had agreed to it in the first place, let alone kept vigil for several hours. The women were speechless and appeared frightened when we arrived with the soldiers. When they looked at us, however, they looked relieved that we had returned safely despite being accompanied by soldiers, and that, at least on the surface, we were unscarred.

One soldier checked the engine while the others continued to point their rifles at all of us, the women, to maintain control of the situation. My body trembled: the effect of the cold air was intensified by wet clothes and the fear of being raped or shot if we disobeyed. They couldn't fix the problem, they said. The soldiers insisted we all go into Barata, where the mechanic would examine the engine. It wasn't clear to me why the Andean women were told to accompany us. They were even more perplexed than I, and when they resisted, they were knocked to their knees by a strike from the heel of a rifle. Sister Tricia and I helped them to their feet and into the back of the military truck.

Returning to town, Sister Tricia and I were escorted along with the Jeep to the mechanic. When I turned to see where the Andean women were, I saw them heading in the opposite direction, escorted by armed soldiers to an area out of my view. By the time a mechanic looked at the engine, it was close to sunset. The Andean women and the soldiers never returned. The mechanic told us that nothing could be done with the Jeep until the morning.

The only light in town was the starlit sky and the moon and I found some solace in that. I had never been so aware of the stars; here in the mountains they were so close I might reach up and touch them and they might protect me.

But Sister Tricia and I were tired, cold, hungry, and disappointed that nothing could be done to repair the Jeep. I felt concerned that we had to stay overnight as there were no hotels to be found.

"Where are we going to stay?" I said.

love and prayers, Kara

"We'll be fine," Sister said.

"And, where did they take those poor women that were with us?" I asked.

"I have no idea," she said.

The soldiers hadn't responded to our inquiry about the Andean women. They were, however, eager to offer us bunks in their barracks. We declined the offer and without delay headed on foot towards the town plaza where we called upon Father Rosas again. The church steeple was easy to find. It made sense to reach out to the Church for assistance. Sister Tricia was sure that Father Rosas, the kind, elderly religious man, would provide lodging. I wasn't confident about anything anymore.

When Sister Tricia asked *Padre* Rosas if he could put us up for the night, he said, "It would be scandalous if a Catholic priest were to give lodging to two young females!" Apparently it would be improper to offer accommodations in the church rectory as suspicions in the small town might emerge. Improprieties of real concern went on in all corners of town, never to be reported, yet Padre Rosas would not allow any woman, under any circumstance, to sleep under his roof. I thought our situation warranted an exception, but the Father's mind was made up.

Finally, thanks to the only doctor in town, we stayed in *la posta médica*, the medical clinic. It was a small, dusty hospital-like center with dim lanterns, five cots for patients, several cabinets of expired medicines and stained bandages. It was drafty and had no heat. But most importantly, the door had a lock. We spent the night on steel-framed cots with no mattresses or blankets. Despite the discomfort, I managed to make the best of it, and I was glad it was a safer place than the army barracks. I didn't sleep much that night. How could I? There was still the ominous threat, the one that had caught the Andean women earlier in the day, hanging over me. Once I convinced myself we were safe, I thanked God and was grateful. On the other hand, I felt badly that other women were not as fortunate. I dozed off a few hours before sunrise.

Early the next morning, we were told that nothing could be done for the Jeep and that we could return to Takana on the local bus. Before leaving, we accepted an invitation to eat a mid-morning meal at Father Rosas's house. He served us a plate of cooked rabbit. Not a piece, but the whole animal sprawled out on the plate, paws, and all. I have never loved meat but this made me nauseous. I mean it still looked exactly like a rabbit with its teeth and skin with fur intact. I had been served similar meat in the pueblo jóven, *el Progreso* outside of Lima two years earlier. The stomach cramps and hours spent on the toilet following that meal were not something I wished to repeat, especially on a long bus ride. I felt a similar fear and trepidation as I had then, but I filled the empty pit in my stomach with what was available. As I could see, there were no restaurants in town. Father Rosas gobbled down his food like a pig and I was disgusted at his lack of manners. But he had lived alone for many years in two small, disheveled rooms off the side of the church, with no one to call him on his habits. He was oblivious. I leaned into Sister Tricia's ear and whispered, "Did he ever learn table manners?"

After we took a bus back to Takana where we enjoyed a good night's sleep at the Marian house, Sister Tricia and I were back on a bus to *Chuqiyapu* the following day, the Jeep having been abandoned in Barata for the time being. *Is it this difficult to get from one place to the next?* I wondered. Apparently, I was learning, in the Peruvian Andes, the answer was yes. It was too late to change my mind and call off my move to the parish. I had agreed to give religious life a chance and I would keep my promise. After an eleven-hour trip due to the rain that day, we arrived at the center plaza.

There I refused to disembark. Sister Tricia, in a soft, reassuring tone, and some prodding, convinced me to get off the bus. The other option, of course, would have been to return to Takana and then to the United States. I had been suddenly afraid: so much unknown lay ahead. In the Andes, one never knew from one day to the next, or even one hour to the next, what was going to happen. Finally I stepped off the bus and proclaimed Chuqiyapu, the Andean town of approximately five thousand inhabitants, to be my new home.

love and prayers, Kara

Chapter 9
Chuqiyapu

The greatest truth is the simplest.

Days after my arrival to the town of *Chuqiyapu*, I learned that its Aymara name means *peace* in English. It seemed a perfect place for me to land. I was glad to leave the congestion of the city of Takana behind me. I was also glad the drive was behind me. One of the locals took pride in telling me that the town was situated in the Peruvian Cordillera, at an altitude of 3415 meters or approximately 12,000 feet above sea level. All the roads were unpaved, and the trip had involved a continuous series of switchbacks, up and down the mountains, often with a roadbed wide enough for only one vehicle. Once *Chuqiyapu* was in sight, snow-capped mountains and deep gorges lined with scattered eucalyptus trees had provided breath-taking scenery nearly all the way to the center of town. Now that I was off the bus, I could be in awe of the view. The town was nestled at the base of a beautiful snow-capped volcano named *Yanajaja*. *Los lugareños*, townspeople, got a kick out of teaching me the pronunciation— ya-na-ha-ha—and I

111

loved saying its name out loud. Everyone laughed each time we said it. The main plaza was surrounded by only a few buildings with a church steeple housing a large bell tower suggesting Europeans had once settled there dominating the plaza landscape. In 1987, *Chuqiyapu* was the main hub of fourteen villages, comprising some twenty thousand people. Of the fourteen surrounding *pueblos*, six could be reached only by foot, mule, or horseback. Others had access roads.

The Santo Domingo parish was under the spiritual care and direction of Sisters Flora and Tricia. The church's white bell tower marked arrival to the center of town; it stood above all else. For months it guided me, leading me back into town any time I strolled into the surrounding countryside. Each Sunday, Eugenio, a young town resident who worked for the Church (whether he received a salary was not clear) would climb to the top of the tower to ring the bell before the morning Mass. I would learn that both the parish and church dated back to 1777. While the original church still stood, the sisters told me that the residential building, soon to be my home, had been built only a few years earlier. It was a seven-room adobe mud structure blending in with the homes of the local residents in a horseshoe shape around a courtyard and garden that provided herbs for cooking.

The convent had a shared room that included space for two large comfortable chairs, several bookshelves, a dining area, and the kitchen. Nearby, but not reachable without exiting the common space, there was an office for business affairs and visits from folks seeking pastoral guidance. One large desk, three tall filing cabinets and several folding chairs, and more bookshelves furnished the office space. Five small single dormitories for the Sisters and overnight guests and one bathroom completed the horseshoe. There was no electricity. The generator was reserved for church ceremonies. There was also no heating except for the warmth from the kerosene lamps and the wood stove in the kitchen. I would soon learn that preparing a hot water bottle every night to keep in bed was a life saver as temperatures dipped below freezing during a good part of the year. I would struggle to get out of bed in the mornings because of the cold air.

My bedroom was sparse in the style of convent living: a single bed, small nightstand, and a desk and chair was all the room could hold. A large wooden cross hung on the wall above the bed. There was a small closet to perch five to ten hangers of clothes. The windowsill stood in as a shelf. I arranged some personal items and books there, then decorated the ledge with shells and stones I had collected from the beach as a reminder of the sea, now many miles away from me in my new home. One drawer under the nightstand held a King James English version of the Holy Bible.

Life in the mountains required new habits not needed on the coast. It was essential to wear heavy clothes until ten o'clock in the morning even indoors, and to change into lighter clothes at three in the afternoon after the sun had warmed the house. Showers were taken infrequently and we depended on the sun to warm the water. Back in the States I never went without hot water and showers but I grew accustomed to short, cold or lukewarm showers and loved those moments of refreshment available only several times a week.

113

February 1987

Dear Mom and Dad,

I officially arrived in Chuqiyapu on February 18th. I have now been here for several weeks! The trip was long, quite an adventure you'll hear about someday. The article I am sending gives you some background about the village and the Sisters that I am working with. Also, I am enclosing a sealed letter from Sister Flora (known as the Mother Superior, or the nun in charge, ha-ha) who wants to assure you that I am well. I think she is a fantastic lady. I am very pleased with the accommodations – simple but clean. I haven't done much yet as I am getting acclimated to the altitude (approximately 3500 meters above sea level). Altitude sickness is not fun. Here it is referred to as soroche. I am feeling the usual effects: headache, gas, nausea, and tiredness, but those that get it bad often vomit for days and need to get to a lower altitude fast because they require oxygen. I am sure that in time I will be ready to work.

The people in Chuqiyapu were mostly of Aymara ancestry. Professionals such as teachers, police officers, and civil workers are Mestizo (from European and Indigenous ancestry). The children's faces are round, and their red cheeks are burned from the cold and sun. They are adorable. Their dark black hair and eyes, inherited from their ancestors, stare at me from under large-brimmed hats stare at me. Adults and children wear sandals called ojotas, made of durable tire rubber. I think I will wear them too, but unlike the locals, I'll have to wear them with socks, otherwise the rubber would rub until my skin bleeds. The local mountain folk build tough calluses on their feet; they have walked miles and have worked in the fields for years. The people also wear cowboy-like hats to shield their eyes from the harsh sun. My eyes and delicate white skin will need protection.

114

love and prayers, Kara

For the time being, I share a room with Ellie, an American volunteer like me. I am not sure what she is really doing here. She doesn't speak any Spanish and she is very unhappy most of the time. She will be returning to Chicago before too long – then I will have my own room! We all must share responsibilities in the house with chores including cooking on certain nights. I will need to learn how to use the potbelly stove; we don't have a gas or electric stove or an oven. I think I'll make soup tonight; I don't know how to make much else. Ha!! I think I need to dig up a cookbook from somewhere.

This morning we had a Mass without a priest, a first for me. The Sisters do everything during Mass except consecrate the host. The same Mass ritual is followed but the congregation receives hosts from a chalice which stores hosts previously consecrated by a priest. I never knew that only priests can officially consecrate the bread shared during communion. The Sisters write and give homilies based on Scripture – something I have never seen a nun do before either. They said that I too will have my turn in the pulpit!!! Imagine that? I thought only priests spoke from the pulpit.

La artesania, an arts and crafts project I envision starting with women, is still up in the air. Making art isn't a priority for the Sisters. They are primarily focused on Catholic ministry. The town is celebrating the Feast of Santo Domingo, the saint for whom our Church is named. I am not sure what he is the patron saint of. There will be a procession honoring the Virgin of Chuqiyapu. All the traditional Andean costumes will come out and the dance groups will perform their folkloric dances. The plaza will be filled with people from all surrounding villages dancing los Huaynos for days. Too bad I can't join in – more Masses will be added to the schedule which means that instead of dancing, I'll be working here at la Parroquia. Sister Tricia seems to be worried about the amount of alcohol consumption during

115

the feast. She hasn't explained her concerns to me, so I'm not sure what that's all about. I'll soon find out.

Love, Kara

Dear Mrs. Grey,

It is time to make your acquaintance. Kara arrived here Monday. I had been alone for a week and was very happy when Sister Tricia brought Kara. Sister Margaret and a young volunteer, Ellie, recently joined us as well. Ellie will be here for a short visit and Sister Margaret will join our ministry. Kara has settled in nicely and seems very happy. We are happy to have her. She'll be a great asset here with her strong command of Spanish. Also, she seems to enter well into our prayer life. We have a small chapel here in the house because usually it is too cold to go to pray in the church, especially at the hours that we pray.

Be assured that we'll be taking care of Kara. We do try to eat well here because of the altitude. This morning Kara was hungry and was surprised because, as she said, she usually eats very little in the morning. She has quite an appetite here.

Because of the rains (it is the rainy season) we can't travel much in the evening. The fog comes right over us. We live right in the clouds. There's no electricity in town, and our motor (which pumps energy into our home on occasion) has not been functioning for a few months. So, early to bed is our custom!

I hope that you are keeping well. Please, remember me to your husband. We pray for our families, friends, and Benefactors daily. May you find consolation in this.

Yours sincerely in Christ, Sr. Flora m.n.d.m.

*

Once arriving in Chuqiyapu, I had to resist the temptation to return to Takana to see friends, call home or find comfort in the coastal climate. As a rule, it was important to get acclimated to the altitude before going down to the coast too soon. At such a high altitude above sea level, one can't do all that one can do on the coast. One gets tired easily in the mountains, even after a short walk the exertion affects breathing. When I first arrived, shortness of breath was a daily reality in the thin mountain air. Life in Chuqiyapu was so much slower and some days all I did was spend hours reading and writing in my journal. Letters to Julie and to my parents also became companions of sorts. I wrote to describe the newness of everything, and perhaps, to divulge my secrets, doubts, and fears.

February 1988
Dear Julie,
Would I walk four hours to attend a church meeting? It is one thing to walk miles each day to do chores, but to attend church meetings, I don't know. We convened in the parish house and it was astonishing to me to see that most people that attended came quite a distance from their smaller pueblo. Many traveled two to four hours on foot to get to Chuqiyapu. I am told they are used to it – no cars, or horses, it's no big deal. Talk about being devoted to the parish!

At the meeting we all ate and prayed together. We shared stories and laughed a lot. It was a beautiful feeling having these people, mostly campesinos, at the dinner table with us. They are quiet, simple, humble, and generous. They know this land intimately; they are deeply connected to the earth and treat it well because it provides for them; they use the land for food, shelter, and clothing. Their knowledge of farming techniques is extraordinary. They speak of their animals as members of their family. I am curious about their ancestors' beliefs in deities of the universe and if they still worship them. I have so much to learn from these people. I have even more to learn from nature.

When I write to you, I feel like you are alive. I wish I could find the words to describe these mountains—I believe that you, Julie, already know their magnificence. This place is nothing like I've seen before. I go walking a lot and always find myself in awe of the scenery that surrounds me. It is expansive and the sky is so big! The air is so fresh. It makes me feel at peace and close to you, and to God. I never feel alone. What might I learn from nature? I don't have a close relationship with Her. And yet, it is here in nature where I draw strength and hope when I am down or lonely. I feel whole when I am in the mountain silence.

Where are you, Julie? I miss you.

I have been away from home for two years now. It does and doesn't seem like a long time to me, but it might feel like an eternity to my family. The folks worry constantly about my health and safety. Unreliable infrequent mail and phone calls haven't helped the situation much, especially for my mother. I received several letters when I was in Takana and in them it was clear that they're afraid I might be brainwashed in Latin America or even worse, by the Catholic Church. The bottom line is they don't want me to become a nun; they can't understand why I would be considering a life of obedience, poverty, and chastity. And solitude.

I haven't yet figured out what I am hoping to find in the convent. However, if I am to discern what is best for me, I must block out their negativity. I will say that I love this place and the people. I would love for my folks back home to develop a deeper understanding and empathy for this country and Peruvian people.

Love and prayers, Kara

March 1988
Dear Dad,

Hi! Thanks for your letter; I was glad to hear from you. I am sorry that my decision to move into the convent in Chuqiyapu upset you and Mom so much. I am happy, you can assure Mom of that. Yes, we do shower here in the convent. I live simply, but not too simply. We have a water tank on the roof with a solar panel. When the sun shines (which is almost always, or at least a part of every day) it heats up enough water for one or two showers. We all take turns. The best shower is after two o'clock in the afternoon, for obvious reasons! I have taken so many things for granted, Dad.

The Sisters are very conscientious and concerned with cleanliness, boiling water, and cooking raw vegetables. We take all the necessary precautions needed to stay healthy while living in Peru. We especially must be careful to only drink boiled water. Did you know it takes longer for water to reach boiling point at high altitudes? The pot has to stay on the stove for about twenty minutes before water comes to a boil. We use a potbelly stove to heat the main room and cook on at the same time. I am getting into the whole process of fetching wood, stuffing the stove, lighting old newspapers and letting the air in to get the fire going. We light it up at about five every night or when we return from the villages. It sure gets cold up here at night! I can barely roll over in bed because of the weight of so many blankets on top of me. I often take a hot water bottle to bed with me as well.

I found it interesting that you mentioned writing another book, with my inspiration. I have seriously thought about writing something myself, if not a book, perhaps articles about my experiences in Perú. After all, I have spent many nights writing in my journal and

119

these letters home. One problem, though, is my English! It has gotten rusty since I am immersed in Spanish. A good sign, depending on one's point of view. With your help on a book, I can do marvels. Do you agree.

You know that we have no electric lights here in Chuqiyapu? Not yet. They are saying they will be on by April – however, they promised the community the same thing two years ago. The parish has a generator they use to light up the church, but it takes an awful lot of energy to run it for only an hour of evening Mass. We are all set though with kerosene lanterns. They are easy to use. Everything is like an adventure for me. It's very cool that I am learning to do everything on my own.

If you and Mom want to write back, I'm just letting you know that getting in touch with me while I live here will be more difficult than when I was in Takana. Mail only arrives twice a week. There is no phone. You could phone Father Ignatius at the Jesuit school in Takana if there is an emergency, and someone would wire me at the post office here in town. Know that you and Mom are in my thoughts and in our prayers (we all pray together). It is so beautiful here in the mountains. The town of Chuqiyapu is heaven on earth!!! You would love it here, Dad. Please ease Mom's concerns and assure her that I am enjoying my experience and independence here in Chuqiyapu.

Love, Kara

*

Except for the older people, and some of the women who spoke only Aymara, almost everyone I met in Chuqiyapu spoke Spanish. Many of the older generations did not read or write Spanish and the majority of those who were literate were men. I learned that many women of the earlier generation had not gone to school beyond the first or second grade. It was mind boggling how many women in *Chuqiyapu* were illiterate. For those who could read, the Holy Bible was the primary text they read.

Chuqiyapu's education system didn't offer the best opportunities for learning, although classes from kindergarten to high school were available. With teachers and supplies hard to come by on a regular basis, weeks would go by when young people had to make do on their own. The schoolhouse would be empty for long stretches of time; young teachers would travel to Takana for a holiday and extend their stay for as long as they liked because there was no supervision, and many young teachers were openly unhappy about the conditions in which they were working. Young people wanting to continue studies beyond grade school would often have to travel to Takana with or without their family. On rare occasions, private schools such as Ignacio Loyola offered scholarships to students from families in mountain villages.

Those children not studying in a classroom would herd cattle and tend sheep and llamas or do domestic chores for their families. Given the condition of the school system, who could blame them? Nature was ripe with lessons for the children, many of those not considered in the classroom. Most of the people in this region were *campesinos* who rested their livelihood on *las chacras*, farms situated on high-terraced terrain on the mountain walls. Farming techniques handed down from their Incan ancestors continued to inspire their work. *Campesinos* rose before the break of dawn to walk to their *chacras*. This might take hours, and for some the hike was undertaken four times a day as many returned to their houses for midday meals. After *almuerzo* or lunch, they would return to the fields until sunset. All of this was done on foot and their work was accomplished with hoes and hand tools as machinery wouldn't work on the narrow terraces.

As the cattle center of the region, Chuqiyapu supplied much of the meat and cheese to the Takana province. This also meant that the finest meats and cheeses were shipped down the mountains to larger towns such as Barata and Takana, leaving slimmer pickings for families in Chuqiyapu. The main staples of their diet were primarily corn, potatoes, and broad beans. Milk was not readily available to drink because it was used to make cheese. The earth's gifts have sustained them for generations.

*

I wished I had packed a few more English books for life in the mountains; as a voracious reader, I exhausted two romance novels and a *Rough Guide of Perú* after the first five days and was left to scout the premises of the parish for reading materials. It made sense that the Holy Bible was everywhere but I wanted other reading material too—the Bible didn't feel like entertainment. Even Takana, a decent-sized city, had noticeably less access to books, especially in English, than I was accustomed to in the States. I was still working my way through *Los Rios Profundos*, the Spanish book I had begun several months earlier. It would take some time before I could read a book in Spanish with ease. In the mountains, schools had no books to loan, and there were no libraries or bookstores in town. The parish selection of books was a far cry from Benton University's library—one of my favorite places to hang out when I was a college student. The shelves in our shared room in the parish residence held biographies of Mother Teresa, Dorothy Day, Henri Nouwen, Jean Vanier, and Pope John Paul II, as well as several versions of the Bible and the mother of all cookbooks, *The Joy of Cooking*, first published in 1931and which my mother had a copy in her kitchen in Boston. I had expected there would be a copy of *Sor Juana Inés de la Cruz en la cocina*, or her biography, but to my surprise the book was not there. I had read that this seventeenth century Mexican nun had been a remarkable poet and writer who had her own library of four thousand volumes in the convent of Santa Paula. It made me wonder where the Sisters stood on women in the Catholic Church. Perhaps Sor Juana's book wasn't on the shelf because of her criticism of misogyny and the hypocrisy of men. How nice it would be if such a book sat on the shelves of every convent.

The parish office at Santo Domingo stored all sorts of publications, mostly in English, having to do with the Catholic Church and the Sisters' pastoral work. Many copies of one non-religious publication were stacked on top of the bookshelf. When I saw the title—*Dónde No Hay Doctor: a Guide for Campesinos That Live far from Medical Clinics*—it struck me as an essential book to have on hand in a remote town. I took immediate interest in the book, not only because it was one of the few Spanish books in the house, but also because it would be useful to me and the people in town with whom I would soon be engaging. With little medical assistance nearby, it was essential reading to stay healthy. I put a copy aside for myself to study later while I continued browsing the shelves.

There were missalettes and songbooks in Spanish and English versions standing beside dictionaries and handbooks. The handbooks spelled out the rules and policies of the Catholic Church. One entitled *The Obedient Ones: A Handbook for Our Sisters of Our Lady of the Angels* caught my attention. Thumbing through the table of contents, I stopped at Chapter 8: On Sexuality. The chapter on sexuality most likely would pique the curiosity of any twenty-four-year-old woman. It sure grabbed mine. Before thumbing through the chapter, I looked over my shoulder to make sure none of the Sisters were in sight. I stopped on a page that read: "Masturbation is sinful….and one must refrain from the urge to perform this act at all costs." Masturbation was a normal part of my life and had become even more so since I arrived in Perú — I hadn't been with a man for over two years. Truthfully, I had never seen the word in print before, and certainly had never heard masturbation referred to as a sin before. *Oops! I am going to hell! I thought. I am not sure I could follow this rule book. I mean, do the nuns follow everything in it? Is this what it means to be "obedient"? Who made these rules anyway? Did the Sisters of Our Lady of the Angels follow this handbook to the tee? And if so, could I? Why does the Church deny we are sexual beings?* Much of what I read in the manual felt unnatural.

I put it down, unable go on reading that garbage. I returned it to the shelf, being very careful to make sure it was in the exact place where I had found it. I felt self-conscious, as if all the Sisters knew my secret and were judging me. Then I felt somewhat embarrassed, although I knew in my gut there was nothing I should be ashamed of. I retrieved *The Joy of Cooking*, made a brief detour to pick up *Dónde no hay doctor*, and went back to my room with the two books. Still in disbelief, I shifted gears to something productive, burying myself in recipes in preparation for the evening meal.

*

After several years living in Perú, being alone no longer felt as lonely; in fact, silence felt comforting. On my long walks to and from villages in the mountains around *Chuqiyapu*, my sense of God's presence grew larger. It snuck up on me in nature, in the sounds of birds, the animals, and while gazing upon *Yanajaja*, and its two siblings whose snow-capped volcanoes painted the majestic landscape. I felt it in the well-kept green terraced pastures and in the worn hands and smiling faces of the Andean people, and close proximity to the mountains, sun and sky. I was no longer impressed by letters from home boasting about a friend's new job or business on Wall Street, an engagement to a real "catch" or a down payment on a first mortgage. That lifestyle seemed far away from my new life, and those life choices no longer fit mine. News of friends back home became less and less important to me. I often skimmed friends' letters and threw them in the trash bin. As harsh as it sounded, the contents seemed trivial, and materialistic in comparison to the lifestyle of the people in the Andes. I buried myself deeper in solitude as I found it difficult to explain the conversion I was going through,. Attempting to capture the essence of my life, I scribbled the words *a profound encounter with God's universe* in a journal entry. I doubted any of my college friends or family back home would understand so I kept the words to myself.

125

love and prayers, Kara

Chapter 10
Nueva Familia

Within weeks of my arrival, there were new members in the parish household. *Una nueva familia*. Australian priest Father Ryan O'Brien, who would serve the parish for four or five months, joined us soon after I moved in. I noticed how handsome he was…for an older guy with graying hair. He was so tall and so white that the people were astonished and a bit frightened of him. I imagined it wouldn't be long before he nursed a bad sunburn. He didn't speak much Spanish, and since he was fifty-eight years old, I thought the chances were slim that he would become fluent during his tenure at the parish. But he was kind and an inspiration to everyone in the residence. He walked everywhere with his Spanish books and dictionary tucked under his arm, studying a little bit each day. An avid marathon runner in Australia, Father Ryan ran several miles a day, not an easy task in the high altitude where the air is thin! I never heard a cruel word leave his mouth. Living with six women in the convent would prove to be tough, as would his limited language skills.

The household also increased with the arrival of two young women from Puno, an Andean town on the border of Lake Titicaca. Their exact motive for leaving Puno wasn't clear but it was obvious that the Sisters were anxious to have Fidela and Hilda join the order—they had good potential and showed signs of promise as new postulants. Fidela was sixteen years old, and Hilda eighteen, although both seemed older, physically, and spiritually. They were perky, intelligent teenagers with experience working in a Catholic parish in *el altiplano* on the shores of Lake Titicaca. Both girls came from working extensively with women and Christian groups near Puno. According to Hilda, they taught women rights and leadership skills to a non-Spanish speaking illiterate population. It was clear why the Sisters saw them as perfect candidates for their religious community. But I wondered what was the appeal for Peruvian women to live with Australian and Canadian nuns? I mean, besides a devotion to God. Was it their mission? Was it a way out of a life of hardships and poverty? Was it the community of women? I wasn't sure. The Sisters would say it all depends on one's "calling." I had to move to a larger room and share it with Fidela and Hilda. It was cramped but not unbearable. I didn't know much about the girls' families or lives or why they had moved to Chuqiyapu, but I hoped that they, too, would trust me with their stories as we got to know each other better. It also gave me an opportunity to gain insight into the Andean culture and people by learning from the girls. I wondered what Fidela and Hilda thought of me. We were so different.

love and prayers, Kara

April 1988

Dear Mom and Dad,

I am writing from beautiful Chuqiyapu. Things are going well. The Sisters and I went out to some of the smaller pueblos surrounding the main town to conduct prayer meetings. I got to meet some people from each charming, unique village. Quilljuana, Doña Juana, Chumpe, Yamata, Yuchami. Totora, St. Pepe, Jirafa, Poquilla. I love the long list of names — maybe I'll get them all straight one day.

I recently discovered Chumpe, which is about a forty-five minute walk away from our parish. Most of the population in Chumpe is young — couples in their early thirties have several kids. They look a lot older than they are, their skin weathered and tough from the sun. I imagine the women are in great shape from all the hard work they do, although one can't tell what's under the multilayered, full skirts called polleras they wear. Everyone looks plump and healthy. I met with some of the young women to discuss how we might use their wool in crafts and knitting. To my surprise the women don't know how to knit with knitting needles. They are gifted artisans with wool and weave on looms, but this method would be new to them. So I agreed to teach basic knitting skills. The basics it will have to be since I am no whiz at knitting.

I have not done very much yet since I arrived in the mountains partly because everything takes so long here and also because our Jeep has been having trouble — heck it always seems to have issues! I have visited the nearby villages, but most take over two hours to get to by foot, and some are as much as six hours one way. Being the spoiled gringa that I am, all this is so challenging — the transportation issue, having to be okay with not doing anything for a day or two or more, etc. I am so impatient. Of course, the people here think I'm silly — they are always walking from village to village. At times they hop on the back of a cattle truck going to or from the roads leading to the coast or to Puno and Lago Titicaca and jump off in pueblos as needed along the way. It amazes me.

Another challenge here is learning to live in our community. After living alone, isolated really, for two years in Takana, I find it tough. Then again, the company is nice. Fitting in with the needs and requests of others is difficult, and there are religious community rules to follow and prayer meetings to attend. I must cook for five other women which feels like work because I don't really like cooking. Thank God I don't have to do it every week – we have a rotating schedule. After the ordeal is over, I feel good that I have contributed in a positive way to the community. Unfortunately, my meals are not always a positive experience for others. My cooking skills are lame and often the food I put on the table is terrible. It's embarrassing. It fills everyone up and keeps them healthy but I won't win any awards for my dishes. I rely on The Joy of Cooking for tips. We need a lot of calories here in the mountains, so I boil lots of potatoes. At least, no one will get ill from my dishes. No one has been brave enough to tell me the truth about my meals, but the expression on their faces says it all.

I finally got a letter from Mercedes in Takana. You might remember her from my Ignacio Loyola days. She was the only other female teacher in the high school. She says that her family misses me a lot. I miss them too. Nice to know that those friends and experiences in Takana were meaningful. I am sure you miss me as well. Don't worry, before you know it, I will be home. Hmm, what would you do if I fell in love with a Peruvian.

Love, Kara

There was a bit of tension in our parish household, as is to be expected with people from different backgrounds and with different personalities and needs. We also had challenges with communication. Only Fidela and Hilda spoke Aymara fluently, so no one in the house ever spoke it to them but I noticed that they had side conversations in their own language. It made me wonder what their impressions were of the foreigners in their midst and what they said about us. As for Father Ryan, he was completely lost when we spoke Spanish in the house but we often spoke a mixture of Spanish and English. Living in a trilingual household was bound to produce some misunderstandings, and it did, but we also sorted them out.

The fresh air, slow pace and friendly residents of the town were good for our health and wellbeing—mountain life was healthy, and the earth provided well for most of the families in our parish. The fresh mountain air and natural foods, some grown in our backyard and some from our neighbors' *chacras* were abundant and kept us all healthy. Despite certain hardship and challenges, all of us were happy. We walked several miles a day doing our visits between villages. I loved accompanying families to the fields to make cheese; it was great exercise. We gardened each morning, we grew our own vegetables, and we washed clothes by hand. I was early to bed at eight-thirty in the evening with the kerosene lantern burning and up at five o'clock in the morning for morning prayer. The silence was awesome and intense.

I attended most prayer meetings with the Sisters at the break of dawn but would skip the daily prayer meeting in the evening. I never loved going to prayer meetings, though. The morning frost deterred me. But not only the cold discouraged me. I wondered why the prayers were only read from the

Catholic prayer books as these prayers seemed to lack emotion, spontaneity, and personality. Their formality and monotonous boredom lulled me back to sleep and I found it difficult to start my day in that manner. I never heard the Sisters talk to God straight from their hearts—Instead everything was scripted. *Who wrote the prayer books?* I wondered. For me, prayer was like talking to God about what's up in life. Like the weather, my moods would fluctuate. Some days I was happy, and other days I felt kind of sad or confused. But when I prayed from the heart, I always felt heard regardless of knowing by whom. Sometimes I would address my thoughts or prayers to Julie, and other days I would talk and listen to the natural wonders around me.

During morning prayers with the Sisters, we would pray for the people of Chuqiyapu in general, and for the congregation's benefactors, but there were never any names attached. Might it have been nice to call people by name? I was curious why Father Ryan never joined us in morning prayer so I asked him. He said that in the morning it was important to set oneself up for the day ahead. His way of doing this was to go for a run on the mountain trails. "I rather prefer starting my day in nature and with a conversation between God and me, alone. There is no agenda we must follow. This puts me at ease." I understood where he was coming from. I was so thankful for Father Ryan and the townspeople of Chuqiyapu who were teaching me about the importance of being down to earth.

Chapter 11
Word of God

"In the beginning was the word, and the word was with God, and the Word was God."

John 1:1−4

Father Ryan wore beautiful vestments, had taken vows, and had the power to change a piece of bread into the body of Christ, but he couldn't express his thoughts fully, nor fluently, in the Spanish language, let alone in Aymara. Heck, he could barely verbally communicate with the people he was meant to serve in this small Andean town. At one of his masses, he brought the congregation to their knees in a fit of uncontrollable laughter when he tried to explain in Spanish the importance of our "interior world." What he intended to say was: "One must tend to one's interior life, or inner landscape." What he said instead was, "*Tenemos que prestar atención a la ropa interior.* We need to pay attention to our underwear." When he recognized his mistake, his pale white skin turned to beet red which made the congregation laugh even harder. Santo Domingo parish was fortunate to have Father O'Brien commit to the parish for several months and the parishioners were, for the most part, convinced that this was an extraordinary opportunity. That is of course, if the priest had a good command of the community's spoken language.

But Father Ryan was honest about his shortcomings and he began to ask me to read the daily Scripture at Sunday Mass. Apparently living in the parish residence was reason enough for me to assist at the altar. It was a challenge to find literate parishioners for weekly Spanish Scripture readings so the duty often fell to Eugenio Quispe, the parish's caretaker and gardener who could read Spanish well. The Sisters also read Scripture at Mass. Everyone in the residence got their turn.

The truth of the matter was, though not a native speaker, I had the best command of the Spanish language in the house—I spoke it even better than most of the Sisters who had lived in Perú on and off for seventy-five years combined. Father Ryan granted me the privilege of speaking to the congregation, although there were days when I wondered if it was a privilege or not. The linguistic challenge was fun, and I was happy to help, but after the first few occasions when I agreed to fill in for the nuns and the priest, the requests continued and continued. In fact, Father Ryan requested my assistance far more than seemed appropriate.

This was part of what led me to be frustrated with the hierarchy of the Church and to conclude there were more reasons for a man to be a priest than for a woman to be a nun.

Priests were scarce in Chuqiyapu, even scarcer than doctors. Due to this lack, the Sisters carried out all the duties of a Catholic priest except for the mysterious consecration of the

love and prayers, Kara

Eucharist—a sacred task the Catholic Church said could only be performed by a priest. But I wondered, if the Sisters could run *la Parroquia Santo Domingo* and tend to the needs of the congregation, why did they need a priest at all? Couldn't nuns have the privilege of consecrating the host? What power was bestowed upon a man that the women could not possess? It reminded me of my childhood days when altar boys got to handle the precious paper-thin wafers, and girls were told we could not. Could the Sisters receive the necessary training needed to perform such a transformation if they wanted.

Every church parish kept a stash of consecrated hosts in a locked storage box to be used between the visits of the priests. The Sisters and I would store the Body of Christ behind the altar and would offer the wafers to the parishioners for weeks or months until another powerful man returned to perform the miracle again. In the absence of a priest, there were days when the Sisters had to corral people like sheep into the pews on short notice to have enough attendance. Sometimes only three or four nuns and a dozen locals attended, barely enough to merit running the generator to light the chapel.

As in other isolated, poor areas of the country, the priest's visit to town was a rare occasion so upon his arrival, the man of the cloth would offer Mass in place of the Sisters, no matter the day of the week. Parishioners were often more excited to attend Mass when a priest was in town, his title carrying a lot more might than the women of the Church. Even though the nuns made daily sacrifices for *los lugareños*, the Mass and the priest presiding over it mesmerized the parishioners, the mystery of the transformation of bread into Christ in the sacrament of the Eucharist dazzling the crowd every time.

But the visiting priest would go back down the mountain the day after Mass and the real work of maintaining the Church and the community's spirits intact would remain in women's hands.

I could care less if I got to consecrate a host or not, but the idea that a nun wasn't qualified or holy enough to do so really made me angry. Anyway, I could make a much tastier loaf of bread from scratch to entice the parishioners than the little tasteless wafers.

If my housemates were annoyed or unhappy about their position in the hierarchy of the Church, they never said so or did anything about it. Why were they complacent? It all came down to the vows of chastity, poverty, and obedience. But how happy were they with their decision? Did they really find satisfaction in the doctrines of the Church? The Sisters who were unhappy took their discontent out on others. This negative energy did nothing to promote the vocation.

Father Ryan cautioned me not to judge all nuns solely on my experience with *Parroquia Santo Domingo* in Chuqiyapu. He was right. Who was I to judge a woman's life choices or her commitment to God? It was hard enough for me to deal with my own choices.

One Sunday, Father Ryan begged me to prepare and give a homily. Offering an occasional homily in a Sister's absence was hard enough. It would be challenging and extremely uncomfortable to do while the priest was sitting at the altar with me. I felt somewhat uneasy speaking to the parishioners in the priest's place, like an impostor at the pulpit, and preferred to be in the pews with *los lugareños,* the residents. I wondered what right I had to give a sermon. Who was I to preach to these people? Why not Eugenio? Why not Fidela or Hilda? It was all very perplexing, but despite my discomfort and uncertainty, I took on the awkward role when needed. In my clear, American-accented but fluent Spanish, I shared a fair number of reflections on the Holy Scripture. No one knew at the time where my inspiration came from, perhaps not even me.

Father Ryan gave me complete freedom and never told me what to say, trusting in me and my ability. (Some of my harsh judgments towards priests began to soften in Father Ryan's presence; he was different, humble, I thought.)

The first time he asked me to preach, I said, "Okay but how...?"

His only advice was that I spend time reading the daily Scriptures, and then allow their message to come through me by listening deeply to silence. "Go off now into the mountains, Kara. There is nothing more sacred to the Andean people than the mountains," he said. "Just listen. Then you will be able to share from the heart."

"And what if I don't hear anything?"

"You will. You will, my dear."

He was right. Soon my understanding of Church, a sacred temple, shifted to a new perspective: being in the mountains, and in nature in general brought me closer to God. I was ready to listen to Nature's silence and respond accordingly. The mountains, animals, and sun kept me company in a way I had never experienced before in my life. The simplicity and quietness surrounding me made everything more vivid, more alive, and more real. I felt awake as never before, certain that the rituals that went on in the Santo Domingo Church were merely a fraction of a larger awareness of God.

On one of those long walks intended to enlighten my homilies, I caught my first glimpse of a majestic Andean condor flying above the hills at the precise moment that I needed inspiration. It was a big deal to spot a condor—not even all locals had seen one. With its ten-foot wingspan it appeared as a messenger from beyond, a symbol of immortality from the ancestors. The bird took my breath away. It was as though I was possessed by its spirit. I wrote ferociously and it offered me the words I needed. My hand recorded dynamic and meaningful sermons in Spanish that I would agree to give to Father Ryan to use as if they were his own. He delivered them week after week while I was his accomplice. Together we created quite the spectacle at the altar. It didn't matter who gave the sermons— what made them special was their place of origin and I was certain that, because of this, they would resonate with the Andean people who were the parishioners.

At Parroquia Santo Domingo, approximately thirty percent of the Chuqiyapu residents were on the books as parishioners. Whether or not they were true believers was debatable and not all attended Mass or parish meetings. Among them, Aymara was their mother tongue and copies of the Bible in their language were nowhere to be found. Non Spanish-speakers didn't understand what was being said at Mass, and those who understood Spanish held a healthy skepticism. I wondered: *what brought these people to Mass? How devoted could they be?*

love and prayers, Kara

However, there were true followers of Catholicism, and the Sisters were delighted to greet the same families week after week in the Church.

I dedicated hours in the evening, crafting sermons by kerosene lamplight, double-checking spelling and the use of words in certain contexts. Mass attendance grew and Father Ryan and the Sisters had me to thank for it but they never told the parishioners that I was the author. It would have been nice to be acknowledged for my work, but I didn't make a big deal of it. I was more than happy to contribute to my new family in this fashion. I put the words on a page, and I believed that I had received them from a spiritual connection beyond my control. What a privilege, I thought, to be a vessel through which the condor's message spoke.

In retrospect, I realize that, in part, I was smitten by Father Ryan. Was I too generous with my effort and time?

Father Ryan also asked me to translate his thoughts into Spanish. I agreed to do so but I preferred using my own words, and for the most part, he trusted in the power of my word. I loved that he trusted me. It often didn't matter what I wrote or translated; Father Ryan's Spanish understanding was limited, and his pronunciation was terrible and often incomprehensible. Somehow he would manage to plow through my handwritten scripts, and project his voice enough to be heard. People were respectful when he spoke although I could tell that some people were getting uncharacteristically impatient each time Father Ryan opened his mouth. To the Aymara-only speakers who attended Mass, the Spanish message mattered less. But they always grinned gently and benefited from the camaraderie of the gatherings. It took some time for Father Ryan to acknowledge my work, but he did in nonverbal ways with winks and hugs.

*

I gave my first condor-inspired homily from the pulpit in layperson's clothes. I trembled from nerves that day. I had been conditioned to believe that I—a woman and a lay person—didn't have as much to offer a congregation as an ordained priest. I hadn't put in the hours of training and hadn't taken vows. Chuqiyapu residents peered up at me expecting to see a man in full regalia. *What am I doing here?* It all made me recall my first stage appearance as the leading lady, Santa Lucia, in a play when I was just seven years old. I felt too small for the honor. Then I wore a long elegant white tunic trimmed in a gold ribbon around the neckline and the wrists. I carried a wreath of candles on my head. I remembered my fear that the lit candles would fall from my head and ignite a fire that would burn the school to the ground. I would be ashamed. But, of course, that never happened. When I finished my few lines, the school auditorium was filled with applause, the audience was on their feet.

That Sunday evening at the Santo Domingo Church, I felt too small for the role again. Though I wasn't dressed for the occasion, I stood at the pulpit, next to the altar, not a hundred percent sure of how I ended up there. But, there I was, Kara George Grey, about to give a sermon to the congregation.

Suddenly I recognized a young woman sitting in the front pew beside Sisters Tricia and Margaret. I had to take a second look, but I was certain it was Julie. *What is she doing here?* The resurrected twenty-one-year-old woman had shown up to alleviate my doubts. It was the first sign in years that she still had my back. I mumbled, thinking that Julie, now with an invisible power, would hear my thoughts. *Do I have anything of importance to say?* "Yes, you do," she responded. Surely the silence, the mountains, the sun, and the condor had transmitted a message of importance. Julie was there to remind me that it was now my job to say it aloud, to share a message that would connect to wise, humble people who had graciously welcomed me into their home. At least I can speak Spanish well, I thought.

Eugenio approached the pulpit first and read from the holy book. I soon followed. There were approximately one hundred devout followers in attendance that day, a healthy number for the parish. It was evident that the parishioners expected to hear from the priest, not me that night; my appearance startled them. Father Ryan took a seat directly behind me in the only ornate chair in the church. Not everyone understood Spanish, but all had learned the Church's calisthenics—on their feet for the reading of the Holy Scripture, back on the rickety bench for my homily, and later to their knees waiting in prayer to receive the Holy Eucharist.

"*Buenas noches, amigos.*" I cleared my throat and straightened the paper I had written on. "It is not only through men in robes and white collars that God speaks. Men and women of the Church have no special powers" I said. "God speaks through ordinary people like you, and me.... and through nature. You know that better than any of us."

As I continued, parishioners seemed to be listening. The Sisters sitting in the front pew next to Julie (though they

141

couldn't see her) shifted their bodies to a new position. I had already gone off script.

"Don't doubt for a second that God lives inside of you, in your neighbors, the mountains, the animals, and the sun, the moon and the rain. I have learned more from nature, and from you, my dear friends, about God's grace than from any priest or nun obeying the Catholic Church.

I paused in silence and took a breath to calm my nerves.

"God resides in all living things. The mountain's embrace protects you from harm. The animals, your brothers, and sisters, provide food and clothing, and the sun gives you warmth on the most challenging of days. This wondrous universe is all the proof any of us needs that God's love is everlasting."

I looked down at my hands and noticed they had found one another in a prayer position.

"Finally, I will end by saying this: God is not found in a church alone, God is found within you. You, my friends, like the mountains and the sky are gods and goddesses."

I bowed before stepping away from the altar and headed toward the front row of the pew to join the others. When I sat down, Julie was no longer there. A young mother with a baby in her arms occupied the space. There was deep silence in the church. Then applause broke out.

After that evening, I felt empowered. I had been given the opportunity to stand in for the priest, and there was no way I would take vows requiring me to be less. Whether he knew it or not, Father Ryan had given me a great gift: I knew after my sermon that I'd never be a nun. After that evening, my connection to the families in Chuqiyapu grew more intimate than ever before. The locals continued calling me *Madrecita* Kara, Sister Kara, which I hated. I wasn't opposed to the word *madrecita* which literally means *dear mother*, it was the connotation that I was a nun that bugged me. "Call me Kara, *por favor*." But, of course, to most parishioners, I was just another white-skinned foreigner affiliated with the Catholic Church. It was my hope that my connection to the locals was somewhat different; we knew more about each other's lives than the Sisters ever would. I began to experience more *cariño*, affection, from the residents in town after my homily.

In contrast, I began feeling more disconnected from the Sisters of Our Lady of the Angels. My message was beautifully executed, its clarity and linguistic finesse evident to all, including Father Ryan, who gave me a "Bravo. Well done, my friend." All the Sisters were in attendance for my first sermon, yet none of them mentioned a word about the Mass or acknowledged my efforts. Perhaps they had misunderstood it, misinterpreted it? It was quite apparent that such a misunderstanding had nothing to do with a language barrier; my Spanish was clearer than it had ever been before.

*

Sister Margaret was also from Australia, a sixty-something, not particularly attractive woman. Even if the Order had permitted nuns to dye their hair or enhance their appearance in some fashion, she would have been ugly. Much of that had to do with her poor disposition. She was the most sheepish of all the nuns and because of this, no one, including other members of the community, ever knew what she was thinking or feeling.

She was very hard to read and rarely smiled. I often felt like I was walking on eggshells whenever I was speaking to her.

Winter was approaching; according to *los lugareños*, June, July and August were the coldest and harshest months in *la sierra*. In late May one could already anticipate an extremely cold winter. The wind and chill were already sinking into my bones. As temperatures dropped, life in Chuqiyapu got more difficult without heating in our house. In preparation and anticipation of the winter months in the mountains, I had bought a new winter jacket in Takana to keep me warm. Red was my favorite color and I wore it well. It looked great with my brown hair and eyes. One evening the heat from the potbelly stove wasn't enough to warm the room above the mid-forties so I came to the dinner table wearing my winter coat.

Sister Margaret was displeased. "Kara, red is the passion color. It is not appropriate to wear such bold colors around Father Ryan."

"I don't understand" I said. I had never heard anyone say this about a color. "Is there a problem?"

"My dear, I'm afraid there are many things about our way of life that you don't understand."

I was quick to respond in a somewhat defiant manner. "Well, this is my winter coat. Would you rather I freeze to death?" She brought the worst out in me.

"Don't be so dramatic," Sister Margaret said. "Please, go change and put something on more appropriate before the others arrive for dinner."

"I don't have anything more 'appropriate.' This is my winter coat."

144

"I suppose it will have to do, but I have warned you," Sister said.

I didn't have a response to that—the comment was ludicrous. Passion color? Seducing a priest was really the farthest thing from my mind. Sure, I was developing a close friendship with Father Ryan but that was because we spent hours together working on sermons and I was offering him collegial tutoring to improve his Spanish. That was all. This comment from Sister Margaret implying that I was a temptation or trying to seduce Father Ryan was nonsense. Not again, I thought. The warped ideas of the Church had followed me to the mountains too.

The Church had its problems with sexuality for sure: I had read the nun's handbook from their bookshelf months before. Although I had never spoken about its contents to the Sisters, all evidence led me to believe that they had not only read it but memorized every word and lived by the book. Nuns were not to acknowledge their sexuality. At least that was the case for Sister Margaret. I felt sorry for her. It was not clear what the issues around sexuality were for everyone in the household, and it was never talked about. However, it was clear that indulgence in the human body, sexuality and sex were frowned upon by the Catholics.

I wanted to celebrate my body through music and dance, and yes, I wanted to be touched and be held, too. How dare they make me feel guilty about my body! What kind of an environment was this for a young woman in the prime of her life and at the height of sexual exploration?

145

In time a nice friendship grew between Father Ryan and me. We offered one another the companionship of a non-Peruvian friend and a bit of sanity we could never find among the Sisters; their hearts were more available to the Peruvians than they were to the foreigners living under the same roof. There were too many taboo subjects giving the Order control over any possible inquiry they weren't willing to address. By contrast, Father Ryan sought out opportunities for engagement on any subject. We talked about our childhoods, our families, our past romances. He asked me about my dreams for the future. He was a normal friend and we talked about normal stuff.

It was a good thing that the Aussie priest was not present when Sister Margaret made the comment about "red" because he would have given the Sisters a piece of his mind—he, too, was growing impatient with the Sisters who had asked him to cover his legs when he went out for his morning runs. He was a sensible kind of guy, and very open-minded for a priest. I began to confide in him about many matters including my uneasiness regarding my status at the parish. I was thinking I didn't see a future for myself as a member of the congregation, that I wasn't sure that I wanted to be there but wasn't sure where to go either, that I didn't yet see my next move. One might imagine they'd find love and acceptance in a convent, but instead I felt judged and inadequate in the eyes of the nuns. Father Ryan and the postulants who were my roommates provided the warmth I missed from friends and family back home.

But Sister Margaret continued to find fault with me. She picked on me for what seemed to be the silliest details, but to her they were serious matters. In the same mean-spirited way she had approached me before, Sister Margaret scolded me again.

"Those earrings are very long, Kara. They make a provocative statement," she said.

"I can assure you I meant nothing of the sort. My friend Mercedes in Takana gave them to me for my birthday. I think she made them herself," I said.

"We don't believe in wearing earrings in our congregation," she said.

"That's crazy. And…I am not in your congregation. I never promised anything to you."

"No, but you are living with us and are to follow our rules. And we wouldn't want the other girls to get the wrong idea," Sister Margaret said.

"Wait one minute here!" Father Ryan chimed in. "Leave this poor girl alone. She has done no harm. Frankly, I am appalled by your behavior towards your guest…and you call yourself a woman of God? Our Lady of the Angels? A woman of substance would not do this. You ought to be ashamed of yourself."

My roommates Hilda and Fidela were quite clever and never stirred up any trouble like I did. And in the Sisters' presence, they kept silent on all sexual matters. But I knew from our conversations that their silence was no indicator of a sheltered or chaste adolescence. The Sisters' desire to protect them was futile. They told me on several occasions of their

147

sexual encounters with men. Both had lost their virginity years before I had. If the Sisters knew half of what they shared with me about their experiences, good and bad, they never would have been invited to join the convent in Chuqiyapu. In the privacy of our bedroom, Hilda, Fidela, and I would shout, "We are all going to burn in hell." And then we would giggle ourselves to sleep.

Father Ryan lost his patience with the Sisters and boiled over. Not long after the earring incident, he wrote a note to my parents, alerting them to the fact that I was being treated unfairly by some of the Sisters of Our Lady of the Angels. Father Ryan's letter was written out of love and concern, but it shook up the Grey household, validating their ideas about the convent.

My whole family thought I was crazy for living with nuns. When I arrived in Chuqiyapu, I responded to my relatives' inquiries by asking them: "What would you do? Disown me?" I wondered what they hoped to save me from. Now I wondered whether they wanted to rescue me from bitter nuns. I would never admit to them—or to myself—that their concern had some merit.

Father Ryan took pity on me from the day he arrived. After he witnessed certain behavior from the Sisters, he took me under his wing. He was eager to show me a gentler side of the Church. Father Ryan thought his letter to my parents would be a kind gesture, but all it did was complicate matters, and add fuel to the fire. I knew it would which might be why he didn't ask for my consent before sending it.

Soon after Father's letter was received in the States, my mother composed a brief note and dropped it in the mail. A personal note from my mom was quite unusual; all the letters she sent when I was living in Takana were signed *Love, Mom and Dad* and their contents only shared mundane details of suburban life. I hadn't heard from her since I moved to Chuqiyapu. However, she responded to Father Ryan's letter. She made no mention of the incident addressed in his note, but it was evident that something triggered her letter and it was the first I knew that Father Ryan had written to my parents. I was disappointed that my mom's note didn't ask how I was doing or how things were in my new life in Peru.

Dear Kara,
I think you are making a huge mistake with your life by joining a convent. Motherhood is an experience you do not want to miss.
Love, Mom.

To be honest, I wasn't sure what to make of her abbreviated note. Rarely in my life had she shared her thoughts or feelings about marriage or motherhood. What was I to make of this now? She was worried her daughter might make the wrong life decision, but it wasn't hers to make. Maybe what I needed from her was something like: "I love you very much regardless of the choices you make. I trust you will do what is best for you. I am always here if you need me." I was no dummy—I had my own reservations about joining a religious order, however, regardless of what my mother thought, I had to make my own decisions. As for motherhood, I didn't know yet if I wanted to get married or have children of my own. I wasn't opposed to the idea, but I just wasn't about to be shamed into deciding what I might regret. Did I have to marry and give birth to a child to prove my worth as a woman? Perhaps my mother's options were limited when she was growing up, but I knew, deep in my heart, that mine were not.

love and prayers, Kara

Chapter 12
Women's Work

I decided that I wanted to form a women's group in the villages on the outskirts of Chuqiyapu, inspired by the women's *Arpillera* movement in Chile. In Chile, poor women and women whose husbands, sons or brothers had been killed or imprisoned by the government met each week around crowded tables in one-room workshops on the outskirts of the capital city, Santiago, where they shared their burdens and stitched small but meaningful tapestries. These brightly colored patchwork scenes were called *arpilleras*. They chronicled of the life of the poor and oppressed in Chile in the 1970s and 1980s during the totalitarian military regime of General Pinochet. I envisioned creating a sewing group with a similar mission. The women's movement was gaining some awareness and momentum in Perú, a country that had its own share of disappearances and injustices. Peruvian women's voices needed to be heard as well.

It was an ambitious undertaking and I had the skills and drive to start these workshops in villages outside of Chuqiyapu but I wasn't sure how culturally receptive the community would be to a white gringa. Fortunately I had my Aymara roommates, Hilda and Fidela, to lead the way. Without the girls, I would be an awkward American do-gooder stumbling to connect. I knew little about the lives of these women, and it was doubtful that the women in our classes would really trust me. Many of them hadn't learned to speak Spanish fluently, Aymara being their first language. Fidela and Hilda spoke both languages. They were also experienced traditional weavers, as well as incredible knitters!

At first, the Sisters were not so keen on our idea; they preferred that we not blur the lines between the Church's teachings and other kinds of outreach, but we moved ahead with our plan anyway.

It took a few months to organize, but with Fidela and Hilda's help, I started a small women's group in the small village of Chumpe on Saturdays. We began by offering knitting classes — it made sense because the women already had a history working with wool and they had expressed interest in learning how to knit. I saw the creative classes only as a pretext for a larger agenda for the women — to educate them about their rights, encourage them to learn to read and write in Spanish, and ultimately develop powerful voices, an agenda that would require more commitment than making garments. Gradually, after meeting for weeks, and growing trust was established, we would share the mission of the *Arpillera* Movement. Chilean *arpilleras* were more than art forms; they served as documents and denounced oppression in a community where all normal channels of free expression were closed. What did the women in Chumpe need to document? What losses and injustices needed to be voiced? Fidela, Hilda, and I wanted to find out.

To be honest, it was my new Aymaran girlfriends who did most of the teaching. For days, Fidela, Hilda, and I stayed up late at night to study new stitches that we would soon share in Chumpe. We had a lot of fun together. At the start we used the skeins of yarn I had purchased in Takana. But Hilda took it further, shearing llamas and alpacas, washing their wool, and making thread.

Prior to class, we experimented with fabrics, and worked long hours making *arpilleras* in our room at the parish house so that we would have samples to show the women during class. We followed the standards used for Chilean *arpilleras* to start. Our samples were the size of a large placemat, a rectangle of about fourteen inches by eighteen inches, but later smaller and larger ones were made as well. I was a pretty good sewer; I had grown up around fabrics, threads and sewing machines, and had even sewed my own senior prom gown. Everything I learned about sewing I learned from my mother and grandmother who were fine seamstresses. Both women made most of the clothes they wore on their backs, and they even made their own wedding gowns.

Hilda's craftsmanship had more to do with how she saw life and the world than with her sewing talents. Nothing was wasted. Every remnant of fabric had its unique place in the tapestries. She also had excellent technique and a natural design sense. Our initial themes for las *Arpilleras* were neutral. The girls and I agreed that although the tradition of *la Arpillera* was one of protest, our samples would celebrate Andean culture rather than reflect a societal or political issue or demand. We did, however, stick to the same techniques used in Chile.

Hilda's landscape depicting Chuqiyapu was spectacular, a perfect sample for providing inspiration to our new students. She depicted the town as if she had been born and raised there—not even a photograph could have captured the colors and textures, and expressed the emotion of a place whose name meant *peace* like her *arpillera* did. I was convinced that Hilda's keen observation of the natural world around her was why she achieved such perfection in her tapestry. The rectangle was laid out in perfect symmetry. Blocks of varying colors and textures of fabrics divided the landscape in such a way that the viewer saw depth and distance in a flat space. She chose flowered patterns and selected fabrics for their grass-like quality. The infamous snow-capped peaks were sewn onto the Yanajaja volcano. On the right side of *la arpillera*, she attached sheep cut out of a white piece of faux fur. She constructed three fabric dolls, each wearing black felt cowboy hats. Front and center in the tapestry were two dolls dancing (most likely at the *Huayno o Carnaval*). The piece was finished off with a crocheted border of wool and a pocket stitched to the back. The pocket was large enough for a piece of paper bearing her signature and the date. All women's work was signed. Hers read: Hilda R. Ancota, Chuqiyapu, 1988.

The ladies attending our classes were supplied with fabrics and thread and were asked what themes they wanted to illustrate. If they didn't have time to complete their work during the meeting, they would continue sewing at home. Few found extra time to finish their *arpillera* at home. The workshop grew to fifteen attendees. Some of the women's work depicted the celebration of *Día de Santos*, and others were simple landscapes with beloved animals. In time, women would tackle a second tapestry, and through an artistic design express disapproval or silent protest. The women in the group were illiterate so visual expression was a powerful means to convey sentiments.

As the women worked, they spoke in Aymara, their mother tongue. Fidela and Hilda joined right in, but, even though I might have wanted to be part of the fun, I stayed in the dark as I didn't want to give either of the girls the burden of translating. It was not that the women couldn't speak Spanish fluently — most of them could — but they were more at ease with one another speaking Aymara and that was important. I understood this comfort from my earliest days in Perú. Falling into conversation in my mother tongue was refreshing after struggling to make sense in Spanish. I accepted the fact that here in the Andean mountains I would always be an outsider, and despite feeling pangs of isolation, I acknowledged what a blessing it was to be in the presence of these women. I took joy in that alone. Fidela and Hilda had taught me some basic words in Aymara. I felt it essential to greet the women upon arrival and departure in their mother tongue. All the women appreciated my effort.

"*Kamisaraki?*" I said.

"*Waliki, jusphajaraña.*"

They responded and giggled at the sound of my American accent and my attempt at pronouncing the Andean language which sounded nothing like Spanish.

One Saturday after the group had been gathering for about two months, one of the husbands came to see what his wife and the group was up to. He smelled of alcohol and his gait was off. He was not pleased with the gathering.

"*¿Qué ideas están poniendo en la cabeza de mi mujer?*" He insinuated that strange ideas were being planted into his wife's head.

"*Nada*. We are sewing and knitting, nothing more," Fidela said.

"Look, I know what you're doing. *La gringa*...her ideas...from her country...women think differently in the United States..."

The man insisted that his wife leave the meeting and go back to their house to prepare a meal. There was little that Fidela, Hilda or I could say as he tugged at her arm. I was in a more vulnerable position to respond as I was the unwelcome American in the man's eyes and his angry tone was directed at me. I remained silent and hoped to avoid a physical altercation. *Was I corrupting the minds of the women?* The classes offered camaraderie and gave the women what was sometimes their first opportunity ever to express themselves. The woman, Elenita, gathered her belongings and left with her husband.

In her haste, Elenita accidentally left behind her second tapestry. When the group looked at it, we all agreed it was disturbing. The background was the idyllic Chuqiyapu countryside but in the center panel, she had sewn two fabric dolls, one female and one male, the male on top of the other in what appeared to be a brawl. The face on the delicate doll on the bottom was in distress, while the man on top had raised his

156

arm above her. At first I thought maybe I was reading too much into it, but others in the class were quick to confirm what I saw. How Elenita was able to capture such emotion in her *arpillera*, we couldn't say but we all understood. Elena never returned to another class.

I did other work in Chuqiyapu. I also had the opportunity to accompany the Sisters as they traveled to organize religious meetings in other towns. One time, I walked with Sister Tricia to Yanajaja where she had been called upon to bless a new church.

As we walked, we talked about the emerging liberation theology movement that was beginning to take hold in Perú and activists had trickled into rural communities. The movement had started in Lima by a Peruvian Jesuit named Gustavo Guiterrez. It sought to empower Christian leaders among poor communities, giving them a voice among their people. The movement also encouraged people to apply their religious faith by aiding the poor and oppressed through involvement in political and civic affairs. In these groups the people were able to question and interpret the Bible. I hadn't seen these groups in our parish or heard the Sisters talk about it, but it made sense to me. In my mind, whatever devotion *los lugareños* had to the Bible, it ought to be lived out on their own terms. They understood their needs better than anyone.

But I hadn't seen a woman leader in the liberation theology circles. Most women were not able to read and write in Spanish, the language used by the Catholic Church to dominate their town, and lives. They were proficient in their mother tongue, but it was seldom written down. Even among the liberation

157

theology circles with their emphasis on the poor interpreting the Bible for themselves, literacy mattered, and excluded women so that their devotion could only be blind faith.

Because of the distance to Yanajaja, Sister and I spent the night in Quillijuana at the home of the Cabral family. Their home had three adobe rooms, each with sparse furniture, and a kitchen with a gas stove and table. They cleared out one of the rooms for us. Although most clutter disappeared, we bunked with caged chickens, hens, and I think guinea pigs. Two goats roamed the space. The family gave us a stack of wool and alpaca blankets for the night. We slept on the bare floor with our coats on and it took five or six blankets to keep me warm. With the weight of the blankets on top of me, I could barely move, but I adjusted and became comfortable.

Soon after we fell asleep, we were woken by the commotion of the family in our space. One of their goats had gone into labor. (I hadn't noticed that any were pregnant.) Within minutes of waking, Sister Tricia and I witnessed the birth of three goat kids. One died instantly, because of the cold, we were told. *La Familia* Cabral was more prepared for the births of the second and third kids. Without hesitation, they grabbed the blankets from our makeshift beds and wrapped the kids in them as soon as they emerged from the mother. The stillborn was wrapped in another blanket. Then, the newborns were brought into another room of the house. Los Cabrales built a small fire on the dirt floor out of the sides of a cardboard box. The room became toasty and agreeable. It was amazing to see the birth of these animals, but then to watch this family orchestrate the emergency recovery of the fragile newborns was even more impressive. One little kid was so weak, I thought I would see a second death but the children rubbed it for several minutes until it breathed on its own. The family was delighted. Cabral children held the kids in their arms. Together they had pumped life back into these two frail animals as if they were one of their own flesh and blood. The father stepped outside. He returned with the mother goat and led her indoors to join the rest of us. The babies sucked their mother's milk for the first time. The family's attitude towards the birth and death of these animals amazed me. It seemed commonplace. They so naturally shared their living space with their animals as if they were relatives or neighbors. It was a special moment for me. All 1 could think of was how back at home in the Boston suburbs we hid behind fences and walls, dividing ourselves even from other humans.

love and prayers, Kara

Chapter 13
To See with One's Eyes

When many families in Chuqiyapu and surrounding towns began getting infected and severely sick with tuberculosis, at first I did not grasp the concern among the nuns about its spread in the villages as well as possibly into the parish house. Tuberculosis was not a threat back in the States, at least not in my circles. I had been immunized against typhoid and hepatitis before flying to South America but tuberculosis was new to me so I needed to do more research. I pulled out *Dónde no hay doctor*, the medical guide I had borrowed from the parish office and found some helpful information in Chapter 14: Serious Illnesses that Without Fail Need Medical Help.

I learned that tuberculosis was quite common in under-developed countries, and it required immediate attention. According to medical definition, tuberculosis (TB) is caused by a bacterium called mycobacterium tuberculosis that usually attacks the lungs but can attack any part of the body such as the kidney, spine, and brain. Not everyone infected with the TB bacteria becomes sick. While not curable, there were treatments for TB but if not treated early and properly, TB can be fatal. TB

161

is highly contagious and the bacteria are spread through the air when a person with TB coughs, speaks, or sings.

After my research, I understood the potential danger I faced if exposed to infected people, especially in the poor communities I frequented. I tucked my copy of *Dónde no hay doctor* in my backpack and brought it everywhere I went. It was extremely helpful in explaining its threat to *los campesinos* and in describing the precautions they needed to take to stay healthy. I appreciated the illustrations in the book because the drawings clarified Spanish vocabulary I had not yet put to memory. In this I felt a kinship to the Aymaran population who, like me, still hadn't fully grasped the Spanish language.

The outbreak was an uphill battle. There was only one *posta médica* in town trying to track the disease and provide antibiotics to infected residents as soon as possible, and the battle was intensified by the fact that the clinic had only one doctor, *Doctora* Ana, who had been assigned by the Peruvian government to work at the clinic for a year. (In Perú, all doctors had to serve populations living in remote areas of the country immediately after graduation from medical school; that meant placing young, inexperienced doctors in *los pueblos jóvenes* on the coast, in mountain towns along *la Cordillera de los Andes* and in *la selva,* the jungle to work with underserved and hard to get to populations.) She alone was expected to serve the people in Chuqiyapu and three hundred surrounding communities. Ana told me that she hated being in Chuqiyapu—and unfortunately, her demeanor with her patients was proof of it—but she had no choice, and the villages depended on *Doctora* Ana's expertise.

Another obstacle in containing a tuberculosis outbreak was that it required early and ongoing treatment and diligence on the part of the infected patient to seek out and administer treatment. This often required patients without reliable transportation to travel long, demanding trips to other towns, or even all the way to the coast, when *la posta médica* ran out of medicine (which seemed to happen all the time) to deal with potentially fatal symptoms.

The first time I was exposed, I was caught off guard and at the time didn't grasp quite how contagious it was. Sister Flora asked me to accompany her to Totora to pick up Fernando Bustos, a middle-aged man exhibiting severe TB symptoms. Sister promised his family that she would transport Fernando to Barata, the nearest town that had a larger *posta médica* and more medical resources and staff. When I initially asked Sister why he needed to see the doctor, she said, "He has tuberculosis. He isn't doing well."

I was reluctant. "I am uncomfortable being in such close proximity to Fernando in the Jeep."

"No worries — he will be sitting in the back seat and we can crack a window."

Despite my well-founded fear of contracting the disease, my young naïvete, trust in Sister Flora, and my sense of duty to the Order outweighed my fears. I agreed to accompany Sister Flora, banking on my youth and health to protect me from the threat of the disease. A one-hour Jeep ride to pick up Fernando was a successful leg of our trip as I enjoyed Sister Flora's company a great deal. She was a sweet lady and cared deeply for the people of the parish. She was very knowledgeable about the villages surrounding Chuqiyapu as she had been one of the first cohort of nuns from the order of Our Lady of the Angels to resurrect the eighteenth-century church in 1970.

Totora was a village with a population of about five hundred. When we got there, Fernando Bustos's wife helped him into the back of the Jeep. The urgency to get Fernando to his treatments was clear: he was coughing up blood, his voice was hoarse, and his skin was as pale and waxy as a candle. Before we drove away, Sister told Fernando's wife to be sure to test the whole of the family for the disease.

Fernando's cough persisted during the road trip. I wondered if he was taking enough precautions to protect us from contagion. He would cover his mouth with the bend of his elbow covered with the sleeve of his wool, soiled sweater each time he coughed. Sister Flora and I weren't masked either. When Fernando first joined us, I opened my window to let in fresh air, but the air was freezing cold. As we moved closer to our destination, I played tug of war with myself as I raised the window to shield myself from the cold and lowered it to protect myself from germs.

All was going fine until the second-hand Jeep, notorious for being unreliable, broke down again in the middle of the *altiplano*. This had been bad enough when the same old Jeep left me stranded with Sister Tricia, but now Sister Flora and I were carrying a sick passenger. The good news was that it was earlier in the day the previous breakdown and the sun was still blazing hot so the cold chill of *el altiplano* didn't get the best of us. My first instinct was to jump out of the Jeep into the fresh air. It was a relief to be outside. Sister Flora looked under the hood of the engine; she knew more about car mechanics than I as it was essential for all the Sisters to know basic mechanics, especially as they relied on a used vehicle and often traveled between remote villages. Fernando was too ill to get out of the Jeep, no longer able to stand on his own.

Sister Flora was in good spirits. "A truck will be passing by any minute and will take us to Barata. I know Our Lord and Savior will make it so."

She tweaked some parts in the engine, but it didn't turn over. A truck did pass by but although the driver saw the raised hood of our Jeep, he did not stop to help. The driver shouted from the window, "*No puedo acomodarlos.*" He couldn't—or wouldn't—help.

Soon after this the sun went down. When the sun sets in *el altiplano*, especially in June, the temperature instantly plummets. The sun burns one's skin all day and within hours a thirty-degree drop below freezing can threaten anyone underdressed. We began shaking from the cold. Hours turned into more hours and no car or truck bailed us out. Sister Flora suggested the three of us pack into the backseat to find warmth from our collective body heat. We had one blanket between the three of us to share.

At first, I refused. "I am not going to sit shoulder to shoulder with a man that has tuberculosis."

"Fine," Sister said, "You have a choice to make: stay in the front seat and get hypothermia or take your chances back here with us."

After a few minutes, I gave in to the second option, sitting on one side of Sister while Fernando was on her other side. The night felt longer than usual. Sister Flora and Fernando fell in and out of sleep, but I couldn't. I was instructed to wake Sister Flora and Fernando several times during the evening so that they could leave the vehicle to keep their circulation moving.

We assisted Fernando to his feet for a few brief steps as he was weakened and incapable of walking on his own. Then I detached myself and proceeded to do a few jumping jacks on my own and took a few laps around the vehicle before returning to the backseat. Fernando had moved to the middle seat position—I wasn't sure if Sister planned the move because he was the most vulnerable but I felt displeased. I couldn't avoid contact with Fernando's shoulder in the car.

As the night wore on, Sister Flora joined Fernando in coughing fits. I grew more concerned and cracked my window but Sister instructed me to shut it. *My youth*, I thought, *will protect me, but Sister Flora is a sixty-something woman, with a weaker immune system and showing signs of decline*. In a matter of hours Sister Flora's conversation with God changed from confidence to despair.

"We must pray, Kara. Pray that someone passes by."

I wasn't sure my prayers had as much clout as the *Madre Superiora*, or if I believed they would make a difference but I humored Sister.

By the time dawn emerged, the Jeep had become an icebox; nothing was visible through the windows covered with ice on the inside. When the sun rose, the sheets of ice began to melt. At about six o'clock in the morning, we heard a truck approaching from a distance. I flagged it down, the others too weak to leave the Jeep, let alone frantically wave their arms. It stopped. The truck driver got out and lifted the hood to investigate the situation. In what seemed a miraculous movement, he jiggled just the right part to get the Jeep started. The man told us to be sure to find a garage immediately upon arrival in Barata.

"*Que dios te bendiga, señor,*" Sister Flora said, blessing the driver.

Until then, I had not driven the Jeep. I had no desire to do so, but in the circumstance we found ourselves in, I took the wheel. It turned out we had not been far from Barata when we broke down. We arrived at *la posta médica* within twenty minutes. I wasn't a stranger to the clinic — it was the clinic where I had spent a night with Sister Tricia. Fernando received his treatment and was met by extended family members who promised to reunite him with his wife and kids back in Totora once he felt stronger. Sadly, we later heard that Fernando never got stronger; he died in his cousins' home in Barata not long after Sister Flora and I left him in the clinic.

By the time we arrived back in Chuqiyapu, Sister Flora felt lousy. We were urged to get tested for tuberculosis immediately. Despite all my worry I managed to escape the disease. Had a higher power protected me? God? Sister Flora did not escape unscathed, however, and she left for the coast within days to begin treatment and recovery. About two weeks later, the Sisters of Our Lady of the Angels got word from Sister Flora that she would remain for several months in Ilo, a small port town to continue treatment and get much-needed rest and ocean air to help her breathe with ease again.

love and prayers, Kara

After almost six months, Sister Flora still had not returned to her assignment in Santo Domingo parish. One of the conditions of a life of obedience was the willingness to relocate as needed and with short notice to another mission or sometimes to another country. I couldn't imagine that Sister Flora had chosen to leave of her own volition as she loved Chuqiyapu and its people. I wrote to her, but if she responded, I never got the mail. When I asked the other Sisters about Sister Flora, I got several responses.

"You know how things are here — letters get lost in the mail all the time." Sister Margaret said. "Never mind about her, dear. She is still resting."

"She may have been assigned to another community. We'll keep you posted as soon as we know more," Sister Tricia said.

When I asked who would be taking charge of the religious community, Sister Tricia said she would be, for the time being.

I felt abandoned by Sister Flora. I never did find out where she had been relocated. This came as a blow to me for, of all the Sisters, Sister Flora was the most attentive and had shown the most understanding and kindness. *At least Sister Margaret won't be left in charge*, I thought.

Chapter 14
Memento Mori

Not by chance
Not by nothing did you pass
by me today
O pain
O day
O night
O death

The apparent threat of death grew more real. My first-hand experience with Julie's death now grew to include new friends and strangers. Since my arrival in Peru, I had witnessed the death of an abandoned child, Soledad, and then Fernando who had contracted tuberculosis. I learned that nothing would last forever. Death and loss were inevitable. Nature was my teacher.

After the evening spent in the altiplano with Sister Flora and Fernando, I was even more aware of the dangers and consequences of being exposed to tuberculosis, and I wanted to help prevent the rampant spread of the disease in the community.

I approached the young Doctora Ana to see if I might be of assistance at la posta médica in Chuqiyapu. Ana was a new acquaintance, a young woman and potential friend. Born in Lima, she had a decent command of English and was one of the few residents in Chuqiyapu to have a vehicle besides the Sisters.

I had thought I might visit patients in the local clinic but I found the place almost empty. The truth was that the residents of Chuqiyapu and surrounding towns rarely went to the clinic and, according to Ana, most patient care was done in people's homes. There was little work for me to do since I had no medical training to offer, so I helped *Doctora* Ana organize her medicine cabinets. The task took all thirty minutes; the shelves were abysmally stocked.

The next day, I returned to the clinic to find *Doctora* Ana packing a medical bag. She asked if I could join her on a few house calls; she said she would welcome the company. With some haste, *Doctora* grabbed her bag and jumped into her Jeep. The first stop, she said, was to visit *la familia* Aguilar in Yanajaja. The whole village of fewer than one hundred people shared the same surname. A pleasant, lighthearted bunch of families had recently lost a family member and were uncertain of the cause of death. *Doctora* Ana had her suspicions but needed to investigate. When we arrived at the house, the extended family offered us a warm welcome and led us to a body that had been dead for just under twenty-four hours. Doctora Ana asked me to wait in the Jeep until she assessed the situation. When she returned, she had a troubled look on her face. It made me unsettled.

"Is it serious?" I asked.

"Several family members are showing tuberculosis symptoms. They most likely have all been infected. I need to be certain."

"What are you going to do?"

"They are asking me to do an autopsy to confirm that the deceased died of TB. It seems like the right thing to do."

"Why?"

"I need to examine the body to confirm the cause of death and to see whether his treatment was effective...to determine the risks of the whole family becoming infected."

"You can do that here? In the middle of nowhere?"

"I have no choice. If it is tuberculosis, it is important to stop its spread in this village as soon as possible."

"But, I mean, *here*? Have you done an autopsy before?"

"In medical school. Obviously, in better conditions...but it's okay, I'll improvise." She looked over at me. "I will need your help."

"Me? How can I help? I've never done anything like this before!"

"You'll be fine. My advice to you: keep this bandana over your mouth and nose the entire time. It is going to smell bad and, you may have the impulse to gag."

Ana pulled another bag out from the back of her truck. This one was more like a toolbox. She removed a saw. "I will need this," she said.

My desire to help at the clinic didn't include seeing a dead body, let alone going inside one. I hesitated, feeling like a chicken. I thought to myself, *What am I doing here.*

"Are you coming?" Ana asked.

"Sure."

Doctora Ana began by drawing some sort of "Y" on the man's chest, marking the lines she would follow to cut the chest open. All doctors have the privilege of dissecting human bodies, but most of us go through life utterly estranged from the stuff we are made of, the bones, muscles, tissues, and organs common to all of us.

She explained as she went along. "I will need to break the chest bone and some ribs first to get into the chest cavity."

She motioned to a bystander and requested another pair of hands. "I need someone with a lot of strength," she said in Aymara. She meant physical strength, but I was thinking she meant the other kind, that inner strength that keeps you in the game when you want to get out. Luckily, a volunteer from the Aguilar family stepped forward. I knew that let me off the hook, at least for breaking bones. The helper was one of the dead man's brothers, they explained.

There were still jobs for me: I needed to hold the body in place and to hand Ana tools when requested. She was right: the stench was powerful, and I quickly became nauseous. *Is this what death smells like?* I thought.

"Are you okay, Kara?"

But I had already fled. As miraculous as our human body is, I didn't want to look at the insides of a corpse. I headed towards the vehicle, hoping to make it to the back of the Jeep before I puked but I only made it as far as the back bumper before lost my breakfast all over my boots.

I yelled to the doctor. "I'm fine," I said.

love and prayers. Kara

But I wasn't fine at all. That night after returning from assisting with the autopsy, I was physically and emotionally drained. I had just had my first encounter with a corpse, and it was shocking. I was not new to death, but I couldn't speak openly about it. I couldn't see the point in telling anyone in Perú about the loss of my best friend, Julie. It wouldn't bring her back. But I continued to search for ways to understand it. There didn't seem to be anyone in my new home with whom I had built enough trust to share my grief.

I returned from the trip with *Doctora* Ana after community supper had already been served and consumed. Leftovers sat on the stove. I was so tired I didn't even heat the food up before putting it on a plate. I was grateful that everyone had already eaten; I didn't want to talk about the day or answer the Sisters' questions about the details, the family, and the prayers over the body. I enjoyed the silence as I ate.

Then Father Ryan walked in. His presence was always welcome as was his warm smile and kind words. If there was anyone in the residence I wanted to see, it would have been him. He pulled up a chair beside me and placed his hand on my shoulder. His touch felt nice.

"How are you?" he asked.

"Exhausted. It was a crazy, long, challenging day."

"I can tell."

I appreciated how well Father Ryan was able to read people; it was one of many qualities he had that made him a good priest, and friend. Weeks earlier, he had said, "You can call me Ryan." When we dropped the formality of his title, we grew even closer.

love and prayers. Kara

"Are you sure you want to hear about my day?" I said.

"Was it that awful?" Ryan asked.

Looking down on the dead body that day had made me think about Julie. I was in my senior year when I skipped my classes and took public transportation to the hospital where she had been admitted near the city of Revere on the coast of Boston. Because I hadn't visited her in several weeks, I was frightened by what I saw; she was almost unrecognizable as she was swollen, pale and connected to tubes. Despite receiving chemo, her brain tumor continued to grow, and it affected all her bodily functions. It seemed so unfair; she was so young.

"I assisted *Doctora* Ana with an autopsy today. Seeing a dead body triggered the memory of the death of my best friend, Julie," I said. "I remember the last time I saw Julie as if it were yesterday."

"Oh, Kara. I didn't know," he said, "Do you want to talk about it?"

"Not really, but perhaps another day?"

"Of course. You can talk to me anytime, about anything," Ryan said.

"Thank you, I really appreciate that."

"How'd you like to take a stroll when you finish your dinner?" Ryan asked. "The stars are blazing tonight."

"That sounds nice," I said. "I'm almost done."

I went to the garbage bin, cleaned my plate, and rinsed it under the faucet. I grabbed a coat, my red one, and left the residence. We headed to the main town plaza. That night, no one was out strolling so we had the plaza all to ourselves. The stars were so bright we didn't need lanterns or flashlights. We sat on a bench in front of Santo Domingo Church. Ryan wrapped both his arms around me as if to shelter me from the cold. We sat there for some time in silence. His presence was comforting, and soothing, like balm on a sore limb. I loved being with Ryan. He was a middle-aged man with graying hair and bald spots, and, despite his morning runs, a bit thick around the waist. But, to me, everything about him was beautiful. His sunny personality and tenderness intensified my attraction for him.

For weeks the sexual chemistry between us had been building. I had denied it was there. *How could it be? He is a priest.* But the dam was about to break — our romantic attachment was undeniable. Now his touch filled my body with electricity, and I reciprocated by placing one hand on his thigh nearest to me. I was a bit shy, afraid to look at him for fear that I wouldn't be able to resist the temptation to kiss him. I kept looking away and up to the sky. Then, he took my face in his hands, turned it towards his mouth and kissed me on the lips.

love and prayers, Kara

Chapter 15
Pachamama

July 1988

Dear Julie,

The winter has been long, but warmer days and diminishing evening frost is on the horizon in a matter of months. El campo is beautiful. The mountains bring a tranquility that I would like to wish upon everyone, to my family, and especially those living amid a noisy city. Can I bring this peace back to the States? Early this morning I went to el campo with Catalina, Fidela, and Ryan to watch and learn how the locals make queso fresco. We eat this cheese every day but I got to see where it's from. I tended to the calves while the others milked the cows. Can you imagine? I wondered if these animals intuited that I am not from here, and that I'm not a country girl. Does it matter to the calves that I am American? Una gringa. That English is my first language or that I grew up in a suburb with an upper-middle class family? Until several months ago, I didn't care one bit about them or any animal or this family, who cares so deeply for them.

Then I got my turn at milking the cows! It was harder than I had ever anticipated – tugging on the udders took all my strength and no milk came out. When Catalina said, "Pull harder," I did, with all my might, and sprayed myself and everyone else in proximity with milk.

Ryan thought he'd learn something from me before taking a stab at it himself, and so he had just bent down over the scene to get a better look as I attempted to draw milk from the udders. I squirted him. Wham! I almost took his left eye out. I completely lost control of the udders and the milk went in all directions, soaking Cata and Fidela. Everyone laughed until our stomachs ached. I ran to tend to Ryan. I was careful not to show too much affection when I inspected his eyes for fear that the girls or Cata would pick up on our connection. Yes, it appears that there are romantic feelings brewing between Ryan and me. I know what you're thinking, a priest. Days later, his eye is still swollen from the impact of the milk.

Anyway, what did I know about making cheese? Nothing. It was a far cry from the Velveeta cheese brick my Grandma would pick up at the food pantry run by her church. That thing could have killed someone, and it was usually a bright orange yellow, not a color I have found here in the natural world. Did you eat it too? Making "real" cheese is easier than I thought, once one knows the secret ingredient: el cuajo, a liquid taken from the cow's intestine that hardens the milk. After buckets are filled with milk, a small amount of el cuajo, the coagulant, is poured in, and stirred. This mixture is then left to sit for at least twenty minutes while the milk coagulates. Meanwhile, more milk is being taken from other cows and the process continues. When coagulation is completed, molds made of woven totora (a common reed that grows in the altiplano) are placed on wooden boards and the thickened milk is dripped into the molds. The milk thickens for hours resulting in a hard, fresh mound of cheese. Cheeses are salted and stored back in the homes until they are ready to be shipped to Takana. They're white, not orange yellow.

I'm turning in now as I can barely keep my eyes open. It was a full and exhausting day out in el campo. I am grateful for the lessons.

Tomorrow Cata assures me that she and her family will teach me how to make el chuño, *the freeze-dried potatoes that all Andean people prepare and store in anticipation of a long cold winter in the coming year.*

I am not sure what to make of my friendship with Ryan now. We spoke little at dinner and retreated to our rooms early. This is a confusing time for me. Did I do the right thing letting Tom go? Will I marry someday? What does God or life want of me?

Love and prayers, Kara

*

What do Andean people have that allows them to live with such grace amid life's challenges and even despair? I wondered. *Is it their understanding and connection to the law of nature? Why has rural life become diminutive to folks back home in my suburb and city?* In *el campo* of Chuqiyapu, I saw incredible beauty and simplicity. It was not easy simplicity — life in the country was hard. But I envied aspects of it. I envied the relationship that the Indigenous people had with the earth, how they listened to and partnered with the seasons, knowing that reciprocity between them would result in a better life for all and for the planet. That is what their ancestors had taught them.

I was in awe of Cata, a mother, quiet leader in the community, a warm, wise woman everyone seemed to gravitate towards. She never spoke of a husband or the father of her children but this didn't matter to me; her grace was not diminished by it. She had been born in Chuqiyapu, as had family generations before her. She carried her name, Catalina Flores, with pride and dignity, exemplifying strength and respect to all who crossed her path. Walking to Catalina's plot of land at the break of dawn each morning took stamina and endurance (at least that is how it seemed to me) and then once she arrived, she would work hours, sometimes in harsh conditions and always some part of the day under a canopy of hot sun. Catalina had grown hide-like tough, dry skin on her hands and feet from years of exposure to cold and sun. After tending to outdoor chores, she would return to town, and prepare meals for the family. Her children were all old enough to fend for themselves, but when they were infants, she had carried them to *el campo* on her back wrapped in a handwoven wool *manta* thrown across her shoulders with finesse.

Despite the challenge of physical labor in the fields, I preferred it over the other responsibilities I had in *la parroquia* and looked forward to my excursions with Catalina. The contrast between being in town and in the fields was like that between suffocating and breathing. I was free in nature. Nature had its own rhythm and in time, it became mine as well. It slowed us down. Cata showed the way, moving with ease through each day. I loved every moment spent with this peaceful woman. She had a pleasant disposition and I felt at home in her presence. Her smile and laughter were as warm as her handwoven blankets. The long black braids that fell to her buttocks were tied together and tucked under her cowboy-like hat so as not to interfere with the work done with her strong hands.

She was a nurturing mother and caretaker of her kids and her animals. She was hardly old enough to be my mother, but she had the tenderness I longed for from mine. Her seven-year-old daughter, Saida, often accompanied me and her mother to

love and prayers. Kara

el campo for daily chores, but there were days when Catalina insisted that Saida go to school. Saida would kick and scream in opposition. Occasionally, Cata would suggest that I go with her daughter to school; that seemed to calm the child down somewhat. Her mother's intuition was always spot on, so Saida and I made the trek a few times. Catalina hadn't attended school past the second grade, and she could not read or write. Her Spanish was understandable. Perhaps because of her lack of formal education, she had decided that she wanted life to be different for her kids, especially her daughters. "They ought to have the education I didn't," she said. So, while she wasn't encouraging her son Edgar and her oldest daughter Maruja to leave Chuqiyapu for Takana, she did support their dedication to schoolwork in the home. Somewhere on the horizon, books and schooling were inevitable for the youngest daughter, but Saida was not the least bit interested.

As I had seen, schools in *la sierra* were inadequate. Unlike the private Jesuit school, Colegio Ignacio Loyola, in Takana, this small two-room schoolhouse in Chuqiyapu had been neglected. Students of all ages, and in first through sixth grades, shared one room. Some families placed little emphasis on formal education. For those still hoping to pursue academics beyond elementary levels, there was a second room for a few older students. There were few older students in the schoolhouse; most teenagers left the mountains for the city of Takana to study, or search for street work in the city. Others dropped out of school all together to work for their family in the fields. The schoolhouse had no books, paper, pens or pencils, and the few cracked blackboards almost never held chalk.

181

I was invited to the school several times to teach religion and art. When I went, I carried all the school supplies we would need in a basket and distributed them to each child. Learning happened there, but it was surely a challenge for any teacher to find ways to motivate children and keep them on task without notebooks and other essential school supplies for practicing lessons. Some children were unable to concentrate on their studies due to domestic problems that lay heavy on their minds. Many children in Chuqiyapu were tending to cattle and those that were not often wished they were. Saida, for example, couldn't sit still in the classroom. She would stare out the window and daydream with her animals until the teacher called her back. She preferred being in the field with the cows and sheep.

When asked to provide some training for the teachers in Chuqiyapu. I felt ill-equipped; I'd only taught for a few years in Takana and was still new to the profession. Nonetheless, I supposed I had something to offer. I taught demo classes and afterwards engaged the teachers in discussions about methodology. But ideas and methods would only go so far; teachers were stuck in a system that offered poor compensation and no incentives to continue living in a remote town. It was not enough to have a desire to teach young people; few were willing to give up a career and life on the coast for what little was offered in Chuqiyapu and surrounding villages. Few residents in town had adequate training to replace or substitute those young teachers who abandoned the school for a new assignment elsewhere. No wonder teachers would disappear for months at a time. How lucky the Colegio Ignacio Loyola students were, I thought. It occurred to me then that I had not fully appreciated all that Father Ignatius had done to provide an excellent education for so many Peruvian boys in Takana. I wished that all children, boys, and girls, could attend such a school.

I did what I could in the school but as a foreigner I couldn't be hired at the school because they were run by the Peruvian government. Besides, I was technically under the care and guidance of *la Parroquia de Santo Domingo* and had agreed to volunteer in the parish. The Sisters weren't too keen on my teaching anything other than religion. On the rare occasion when I taught English to the second-grade boys and girls, I was excited to see how they absorbed my every word. Their big brown eyes lit up with wonder and when I asked questions I could barely control the enthusiasm of their replies. Their arms shot up like a rocket ship heading for space. I liked seeing girls in class and to see them as engaged as the boys. Were my classmates and I this enthusiastic when we were in grade school? Perhaps, we had taken our education for granted. As was to be expected, my involvement in the Chuqiyapu school was short-lived as the Sisters intervened and requested my presence at the parish.

*

When Saida was in *el campo*, there was a twinkle in her eyes. The natural world, the mountains and the sky made up Saida's real classroom. Any day that Saida got permission to join her mother in *el campo* was a great day. One special day in late August, Saida was elated to get permission to miss school. There was nothing being taught in the school that was more

183

important or useful than her participation in their Andean ritual.

An essential part of the Peruvian diet, large, versatile potatoes are separated at harvest to use with daily meals and smaller ones are put aside to be freeze-dried later. The preparation for *el chuño* takes place months after the day of harvest. Potatoes harvested in March or April would be stored in sacks for several months in anticipation of the first frost, an invitation that the process of making *el chuño* was about to begin. June, July, and August were the best time of the year to make *el chuño* because it was during those months that the mountains had the biggest frost. Numerous bags of carefully chosen smallish potatoes sat on hillsides overnight for several days until each one had frozen as hard as a rock. Once the potatoes were sufficiently frozen, the family would proceed to the most important step in making the freeze-dried potatoes.

Along with Fidela and Hilda, I had the honor of attending the ritual with Catalina's family.

"*Las papas son una bendición de Dios*," Cata said. The potato was more than a staple to Andean families: it was a blessing, it was their survival.

Pachamama, Mother Earth, was generous and provided over four thousand varieties of different sizes, textures, and hues of potatoes. While a harvest may produce over one hundred varieties of potatoes in each season, Catalina, Saida, and other family members selected only five different types of potatoes to prepare for *el chuño*. Catalina and her fellow *lugareños* took none of them for granted and treated each of them with great care and attention.

"We store them for up to five years," Cata said.

Before the annual preparation could take place, it was imperative to pay tribute to Mother Earth. All families performed a ritual to *Pachamama*. A large hole was dug. Then gifts were offered and buried in the ground before *el chuño* was made. Catalina began the ceremony by acknowledging Mother Earth's greatness. She placed her hands on the ground and gently rubbed it in a slow rhythmic motion. She recited several phrases in Aymara, and proceeded to offer seeds, grains, fruits, *chicha* (an alcoholic drink made from fermented corn), and prayers scribbled on coca leaves, to the earth. She then briskly kicked enough dirt over the hole to cover it. Cata gave praise and thanksgiving to *Pachamama* for all she had provided.

Then the stomping party started. Catalina removed the sandals from her feet and was the first to begin the dance.

"Stepping on the frozen potatoes needs to be a delicate balance," she explained. "It will remove the skin and remove any water. If you step too hard, you destroy the potatoes, if you dance too lightly, you do not remove all its water."

Catalina's son Edgar brought a boombox to the field to inspire the dance. It blasted *la choquera,* dance music, for a good part of the day.

"Kara, take your shoes off. *Ven.* Come try," Catalina said.

"I am not sure about this," I said.

"Join in the fun! What are you afraid of? Look, everyone is doing it," Catalina said.

That was a good question: what *was* I afraid of? There were many families on the hill that day, each one separated by sacks of potatoes designating their territory and containing an array of different sized potatoes awaiting impact. Family members of all ages began stomping in their bare feet and dancing on the potatoes. They laughed, sang, and celebrated. I am not sure why I had decided to wear my hiking boots that day. As I watched, I thought, *oh, how amazing it is to see their bare feet so intimately connected to the dirt*. I wondered if it was time I tossed my hiking boots for good and replaced them with a pair of *las ojotas*. I removed my boots and socks. As my bare feet impacted the potatoes and the earth, I smiled from ear to ear. I was at peace.

Chapter 16
Winter

It is difficult to avoid disease in Perú. The threat of tuberculosis never caught me but that winter, typhoid fever did. I had no sooner escaped two tuberculosis scares when I fell ill and had to leave for the coast. It wasn't fun: I had a high fever, stomach pain, severe diarrhea, and vomiting. And yet, on some other level, I thought, it wasn't awful. Getting sick made me more aware of the reality of the country and the constant threat of disease. Somehow, I felt in solidarity with the plight of the people while lying in my bed for days.

Convalescing brought thoughts of Julie. I felt horrible, but I knew I would recover. Julie gave me courage. For most of the month of July, I temporarily relocated to Pico, a town near Takana, where I would stay for six weeks, the time it took for me to recover. I remained under the care of the order of Our Lady of the Angels. I wrote a brief note home to tell my parents what had happened but I downplayed the disease and my condition. I didn't want my family to worry and, even more importantly, I didn't want them to use the information to further reinforce their beliefs and the narrative that American newspapers pushed about South America, portraying it as a dirty, dangerous, savage continent. I did everything within my power to get better. I slept a lot during those weeks. I also thought a great deal about Ryan and all we had not said. Perhaps I could say it in a letter.

July,1988, Pico, Peru

Dear Ryan,

How are you? I didn't feel well enough to write before now. Anyway, with the mail strike nothing was moving. The Sisters' house in Pico, a small port city to the south of Takana, is okay for now. They are taking good care of me. Please don't worry.

The provincial priest has been here for a few weeks because the first Peruvian girl to enter Our Lady of the Angels mission this year made her final vows last week. So mail will be sent back with him and then onto the States.

I have had good and bad days. I won't bore you with the details. By the time you get this letter, I will be fully recovered. I am pretty sure I got typhoid from a brook on the outskirts of Chuqiyapu where I drank the water when my water bottle was empty and I was really thirty. I really didn't have a choice; it was either that or dehydration. It's possible that heavier rains than usual this year made already contaminated water even dirtier. Or, I might have contracted it when Sister Tricia and I stayed overnight in Quillijuana. I'm not sure. We had a meal there, slept near animals and used the outdoor latrine. As you know, the disease comes from many sources.

Before getting sick myself I rarely thought about how so many people get infected with typhoid and hepatitis; those who don't know how to prevent disease often die. Poor hygiene, dirty latrines, or in some cases where there are no latrines, human feces are transported by

188

animals or children. That doesn't make me feel any better, but it's true. Anyway, take good care of yourself.

I've spent a lot of time reading, writing…I have read many books on spirituality because those are the ones to choose from on the shelves in the convent. I read a journal by Henri Nouwen, a Dutch priest, called Gracias. It was written during his time living in Latin America. Very interesting. I also found a biography of Mother Teresa on the shelf. How she was able to love the dying. Wow! Very humbling. I suppose it would be nice to read a trashy romance novel, now and then…forgive me…ha-ha…but they are nowhere to be found!

My time in repose has put some things into perspective for me. I realize how fortunate I am to be alive! Living in Perú has been a blessing. And how lucky to have been born in the United States. Such a privilege. Do you know what I mean? I am certain that you have similar thoughts. I will never be the same person after living here.

I can't wait to get back to the mountains and breathe the clean air. And life is much calmer in Chuqiyapu than Pico. This city is not huge, but the streets are crowded, there's lots of noise and traffic, and the poverty surrounding downtown feels sad, sadder than the poverty in the mountains (if that is possible). I am getting stronger every day – before long I'll be in good shape, and we'll be back under the same roof. If the doctor gives me a thumbs up, I'll be back to Chuqiyapu in about two weeks. We need to talk. I miss you terribly.

All my love and prayers, Kara

*

While in Pico, I was fortunate to receive a few visitors from Takana: two former Ignacio Loyola colleagues and Sister Sarah. They helped lift my spirits and that quickened my healing. I returned to Chuqiyapu ten pounds thinner and still somewhat weak.

189

Fidela and Hilda were thrilled to have me back. Not only had they missed my company but the Sisters had piled on them more chores and duties to fill the gaps left in my absence. The girls were willing to cover for me and did so with a more cooperative attitude than I might have. They also had maintained the Saturday morning women's group while I was away.

It was also great to be back in Ryan's company. Even though he and I hadn't spoken about the evening when we exchanged a kiss, it had never left my mind. Finally, after six long weeks of anticipating how the conversation about our feelings for each other might go, we met in the gardens behind the church and talked.

"I am so glad to have you back," Ryan said. "This place wasn't the same without you."

"I missed you too," I said.

"Where to start?" he said.

"How about we talk about the night you kissed me on the lips."

"Oh, yes, that," he said.

We were both unequipped to speak about such intimate matters, Ryan more so than I for he had lived many years as a celibate priest and had never had to confront such emotions, but I was very nervous, too. It was important we address what had happened. I waited patiently for him to find words to articulate his thoughts.

"Kara, I have strong feelings for you. I can't deny it. But...."

"But?"

"Look, we've had the conversation about taking vows. You know what a difficult decision it is. It is precisely the reason why the discernment process is so difficult....and important. I want you to be as sure as possible, if and when you take those vows."

"I have not yet decided to take the vows," I said.

"I understand. And I don't know if you will. But the thing is, Kara, I did take the vows. I did so many years ago when I was about your age. If I am true to that agreement I made, I need to honor it. Even though my heart is aching for you. If I am honest, well, I want you all to myself."

"You could have that," I said. I sighed. "It's all so confusing."

"For that I am sorry. I should have used my better judgment," he said. "I never meant to confuse you. Forgive me."

"So what was the kiss about?"

"It was a beautiful expression of...our love. You agree?"

"I certainly would have kissed you if you hadn't kissed me first. It was bound to happen."

"We're human," he said. "Old orthodox ways would have us deny our feelings. I don't think that is healthy. Do you?"

"It's not healthy, but it makes things more difficult because we can't have it both ways."

"No, you're right. I apologize. If I have overstepped or abused my position in an inappropriate way, I am so sorry. I really care for you. I really do."

"You don't need to apologize. The kiss was beautiful," I said. "I don't regret it. The feelings are mutual. You know, we are not the first two people to find ourselves in this predicament."

"I suppose not," Ryan said.

"I am disappointed, because I love you," I said. "But I would never ask you to break your vows so it's for the best. Anyway, you are too old for me."

"Is that so?" Ryan said with a smile. "I bet you couldn't keep up with me on my morning runs, but you're welcome to join me at five thirty tomorrow and try."

"I think I'll skip it for now…until I build up a bit more stamina."

Before we returned to the residence, we took a walk into Chuqiyapu's magnificent countryside. When no one was around or looking, we walked hand in hand. The sun was bright and the sky was blue. We passed a few locals on the dirt road, released our clasped hands, and exchanged nods and a *buen día* with them. Around the bend in the road, Yanajaja came into sight. We repeated its name several times, like kids, and burst out laughing. We continued walking in silence, allowing the presence of the volcano to wash over us. Neither of us had anything more to say; we trusted that we would receive what each of us needed from Mother Earth.

Chapter 17
Winter Birth

Since the day of its inception in the year 1777, Santo Domingo parish had prepared numerous families for the holy sacraments. But when the Sisters asked me to prepare the children for First Communion in 1989 I told them I wouldn't do it.

"I am hardly qualified to prepare children for this sacrament."

"My dear, if you have received the sacrament yourself, and you are a devout Catholic, that is enough preparation," Sister Tricia said.

"I disagree," I said.

To be honest, I was conflicted about what the sacrament represented. I recalled how at seven years old, I wore a white dress, and veil on the day of my First Communion as a symbol of my marriage or union with the Church. I went along with it then because I didn't know any better, but I could no longer carry on the charade. Marriage to the church just didn't make sense anymore.

I managed to escape the assignment to prepare kids for First Communion by offering, in exchange, to prepare the teens for Confirmation. I wasn't thrilled to do any pastoral work but I figured that at least I could hang out with the teenagers; I enjoyed that age group and was at ease in their presence. I vaguely remembered the preparation or intent that went into my own Confirmation ceremony although I was not convinced many young people did.

The sacrament of Confirmation traditionally takes place when a child approaches thirteen years old. My understanding of the sacrament of Confirmation, from being raised Catholic, was that at about this age, the teenager can take on more responsibility and therefore is ready to make a deeper commitment to the Church. In the Church's eye, once a teen was confirmed, he or she ought to be able to make better informed moral decisions. But I still grappled with the same question— *What does it mean to accept responsibility for one's destiny or life?* — at twenty-six years old, long after having been confirmed in the Catholic Church.

Most American parishes would require a child be baptized and receive Holy Communion before receiving the sacrament of Confirmation, however, the Santo Domingo parish, deeply embedded in the mountains of the Andes, made many exceptions to this rule as the future of the parish depended on the attendance and participation of the younger population especially as many young people left Chuqiyapu in search of new opportunities and education, and few teenagers freely chose to stay behind.

Traditional preparation for Confirmation included memorization of biblical verses and pages on the holy sacraments from the Church's manual but the Church's proselytizing efforts had little appeal to the teens. I considered: *what would attract the younger population?* I decided my approach would be to encourage the young people to share personal stories that built connection and trust within our study group. When the Sisters checked in periodically about my progress, they showed disapproval with my methods.

"How are the young people progressing in their faith, Kara?" Sister Tricia asked.

"That's tough to gauge. Not all kids are ready to talk about their faith, the Church and commitment to it right away. We need to build trust with them. They're doing icebreakers."

"Icebreakers? They don't need ice breakers. Please, prepare them properly by studying Scripture," Sister Tricia said.

"They need to have fun too," I said.

"Yes, as long as they get through all the material in the manual in time for the ceremony. Remember they need to be prepared by the end of the year," Sister Tricia said.

"They also need room to explore their own lives. Isn't that what it means to be a responsible adult capable of making important decisions?"

"Oh, darling... Kara, you have high expectations. Just follow the manual, please."

It was difficult working with the Sisters as they were inflexible, especially when it came to teaching the Gospel and preparing parishioners for the sacraments. I got it: they had to justify the importance of their doctrines. I saw the importance of Scripture, but I knew I would lose the teens if I couldn't personalize the teachings. When I asked Ryan what he thought about how the kids ought to be prepared, he said, as he always did, "Kara, trust your instincts, they are good." My instincts told me that being a young lay person might allow me to build more trust with the youth.

One day, the kids confessed that the nuns' presence made them nervous, turned them off and that they had a hard time sharing with them. I had felt the same way in the residence. I wondered if the Sisters had ever dated, had they ever fallen in love, or had sex. They rarely spoke of themselves or of relationships, family, or romance of their past. Had they experienced heartbreak? Had they had affairs? Then there was the issue of sexuality, an issue that the Catholic Church never got right. Adolescence is a time of sexual discovery, and while the Church and its leaders pretended it was not so, denying its healthy existence only distanced the young people, made them feel confused and badly about those parts of themselves. I could empathize with them. At one meeting, the kids told me they were afraid to be judged by the Sisters for sexual thoughts.

"I don't think the Sisters like us."

"That's not true," I said. "They just don't know how to show it."

What was it about the Church titles Father — *Padre* and *Madre* — that was so intimidating to me and others? I wanted no part of it. It was hopeless to expect that parishioners would stop calling me *Madrecita*. I lived in a convent. Once I oversaw their children's preparation for the Holy Sacraments it seemed more than appropriate to the families. My Confirmation students understood my aversion to the religious name-calling and never called me *Madre*. They also knew that, with me, no subject was off limits. This led to a mutual and trusting bond between us. My students invented nicknames for me, which I took as terms of endearment. Amiguita, Karina, Charito. Each time I heard my nickname, I felt accepted into their circle of friends.

*

Diaz Condori was the president of the Santo Domingo parish youth group. He was only a kid at eighteen years old. His muscular body stood just over five feet and four inches tall. He was never on time for meetings, and he often smelled of alcohol when he arrived. His short stature suggested he still had some inches to grow; his facial hair and irresponsible behavior further confirmed he had not yet arrived at manhood. His behavior bothered everyone and really infuriated Sister Margaret, and she wasn't shy about speaking her mind. In her eyes, Diaz was a failure and not worthy of receiving the sacrament of Confirmation.

"Why didn't you do something about him, Kara?" Sister Margaret said. "He doesn't deserve to be the president of the group, let alone be confirmed."

Sister instructed me to tell Diaz that he was no longer welcome at the parish. One evening I found an opportunity to talk to him about the situation. I asked him why he always came to the parish with alcohol on his breath and left most meetings early. I felt badly for the young man trapped in a cycle of alcoholism but at first, it was hard not to judge him. When I learned of the circumstances that contributed to Diaz's behavior, I saw him in a new light. As I had expected, I learned that his life was more complicated than I'd imagined

"I am the oldest, and only son in the family. I have a lot of responsibilities," Diaz said, "Sometimes it feels like too much."

"And, what about your *padre*?" I asked.

"*¿Mi padre? No sé nada de mi padre.*"

He did not know his father. Along with his mother, and seven siblings, all girls between the ages of three and fifteen years old, he lived in a two-room adobe house off the main plaza. As the oldest and only son, Diaz assumed the role of head of the household. The family had already buried two infants and his mother was pregnant with what would be her tenth birth. The infant was due to be born within a matter of weeks. Women in *la sierra*, gave birth with the help of relatives or a midwife. Some had hospital births but the majority were in homes. Diaz felt confident that his mother would have the support of several neighbors at her birth.

I didn't follow Sister's advice to scold the young man.

It appeared that our chat had carried some weight: for three consecutive weeks, he made every attempt to arrive on time and was a respectful participant in the confirmation meeting. Week four, when he didn't show up at the parish, I was concerned and went to his family's home.

As I approached the entrance, I could hear a woman screaming in agony. A little girl, one of Diaz's sisters, greeted me at the door. I entered the house to find all the sisters gathered around their mother, the mother clutching the eldest daughter's hand each time a contraction came. Diaz was on his

love and prayers, Kara

knees and seated in front of his mother, her two knees up and legs spread apart.

I didn't know what to do. I had never witnessed a birth and I had no training in midwifery.

"Are you going to deliver the baby?" I asked.

"I have no choice, the neighbors are away, and my mom's water has broken."

Despite the little I knew about births, I knew that after the amniotic sac bursts, delivery is not too far off. Plus, this woman had already given birth many times; most likely she would have a short labor. I asked myself: *How am I here in this mess and can I be of any help?* The younger sisters seemed to know more than me about this life passage and they were already boiling water on the small gas stove. There was little room for pots on the stove and I wondered how they would supply sufficient clean water to last for an extended amount of time. One sister delivered a not-so-clean sheet to her brother who gently rolled his mother on her side and placed the dry sheet where her water had soaked the bed. It was not enough to absorb all the moisture and the poor woman had to labor on a wet surface.

From my point of view, nothing about the scenario looked safe for the mother or the newborn. The sisters had cleared a table next to their mother for the water and sheets, but there were no clean scissors, cord clamps, cord tape, fetal stethoscope, kidney dish, gauze, forceps, cotton swabs, on it, all the minimal number of instruments needed for a safe delivery. *This is an absolute nightmare,* I thought. *What if the baby or mother has complications.*

"I will go for help," I said.

La posta médica was not that far from the home. There was little probability that *Doctora* Ana would be there, but I thought I was useless with what was unfolding, so I took my chances and ran for help. By some stroke of luck, I found Ana at the clinic. When we returned, Diaz and his mother were still doing fine. His mother was drenched in sweat and there was an odor in the room. According to Diaz, the pains were coming every three minutes, and the baby would soon be on its way. I was surprised at how confident and in control Diaz was, it was as if he had done this many times before. With the next contraction we saw the baby's head beginning to emerge. *Doctora* quickly put surgical gloves on and changed places with Diaz. She then encouraged the mother to push. I felt so much better once a doctor was between the mother's legs, but Diaz was not far from her side either. With animal instinct, his mother began pushing, but Ana tried to control the pushes so that there would be a slow delivery of the head.

"Breathe deeply…yes, carry on like that," Ana said.

Diaz chimed in to coach his mom.

"Breathe deeply, push a little; not too hard," he said.

I watched in disbelief. *How can a woman endure such pain*, I thought. *How do any of us survive this ordeal and make it into the world? Truly a miracle.* The mother's agony was focused; her pain didn't seem to matter anymore.

"Just a little bit more and soon you'll have your baby," *Doctora* said. "I have the baby's head in my hands. With the next contraction the baby will be born. You no longer need to push. Try to relax, and pant like crazy."

Relax? Are you kidding me? I thought. I saw the baby's head, shoulders, and then whole body slide out of the woman's vagina effortlessly. The baby was blue and covered in mucus and blood. I didn't think the sight was beautiful at all, but I couldn't believe my eyes. It was as if I was having an out-of-body experience. *Doctora* checked the heartbeat. All was well. Then she clamped the umbilical cord in two places and cut between. She held the baby — a boy! — upside down to ensure no mucus was inhaled. When *Doctora* Ana placed the baby in the mother's arms he was still slimy and ugly, in my opinion, but when Diaz and his sisters gathered around to gaze upon their new brother they were ecstatic. Their mother cried tears of joy. The family relished the life of the new baby.

There was still work for the doctor to do, but I felt it was time for me to leave. I had offered no more than moral support, but I was exhausted all the same. I didn't envy my friend Ana at that point; anything could still happen with the mother and a hospital was nowhere to be found. As for me, I knew I had just been given the privilege of a lifetime to witness a birth. I was astounded and grateful.

With Diaz's help, his mother was back on her feet in no time. He continued to assume the role of head of household. Unfortunately (or perhaps not), Díaz fell far behind in his Confirmation class preparation. In fact it became evident he wouldn't be able to catch up in time to receive the sacrament at the end of the year. So, the leader of the youth group had to drop out of my class. But with or without the sacrament of Confirmation, Díaz had been ushered into adulthood. He did not need the Church's teaching for that. His initiation into

201

adulthood wasn't something any institution or sacrament could teach him; he lived it. It made me question what the purpose of Confirmation was after all. I had seen how life took the upper hand and asked a lot of Diaz. He had accepted responsibility for his destiny, and he demonstrated to all of us that he was more than capable of doing so. In my mind, Diaz was making the utmost sacrifice for his family.

*

For as long as the town of *Chuqiyapu,* and *la parroquia Santo Domingo* had Father Ryan as their visiting priest, he was my best friend. Our friendship was solid, and we were thankful for it. After returning from the Condori home, I knocked on his bedroom door. Thrilled to have witnessed the birth of a child, I had to tell Ryan. We had a secret code at his door—two strong knocks, and then three rapid taps in succession.

"Kara, hello, what's going on? Come in."

"Ryan, I just had the most amazing day!" The whole story spilled out from me. I could tell that Ryan was making an effort to feel my excitement but it was apparent from his face that he was not in as good a mood.

"What's wrong? Are you okay?" I asked

"Actually, I have some bad news," Ryan said.

I moved closer to him, took his hand and we both sat down on his bed. I noticed there was a telegram on his desk. "What's going on, Ryan?"

"It seems that I will be leaving Perú sooner than I anticipated. It's my mother," Ryan said. "She had a stroke…she's in critical condition. I will know more once I can call from Barata or Takana. I got a cable at the post office, but I have few details."

"I am so sorry to hear this," I said. "How are you doing?"

"To be honest, I thought something like this might happen while I was away. She is eighty-eight."

"The news is harder being so far away from your home," I said.

"She could be dead long before I get back to Australia."

"Don't say that. Let's be hopeful." There was a long silence. "When will you leave? Have you told the Sisters yet?"

"I did, earlier this afternoon. I'll be on the six o'clock bus to Takana tomorrow."

"It will all work out. It's out of our hands."

"Yes, it is in God's hands, Kara," he said.

What a rollercoaster of emotions! First the joy of birth, then the fear and sadness of impending death. We embraced and I started to cry. I should have been consoling him—after all, his mother was gravely ill—but he consoled me. Within days he would be back in Australia.

I knew, in my gut, that I too would soon be leaving Perú and that we would likely never meet again. Our time together, our affair, had come to an end. At least we had been spared heartbreak. Thank God we dodged the temptation to make love. It was getting harder and harder to say no. But, oh, what a beautiful consummation of our love it would have been.

How pathetic I was. He had just heard that his mother was in intensive care and that he might not have the chance to say goodbye to her, and all I could do was focus on myself. My heart was aching at the thought of saying goodbye. I should

love and prayers, Kara

have been grateful for the time we had. That was all. It was out
of our hands.

Chapter 18
Eduarda Quispe Mamani

"Blessed are they that mourn for they shall be comforted."
Matthew 5:5

Eduarda Quispe Mamani had given birth to nine children but by the time we met in Chumpe at the first women's gathering, the young Aymara woman had already buried four children. Eduarda lived with her husband and five living children who ranged between two to ten years of age. Her ten-year old daughter, Luz, was a great help to her mother; she always attended the meetings and provided caregiving for her younger siblings while her mom's hands were busy knitting socks and sweaters or designing *una arpillera*. The arrangement appeared to work out fine.

Even though the whole gang, minus the father, was at the women's gatherings every Saturday, I knew little about Eduarda's family. I assumed that the children showed up each week because there would be no supervision if the mother was not home. On weekends, many husbands were unreliable babysitters or caretakers. For the most part, they were at Bible study or putting the week's work behind them by consuming alcohol with their buddies. Women needed periodic breaks from domestic responsibilities on the weekends, but being strapped to the children meant the kids always came along. The women rejoiced in the freedom at the Chumpe women's group, no domestic chores for a few hours. And they always lingered after their instructors' last wrap up as chores would be waiting for them when they returned.

Eduarda was one of the best knitters in the bunch. She could knit an adult sweater in the time it took most people to knit a pair of infant booties. She was also the most boisterous and well-liked by the other participants. I rarely knew exactly what all the laughter among the women was about, but it was obvious that Eduarda's jokes were the cause of the merriment. Eduarda had a warm and generous personality. One Saturday meeting in Chumpe, she and her daughter Luz carried a large pot of boiled potatoes with hot sauce to the meeting. Sometimes she shared a bottle of *chica*, a homemade fermented corn drink. I wondered why she didn't just invite the group over to her house; it would have been much easier. Eduarda must have had her reasons, but we never heard them. She had a knack for bringing people together and with one pot of food created a celebration for her friends. The women knitted, ate, talked, and laughed. It was due in large part to Eduarda that those Saturdays were joyful.

It came as a surprise some months later when Eduarda told me that her family was moving to Chuqiyapu from Chumpe. She gave little explanation. All she said was how nice it would be that we would be neighbors.

I had heard from the Sisters that she had gone to the parish weeks earlier to speak with them about domestic affairs. Domestic abuse. The situation never improved so, as Sister Tricia explained, Eduarda decided to leave "to protect the children from their dad." She left her house with her children and all the belongings they could carry and walked to Chuqiyapu in the middle of the night while her husband was out cold for hours from an overindulgence of alcohol.

Always one to see the lesson in all things and demonstrate optimism and courage, Eduarda did not dwell on the situation. The morning she knocked on the parish door for help, she never uttered a bad word about the father in front of the kids, but we came to learn the urgency with which she sought temporary refuge. The family installed themselves into the parish office for a few days, until Eduarda and the Sisters could contact her extended family. Eduarda reconnected with relatives she hadn't spoken to since her marriage; they eventually agreed to take Eduarda and her family in. They settled into a small room in the back of their house.

Once Eduarda and her children settled in their new life in Chuqiyapu, Eduarda and I saw each other with more frequency. She couldn't attend the Saturday meetings in Chumpe for fear for running into her "ruthless husband" and her brilliant presence was missed by all. I took full responsibility for forming the group and pushing the *arpillera* agenda but I was naïve and oblivious to the true impact it might make in the lives of *los lugareños*. Surely, I didn't want to put any woman or child in harm's way but the women's gathering

207

had stirred up insecurity in other households and the husbands grew more controlling.

I turned to the Sisters for some advice. They didn't offer much; they told me to discontinue the meetings in Chumpe as soon as possible, and so we did. Several of the women from the group walked ten miles on foot for one last Saturday meeting in the parish office in Chuqiyapu. Eduarda would reunite with friends. The life of the party showed up with another pot of potatoes and corn, and more *chicha* for all to share.

*

One Sunday in August after morning Mass, Eduarda appeared alone and unannounced at the parish house asking me to accompany her on *un paseo,* a stroll through town. She and her children had been living in Chuqiyapu for several weeks by then and were adjusting well, she said. She was thankful for the assistance from the parish and for family nearby to help with the children. She had acquired several cows and soon began making cheese. That Sunday, she came to the residence alone.

"*Hola, Señorita, ¿me puedes acompañar un ratito?*" Eduarda said.

"Of course. Where are we going?"

"Al cementerio."

I asked why but Eduarda didn't answer me until we arrived at the entrance to the cemetery. Months earlier, on a day in November, I had been to the cemetery in Takana with Sister Sarah. It had been a sunny day and the cemetery was packed with Takaños celebrating the annual All Saints Day celebration. The cemetery was decorated with bright colors and altars were adorned with food, flowers, and items celebrating the lives of those who had died. Burial sites were marked by a range of tombstones, some engraved marble or cement placards. Other graves were dug deep in the ground or in walls lay beside mounds of dirt, graves marked only with plain wooden crosses. This reflected the vast economic disparities in town. But all families, regardless of status, remembered loved ones and rejoiced in the same way on All Saints Day.

This visit to the local cemetery, where all the families from Chuqiyapu and surrounding villages buried their dead, was different. It was an overcast day; there were no celebratory colors. Each gravesite resembled the one next to it. How could anyone find their loved one in this open field where almost all were identical? Eduarda and I were the only visitors that Sunday morning. She led me to a plot of dirt in the cemetery, saying she recognized it by the unique shape the earth took after a rainfall, a puddle of water still there. She knelt in the mud and began to recite what seemed to be a prayer in Aymara. Turning to me, she said, it was a special day.

"*Hoy es el día santo de dos de mis bebés.*" She came there to pray and place flowers on her children's birthdays, she said.

"Two of your children were born on August 30th?" I asked.

"*Sí, gemelos,* twins. They died three months later."

"They died? How?" I asked.

"*Mis bebés fueron muy débiles...*they were weak. I didn't have enough milk to feed them, and we had little food."

I remained silent. What to say to a mother who had lost twins to starvation at only three months old? Eduarda stood up, signaling for me to follow. We proceeded to two other plots of land, similar in appearance to those where her twins had been buried. The two unmarked graves, not far from the twins, were also small mounds of dirt, about three feet long with simple wooden crosses dug into the ground at the point where the child's head might have been.

The tiny graves made me question whether Soledad Mamani Esperanza had had a proper burial. Who had buried her and where? Did anyone visit her gravesite.

I still couldn't accept the loss of loved ones. How could this woman still be standing after her losses? I had not attended Julie's burial and I had refused to attend the wake because it seemed to me that the well-groomed, decorated corpse in the open casket was not Julie. More likely, I was in denial. The church funeral was enough to put me into an emotional spin and I couldn't bear to see what they told me was Julie's body, go into the ground. I opted out of following the caravan of cars to the burial site. My heart hardened that day and regardless of good intentions, I couldn't accept any condolences that came my way. It was many months later that I returned to the cemetery where Julie had been buried. By then a large marble gravestone had been installed, and sat among others, on a patch of freshly cut green grass. That day the sun shone brightly. For the first time, I read the inscription engraved onto Julie's tombstone: *Dwell not on the shortcomings of others, instead, rejoice in their goodness.*

Standing in the small cemetery in Chuqiyapu with Eduarda, the words on Julie's tombstone hit me like a lightning bolt. I had crossed paths with many people in Perú who embodied Julie's message but no one embodied these words more than Eduarda. I aspired to live up to them, as well, but knew I still had much to learn. Eduarda continued to lead me through the full length of the cemetery, pointing to other dirt mounds, plots where her other children were buried on a different date. To her left were all the gravesites, and to the right, a spectacular view of the Yanajaja volcano. Eduarda chose a spot on the far end of the graveyard and invited me to sit with her on a large rock. From there she introduced me to the other children she had buried.

"Here are my other babies, one boy and one girl. *El niñito murió durante el parto,* my little son died during childbirth. I never even got to name him, *el pobrecito. Mi bendita hija,* Estrella, she died just before she turned two years old," she said.

Eduarda shed no tears while she spoke about her babies. She seemed happy to be there, as if being at the children's gravesites enabled her to watch over and protect them. She broke into the local language again, I assumed, to speak to her kids. Then she spoke in Spanish to me.

"They were so beautiful…beautiful little dreams," she said.

"How did you survive this?" I asked.

"*Mis hijitos,* all of them, are in heaven with God. My little ones were so precious …. I was blessed to have had them for a time …. that was a gift. For this, I am forever grateful. *Bendito sea Dios,*" she said.

I knew that I was witnessing something remarkable. I was in the presence of something holy, sacred. I wanted to fill the space with words, but silence was all that did the moment justice. The sound of wind and emptiness filled us. Why was I in that spot at that time with Eduarda? I felt sad, awkward and awestruck all at the same time. I had a difficult time keeping my emotions in check as I recalled my own loss. I was still trying to pull myself up from grief. Julie's death had been devastating; she was too young to die. *Too young to die*, I thought. I braced myself for some emotional outburst from the woman I barely knew, whose children had never even lived, and I was afraid that I wouldn't be able to handle it. But Eduarda never had an emotional outburst that day. Eduarda's composure was calm, kind, and at peace during the entire visit.

I was again overwhelmed by the power of love. I didn't fully comprehend a mother's love, for I did not yet have children of my own, but regardless, I felt this woman's pain and love for her offspring like I hadn't before. I knew Eduarda as a kind, optimistic, and generous person; how had she not become depressed and bitter after all she had suffered? Eduarda remained unshakeable during our visit to the cemetery. If anyone had the right to be sad, negative, or bitter after suffering life's blows, it was Eduarda. What had lifted her above grief?

I tried to make sense of what I had witnessed. Sadly, the reality was that life in the mountains could be harsh. Children die more often in those parts of the world than in my country. They lived closer to nature, and closer to death. Perhaps, that made it easier for Eduarda. Or did it? A loss is a loss. By the grace of God? Whatever the reason for Eduarda's gentle acceptance and quiet amid tragedy, it brought me to my knees, bowing my head to the unknown. I implored higher awareness: *Help me, God. Grant me the peace and grace that I have witnessed here today in your child, Eduarda, the mother of nine beautiful children.*

*

The contrast between the daily lives of the people of Chuqiyapu, and the religious life of the Sisters was striking. Not all residents could see the conflict of interest between the Catholic Church and *el pueblo*. I doubt all the nuns could either. The Santo Domingo parish did great charitable and pastoral work with the communities but their primary goal aimed to change spiritual lives according to the Catholic Church's beliefs. This meant that the Church exploited the most vulnerable residents in the name of God. How could uneducated, illiterate people follow a book that they had never read? And, why? The non-Spanish speaking women took it on blind faith that the Catholic Church would improve their lives; literate men read Scripture supporting and reinforcing the value of its claim. And, whose God? Indigenous beliefs in the power of natural elements, the Sun, the Mountains, and the Rain were replaced by a white man in a robe they would never wear. How did that happen?

It bothered me that many people relinquished their own personal power to the Catholic Church, and that the Church took advantage of them. No belief is formed without some need attached to it, I thought. And, no doubt, there was much need in Chuqiyapu and in Perú in general. Many parishioners of *la Parroquia Santo Domingo* were in financial distress, and it was eased by the Church: there was money to help the most desperate families with food and clothing, transportation for the most elderly and sick, and money to construct homes and erect walls for worship. The Church offered a belief system that gave hope for improved lives. All that could be done in the

213

name of an idol. The country's own government didn't offer much hope. Could foreigners working with the Catholic Church fulfill such a promise? I questioned the Church's power, not the existence of a higher power, God. I had more faith in the people of Chuqiyapu, and in life itself, than in the Catholic Church.

Chapter 19
Lost Sheep

And he spoke this parable unto them, saying:

What man of you, having a hundred sheep if he loses one of them,

Doth not leave the ninety-nine in the wilderness,

And go after that which is lost, until he finds him.

And when he has found it, he lays it on his shoulders, rejoicing.

And when he comes home, he calls together his friends and neighbors and says to them,

Rejoice with me; for I have found my sheep which was lost!

-Luke 15: 3-6

Children in Chuqiyapu, if they were old enough and not sitting in school, were often out herding cattle and tending to sheep and llamas in surrounding villages for their families. Pantaleón Campos was one such child. The extra pair of hands was a tremendous help to his family, a family I knew little about. I had not seen the child's name on the parish rosters, nor would I recognize the boy from the pews at Mass. We would have known if his family were active parishioners; most in the small town of about five thousand residents attended Sunday Mass, and the Sisters made sure all followers knew one another.

One afternoon just before sunset, at the end of an unpaved road that connected the town plaza to the countryside, I bumped into the boy and his lamb. Pantaleón was around eight years old. The boy's face had round rosy cheeks chapped from the wind and cold. His torn brown sweater and pants matched the color of his skin. The lamb, so small, and as soft as snow, was attached to a rope around its neck, like a dog on a leash. The boy had been crying and wasn't watching where he was going. The lamb needed guidance, as well. We collided.

I said, "Careful, watch where you're going."

When I realized he was crying, I felt badly for scolding him. He was barely able to speak through his tears and dripping nose. The sleeves of his sweater were hardened from him wiping his nose so much.

"Are you all right?" I asked.

The boy said in Spanish, "I lost my sheep. My father is going to kill me."

"What do you mean you lost your sheep? You have one right here."

"The others…I can't find my herd of sheep. I left them on our plot for a short time. When I returned they were gone."

"Why did you leave them unattended in the first place?"

"I had to. This lamb wandered off. I had to find him."

"How many sheep are lost?" I asked.

"*Veinte.*"

"Twenty? Well, they couldn't have gone far," I said.

I didn't know what I was talking about. The truth is I knew nothing about a shepherd's life. There was an awkward silence and the boy gazed down at his sandals. Was he embarrassed? Was he ashamed? All I wanted to do was help in some way. I knew a bit about feeling lost. He raised his head, and when I saw his tear-filled eyes, I had to act.

"Let's go. I am going with you to look for the sheep."

"*Mi padre me va a matar. Mi padre me va a matar,*" Pantaleón repeated, his fear of his father's anger was clear.

"Don't worry, we will find your sheep. *Vamos*, let's go," I said.

My father is going to kill me. What is he saying? Why is he so afraid of his father? I temporarily let go of that concern and left town with Pantaleon. There was utter silence between me and the boy as we walked side by side in search of his herd of sheep. He mumbled something to himself in words that I couldn't understand, and I decided not to let it matter. Pantaleón took the lead on the dirt road, the one lone lamb dragged behind on a leash. The boy skipped over rocks and set a pace far beyond what I was used to or able to keep up with. The lamb couldn't keep up either. I took the lamb in my arms. It was not heavy but not too light either; any extra exertion would have been a challenge for me. The air at 11,700 feet still made it difficult to breathe, even though I had been living in Chuqiyapu for months. Soon darkness would blind our path, and I feared we would not find our way back before nightfall if we were to wander far from town. And, how would we locate the herd of sheep in the dark? I hadn't prepared for this unexpected trek: I didn't carry water; had no extra layer of clothing, and no flashlight.

Wandering outside of town after dark was not a good idea, the Sisters constantly reminded me. Because there were no streetlights, dimly lit homes in town were the only source of light to guide the way. Unless of course there was a full moon. How wonderful it would be if I could coordinate the cycles of the moon so that its light could watch over me in moments of need. How could I arrange that? I thought. Pantaleón was a lot further ahead of me and his silhouette began to blur with the night sky. I became more nervous. When I caught up to him, we paused to catch our breath.

In the end, after several hours of searching it was too dark, too cold and dangerous, and we had no luck in finding his sheep. I decided to call the unsuccessful search off. In the most reassuring voice I could muster I said, "We did our best. You'll have to return at sunrise."

The boy was noticeably disappointed and concerned. "Mi Padre me va matar."

I felt as if I had failed the boy, giving him hope that ultimately wasn't realized. It would always be a hard lesson: how to balance enough hope to keep going and accept reality as it is. Some things are simply out of our control. As we headed back into town, I suggested we move at a slower pace; the boy complied with little insistence from me. He was no longer in a hurry. I passed the lamb to the boy.

As we approached Chuqiyapu, I offered to accompany Pantaleón to his house. At first he adamantly disagreed but as we came closer to his house, he begrudgingly agreed. Señor

Campos, the boy's father, answered the knock on the door in a fit of rage.

"Where have you been? The sun went down over an hour ago!" the father screamed.

The boy was speechless and shaking. I thought I could speak on behalf of the boy and blurted out in Spanish,

"Before you punish him, you should know that we did everything we could to find the sheep. We searched everywhere."

"¿Cómo? ¿Qué dice?" The father said. "How could he return home without the sheep?"

With that he grabbed the boy and slapped him on the side of the head with the back of his hand. Pantaleón lost his grip on the lamb. I caught the rope around its neck. The father threw his son into the house by his hair before grabbing the only sheep saved that day from my hands, entering the house, and slamming the door in my face. Before I could react, I stood there long enough to hear the father's anger grow into more assaults on the boy. Through the cracks in the wooden door, I could hear the boy screaming and sobbing. He tried to tell his father that he didn't mean to lose them. Señor Campos paid no attention.

I arrived at the parish residence late and shaken. Supper had already been served. Luckily it was not my week to cook for the household. I offered a quick apology and sat down. Sister Margaret shot me a mean stare. I remained quiet and debated whether I ought to explain why I was late and if so, how I would go about it. For the time being, I said nothing. After supper was over, I cleared the table and helped with the dishes. Sisters Tricia and Margaret and I lingered in the kitchen.

Sister Tricia inquired about my tardiness. I searched for an opportune moment to share the story.

"Who is the family? Have we seen them at Mass?" Sister Tricia said.

"Família Campos," I said.

"Campos!" Sister Tricia said, "Do you know how many families there are with that name? Where do they live?"

That would also be difficult to describe since so many of the houses looked the same and were unnumbered — one would need to know its location in relation to signposts not yet so evident to someone like me who was not from these parts.

"It was close to the road behind the church, one of the first wooden doors as we headed into town," I said.

"What in God's name were you doing out there after dark? We specifically told you not to be out at that time," Sister Margaret reprimanded.

"Kara, tell us what happened," Sister Tricia said.

"Well, to make a long story short, I went with Pantaleón Campos, the eight-year-old, to look for his lost sheep."

"And you thought you could find them in the dark?" Sister Tricia said.

"It wasn't dark when we left. The boy was really upset. I wanted to help," I said.

"Help? The boy lost his family's sheep….do you realize the value of one sheep to that family, Kara?" Sister Tricia asked.

"Well, he did have one. He lost the other twenty because he went looking for the lamb," I said.

"Like the parable of the lost sheep," Sister Margaret said.

"That's beside the point. Kara, the loss of twenty sheep is devastating to a family. Do you see that?" Sister Tricia said.

"I guess I don't quite understand. But does that give the father the right to beat his son? The father beat the boy when we returned to his house with only a lamb."

"The father's reaction is not our business, Kara. The family depends on these animals for their livelihood in a way that you simply cannot understand," Sister Tricia said.

"But how is the father's reaction not our concern? Why wouldn't we do something to protect this child," I said.

Was the value of one sheep equivalent to a new bicycle or more likely a car back home? It was impossible to compare the two distinct realities of Perú and the United States. Were the animals like members of the family? If the family lost a sheep, let alone a whole herd, might that cost them the food on the table and clothing on their backs. Was it an even deeper relationship? Was it like a death in the family?

"It is a real shame that the boy lost the sheep. Perhaps they will turn up at daylight. But, Kara, we need to stay out of their business," Sister Tricia said.

"What a shame the family doesn't attend Mass." Sister Margaret said.

Sisters Tricia and Margaret refused to contact the authorities. I felt so confused, angry, and helpless. What could I really do? What right did I have to interfere with a family? I was concerned for Pantaleón's wellbeing, and I wondered if there was ever a justification for beating a child. Before blowing out the kerosene lamp, I flipped through the pages of the Bible and located the parable of the lost sheep. In the story, Jesus shows that the Kingdom of God is accessible to all, even those who are sinners or strayed from God. What did it mean to stray from the flock? Where did Pantaleón stand among God's flock? What about his father? Or me? I often felt unwilling to join the followers. I suppose that's why I wanted to reach out to Pantaleón. I wanted him to know that no matter what he would be accepted and loved.

Who was at fault in the Campos family? Pantaleón? His father? Might the father have used another means other than violence to reprimand the boy? Who was guilty of a greater sin? Did it matter? Was sin even the correct word to use in the situation? Sister Margaret believed that had the father and his family attended Mass each week, the family might have avoided the situation altogether. Were devout Catholics better people, better families, and better citizens? As for the father, all I could extend was my forgiveness. I knelt beside the bed and prayed for the Campos family, especially Pantaleón that evening. My heart went out to the child because I could identify with him. I felt like a lost sheep. Then, a revelation came over me: the Church doesn't change one's behavior, or one's heart — love does.

I had seen the Church's willingness to turn a blind eye to abusive behavior before. In the morning I asked the Sisters if they could contact the authorities and report child abuse. I would testify, I said, to what I had witnessed. They reiterated they couldn't do anything, that "it is not the work of the Church." How was it not the concern of the Church to show love for one's neighbors? In my mind, the children, and the families in Chuqiyapu were our neighbors, not subjects of charity or pity. I questioned whether the parish's inaction justified Señor Campos's behavior.

In my close encounters with the Catholic Church, I had observed actions (and inactions) that led me to question the Church's doctrines and perspective on life. The Church had its share of contradictions, and a history of patriarchy and misogyny. Its missionary role in the lives of the Indigenous people was questionable, too. Missionaries? Saviors? What was the Church saving "the natives" from? I could no longer see aligning myself with the Catholic Church's mission for the rest of my life. I was fully aware that the invitation to live with the Sisters rested on me exploring a religious vocation. I would soon need to decide whether to stay in Chuqiyapu or to leave. I had denied red flags in order to get an experience of a lifetime. They became harder to dismiss but selfishly I didn't want to leave Chuqiyapu, its beauty and its people.

love and prayers, Kara

Chapter 20
Awakening

In September, not long after Ryan's departure from the parish, I received a letter postmarked from the capital city. That I was aware of, no one in Lima, besides Augusto Benicio and Brother Andrew from the monastery knew of my whereabouts.

Dear Kara,

Greetings from Lima. About a year ago, I applied for a scholarship to study Third World Economics at la Universidad Católica in Lima and got accepted. I've been in the country for a few months now. I have been in touch with John at Colegio Ignacio Loyola, and he invited me to visit the Jesuits and the school in Takana to check out their work. I will be arriving in Takana at the end of the month. I asked about you, and they said you no longer work in the school but are still living in Peru, in a small town in the mountains. Kara, I would love to see you and catch up on our lives. It certainly has been a long time since Benton University. I would also like to see where you are living and learn about the Andean lifestyle. Let me know what you think.

Be in touch,

David

David Truro had been a year behind me at Benton University. Though he and I had never officially dated, we had hooked up during my senior year in college. Memories from that year were foggy at best, with Julie's death and all, but I did remember an evening David and I had spent together after a party and drinking. Following Julie's death, I had engaged in more reckless behavior than I was proud of, or was willing to admit to myself. During that last year in Boston, it was a way to anesthetize my grief. I couldn't recall details, but I was certain that David had helped alleviate my pain after her loss.

Upon reading his letter, my mind spiraled into memories of one night on my apartment floor when David and I had sex. Those college days seemed so distant from my new reality in the mountains. My body had denied any pangs of lust for months; I hadn't allowed myself to satisfy any urges. I had been aroused in Ryan's presence but I had learned to suppress it. I no longer could.

I welcomed back my sexual thirst as I would an old friend, greeting the recollections with open arms. This would affirm there was nothing wrong with me. Once again, my fingers wandered down into my panties at night. *I am still a normal, sexual being,* I thought. *It's natural and it feels good. No belief has power over the law of nature. Faith is bigger than rules.*

I was certain that if the Sisters could intuit or read my thoughts about masturbation or sex with a priest, they would be enraged. Sex for personal pleasure. Sex before marriage. I no longer thought of Tom sexually. I had daydreamed often about how extraordinary sex might have been with Ryan. A real shame we never acted upon it; I regretted that. Not all, but most of the Sisters would consider such fantasies perverse and would take immediate action to erase them from my brain, maybe lobotomize me, and remove me from the premises. *Sinful thoughts. Sinful. You are going to hell, Kara.*

I couldn't resist the temptation to invite David to Chuqiyapu—after all, he was already in the country, too close to dismiss. Soon after receiving his note, I made the conscious decision to welcome him. It wasn't to hook up—it couldn't happen in the convent—I was genuinely excited to connect and see how he was doing. He arrived several weeks later in the late afternoon with a small backpack and a camera flung over the shoulder. He looked the same as in college, maybe better. He was blond and blue-eyed, tall, and muscular, an anomaly in the Chuqiyapu. I was taken aback by his youth and vibrancy.

When I had asked permission to have David as a guest, the Sisters reacted poorly. I had grown used to ignoring their reasoning. It no longer made sense to me. I really missed male companionship, perhaps, also, I yearned for physical intimacy, and there was no way at this point that I would take no for an answer.

"Where would he stay?" asked Sister Lila, a new postulant from the Philippines.

"Your request is rather unusual," Sister Tricia said.

"He can stay in Father Ryan's old room, where all the male visitors stay," I said.

I didn't see any problem; he would stay in the special room set aside for priests on the rare occasion they visited, which was almost never. Father Ryan's departure three weeks earlier was fortuitous; after almost three months, his impression left the space cozy and warm. The room designated for "men only" was unoccupied.

"I am not sure I am comfortable with this," Sister Margaret said.

"Father Ryan stayed with us for almost four months, and it was fine," I said.

"That is different. He is a *priest*," Sister Margaret said.

"I really don't see how that is different. And David is a very nice person. He won't be any trouble at all," I said.

Our male guest stayed for three nights in Ryan's old room in the parish residence. Other than Ryan, there hadn't been a man on the premises in years, so the Sisters said. Perhaps that was why they were so skittish at the thought of it. David and I spent the days walking around town and talking to the locals. David had enough Spanish to converse with the people and he was wonderful with them. Of course, he stood out like a sore thumb, like me. I was willing to share the stage. It was comforting to have another *gringo* around. David was adamant about documenting his visit with photographs. I made him promise to ask *los lugareños* for permission before snapping a shot, as I had always done, out of respect. He was great company. In the convent during evening dinners, few of us around the table conversed much, if at all. It wasn't clear whether the Sisters were shy, lacked social skills, hadn't interacted with handsome, young men or whether exhaustion from long days got the best of them. David made every effort to engage them in chatter, but they weren't interested.

After eating dinner, everyone helped with the dishes, and as usual turned in very early. Everyone grabbed lanterns and went to their designated rooms. I waited until all the Sisters had used the bathroom and doors were closed before sneaking into David's room. It was as if I was back in middle school on a camping trip trying to outsmart my chaperones. I tiptoed from my room into the bedroom that still smelled like Ryan.

It was a relief, and comfort, to know that I still had a healthy sexual appetite and drive. And David went along with it. I was eager to satisfy and be satisfied. The physical intimacy that had been lacking for years erupted in warm caresses and kisses. I was easily aroused, my sexual hunger heightened by the fact that we were having sex behind the Sisters' backs, in Ryan's bedroom, and in the quiet embrace of the Church. Luckily David had a condom stuck in his wallet; nowhere in the convent would one be found. We sealed the deal in a missionary position although, to be completely honest, it was just sex, not lovemaking.

In the morning, the rooster woke the household at five o'clock in time for morning prayers. I quickly returned to my room to prepare for prayers. David declined the invitation to join the Sisters in the morning prayer meeting, but I attended, exhausted, trying to act as if nothing had happened.

There are many ways to love and serve God, I concluded. All three vows deserved serious consideration and would be difficult to make, but it seemed to me the hardest would be the vow of obedience, for it affected all the others. Any marriage, or union, whether it be between man and woman or the Catholic Church required a certain surrender. Although my gut told me months earlier I would not be a nun, my decision not to join Our Lady of the Angels religious order was now decided. I was not yet willing to surrender to the Catholic Church or to one man. My hope was that one day I would be able to surrender to God alone.

Chapter 21
Adiós

Tensions between Sister Margaret and me escalated after David's visit. Sister Margaret had unleashed denigrating comments, some under her breath and others right to my face, for weeks. She disapproved of many of my actions and strove to diminish my self-esteem. One evening she called me into her bedroom.

"Kara, there is something I would like to talk to you about," Sister Margaret said.

"Yes, of course," I said.

She was clever to ask me when no one else was around. I wondered if David and I had made too much noise when we were going at it. *Had we been caught? So, what if we had?* Casual sex was normal for a young single woman. I was an adult and able to make my own decisions. *Had the affection between Ryan and I seeped out into the residence?* I was not beholden to Our Lady of the Angels, or the Catholic Church or to anyone but myself. I opted for freedom over obedience, sex over chastity.

"Please, come in and take a seat. I wanted to ask you about your intentions with us," Sister Margaret said.

"My intentions?"

"I mean, what are you doing here living with a religious order? A young, beautiful girl like you? What could you possibly have to offer at this parish? You ought to be back in the United States getting married," she said.

There was a long pause. I wasn't clear what she was getting at; if she had wanted to address my fling with David or my emotional affair with Ryan, she didn't. She managed to make me feel small and uncomfortable.

"I am not sure what you want me to say."

"Just what I said, what are you doing here…what are your intentions?" Sister Margaret said.

"I am here because I have made a commitment to assist the parish and serve the communities in Chuqiyapu."

"And what are your intentions regarding taking vows in the Church? It seems to me that you are wasting your time with us if you are not, in fact, serious about a religious vocation."

"There are other reasons to be here besides taking vows. I never promised Sister Flora anything," I said.

"Is that so?"

"I don't need to be a nun to do good work with the people and the Church," I said, "Sister Flora knew this."

"How could you possibly care about these poor people? Someone like you….What do you know about the poor? You are better off at home in the States with a boyfriend and family."

"Someone like me? I don't think you know me very well, Sister. How dare you treat me like this," I said.

In the past, in such a circumstance my eyes would have filled with tears, my feelings hurt, but I was way too angry. I stormed out of the bedroom. Before I could leave, Sister Margaret interrupted.

"Wait.... Please think seriously about what I have said. And do not tell anyone in the house about this conversation — it would only cause unnecessary misunderstanding in our community."

I was appalled and shocked by the words that came out of the nun's mouth. This was beyond disturbing — *such hypocrisy*, I thought. *God's love. Bullshit! What point were vows, the morning prayers and blessings if people were not going to live by them*? It was easier to extend kindness to the Peruvians than to those living under the same roof. It was all about control, hers not mine.

I didn't speak to anyone in the community of Sister Margaret's cruelty; I wasn't a tattle tale. Despite being hurt by this mean, bitter woman, I knew if I said anything, it might come out wrong and I would be sorry for the comment later. I didn't wish harm upon Sister Margaret. I felt sorry for her. Perhaps she was unhappy with her decision to join the convent. Maybe denying her sexuality was harder than she could admit. Maybe she regretted not marrying or having children. Or, maybe she resented being treated as a second-class citizen by the hierarchy of the Catholic Church. I couldn't answer for her. But for me, honestly, well, these had been my questions too.

My fling with David confirmed what I knew was true: I had come to my own conclusions about the Catholic Church sometime before. I didn't need my attraction for a man as proof that I didn't want to be a nun — the Church had already displayed enough transgressions to deter me. The Church's misogyny, and its mistrust of women and her body were reason enough to move on. I couldn't align myself with their dogma; their demands imprisoned me. At first I thought that David had brought me to this awareness and saved me from making a terrible decision. However, it didn't take me long to acknowledge that I had saved myself from becoming a nun.

Sister Flora, who was the most approachable of all the nuns in the house, never returned to Chuqiyapu after contracting tuberculosis; Fidela and Hilda, my young female companions, had decided not to join Our Lady of the Angels religious order and had recently returned to the *altiplano* of Puno to continue their work with faith communities on the shores of Lake Titicaca. My dear friend, Father Ryan, had left prematurely to be at his dying mother's side in Australia. With those departures, the house wasn't the same; there was no more joyful, carefree air, no one with whom to share a heart-to-heart chat. Without Sister Flora's kindness and reassurance, the girls' laughter and Father Ryan's warmth in the household, there was no reason to stay. Soon after the unpleasant encounter with Sister Margaret, I broke the verbal agreement I had made with Sister Flora to serve the parish for a year in Chuqiyapu, and let the parish know that within weeks, I would leave *la Parroquia Santo Domingo*.

Living in Chuqiyapu was phenomenal; it was living in the parish that was becoming unbearable. I was certain I wanted to live in Chuqiyapu, I just wasn't sure how to make that happen without the Sisters and the Catholic Church. Awkward moments at the dinner table continued for days even though no one except Sister Margaret knew the details of the rift between us. I suspected that Sister Tricia's keen intuition told her what was going on. While we never spoke about Sister Margaret, her strong character, or her behavior towards me, Sister Tricia must have known and would allude to it in a future letter, a letter that showed her appreciation for my contribution to Chuqiyapu.

Did I need to give an explanation to the Sisters in the house for my final decision? They probably saw it coming. And would they even care? That no longer mattered to me. I was more concerned about the promises I had made to the people in the Chuqiyapu community. In my heart, I knew that Sister Flora would understand my decision to leave early, and Sister Tricia, being the surrogate mother now, would be supportive in her own way.

Life in the convent was not for me; it stifled the person I was meant to become. I had blamed the problems of the Catholic Church on its male dominance and its power over women. There was that, but I learned that it was so much more complicated and nuanced. Did women themselves perpetuate a sexist agenda by following Church's doctrines? I would leave Chuqiyapu with more clarity about the Catholic Church than I had understood before. For me, true obedience was to the self, not to the Church.

When I announced my departure, it came of little consequence to the Sisters. I thought it strange that there was no sign of disappointment, no words of coercion to change my mind, no discussion, no inquiry, or intention to improve communication within the home. No thanks. They had taken those steps with the young Peruvian women, but not with me. Old doctrines continued to stifle the parish's ability to think with an open mind, and the women's rights movement had made less impact within the Peruvian convent walls than in other institutions and parts of the world. As in all families there were flaws, and the Sisters' residence was no different. It was time to leave home, again.

*

In early December, I was preparing to board the same bus I had arrived on, this time, I thought, *for my last time*. Packed and ready to depart at six o'clock in the morning from the main plaza, the sun had not yet broken through the morning fog and frost covering the fields and terraces. Just as it had been on my initial trip from Takana to Chuqiyapu, the bus was filled to the brim with passengers, packages, and livestock. It no longer bothered me that I might share a seat with a stranger, chickens, a box of fresh cheeses, or even a goat; it didn't matter that every inch of the bus would be packed with bodies and produce from *el campo*. I now understood where the produce came from. I appreciated the labor that went into caring for animals and planting and harvesting crops. I welcomed them all. I was grateful to Pachamama. I was grateful for Chuqiyapu.

One by one, all my friends and acquaintances appeared in the plaza to bid farewell. The Sisters, out of obligation, were the first to gather. *La familia* Flores arrived next, followed by Eduarda, Díaz, Doctora Ana, Eugenio and other parishioners. Many other *lugareños* gathered out of curiosity, or en route to their plot of land in the pastures. It was a strange sight to see so many people congregating in the plaza to say goodbye to me, but then again, I wouldn't have expected anything less from those I could, after eleven months together, call friends.

As I stepped onto the bus, Catalina and her family, Edgar, Maruja and Saida approached and called me back down to the curb. Catalina presented me with a handwoven wool tapestry, and she indicated where my name, Kara George, had been woven into the border design hidden among triangles and llamas. I gave Catalina the pair of *ojotas*, sandals I had worn while living in Chuqiyapu. "They'll get more use here in Chuqiyapu than in Boston," I said. She broke out in laughter. We exchanged hugs. Several women had walked all the way from Chumpe at sunrise to make it in time for the bus's departure. They had been chatting with Eduarda before she approached the bus. She carried a large basket filled with fresh cheese, eggs, potatoes, *el chuño*, and a bottle of *chicha*. Eduarda passed the basket to me, and said, "Aquí ... .toma, es para ti. Lleva a tu casa.... a tu mami."

For my mother. I knew the gifts would never make their way to the United States as Eduarda wished; I knew my mother would never taste the Indigenous foods cultivated and harvested in the region on my new friend's land. That would have been nice. What a beautiful gesture. *For my mother.* The immensity of Eduarda's generosity was enough to move me to tears. The food would stay in Takana. I was so touched by her offering that my immediate impulse was to reciprocate such kindness. I had bought a cowboy hat from the only haberdashery in town when I first arrived months earlier; I had worn it every day in solidarity with the residents of Chuqiyapu. Eduarda had told me, on multiple occasions, that she intended to replace her beat-up, weathered cowboy hat but she didn't have the money. I removed mine and placed it on Eduarda's head. Eduarda fell to her knees, slapped her hands together in a prayer position, and bowed in front of me.

"*Madrecita, Madrecita, gracias*, may God bless you," Eduarda said.

I wished Sister Flora were at the bus stop for me to thank her. If not for her, I never would have known that Chuqiyapu existed. Because of her invitation I learned about the Aymara lifestyle, and I was introduced to another Peruvian reality. The ill will of an unhappy nun didn't tarnish the value of my experience in Chuqiyapu—instead, it helped clarify and redirect my life's journey.

My Aussie companion, Father Ryan, and I had continued corresponding after his departure. In his letters, he'd describe the beauty of his country, and now and then, give me advice about how to interact with the Sisters. Ryan's intentions were always good. He was an honest, generous, and kind man who understood the situation I had found myself in. He also understood the shortcomings of the Church to which he took vows when he was in his twenties. He never denied the Church had issues. He butted heads with the Sisters and had his own quarrels with Sister Margaret. That Ryan and I shared a deep connection was our secret. There was no doubt that Ryan and I loved each other, but whether we could have sustained a romantic relationship or have a marriage, we would never know. The Church held constraints that the heart does not know.

I had written to him as soon as I decided to leave. Just before I left, Ryan's response arrived from West Australia. Enclosed in the envelope were two dried wildflowers from the bush near his home. He had carefully protected and pressed two spider orchids, and an everlasting, between tissue paper. The everlasting flower, "a symbol of our love," he said.

My Dearest Kara,

I thought I should immediately respond to your letter. Thanks for sharing so much of yourself; I feel privileged. And I really do feel for you being hurt as you have been. I know you are very sensitive; it's what makes you so special. You are quite important to me. You did keep me sane in Chuqiyapu, you know. And you did help me to believe that I was not completely self-centered and crazy when my opinions differed from the Sisters. I am sorry that you had a bad exchange with Sister Margaret. But, as most things do, it may yield clarity for your future. You deserve better.

In your next letter, tell me how your visit with David went. I was praying on the plane that you'd have a wonderful time, and that, who knows, you would be happy together. I think you would be happy with a man in your life. I see that you may have come to the same conclusion. Maybe you are having a passionate love affair with him now? If only I were not almost sixty years old…and a priest…and living in Australia! I can't say more…

As for me, I have come to realize that it seems to be the Lord's will for me to be here and to blossom where I am planted. I might have been happy in Peru, but I am glad to be back here and to see this place and its people with new eyes. My beloved mother passed on to the other side last week. It was a peaceful death. I am pleased I was able to be present. God's design is not so bad after all.

Please write more when you can. I hope you like the flowers.
I love you,
Ryan XO

As for the bond with the Sisters, none of the Sisters had much to say in way of goodbye, nor did I. No hugs were exchanged. Like the Sisters, I was able to harness more love, kindness, and acknowledgment outside of the home. It was clear that in a short period of time, I was leaving a huge piece of my heart with the people of Chuqiyapu. As I boarded the bus leaving for the coast that day, I started, again, to get weepy. Catalina approached and hugged me.

"*¿Por qué lloras, mi niña?*" She asked why I was crying, saying I should not be sad, that I was going home to be with my family in the great United States of America.

Cata had never traveled far from her hometown. She'd never even been to Takana. She was born and would die in her beloved Chuqiyapu. She knew of, and acknowledged, the wealth and opportunity found in the United States, but she had no desire whatsoever to travel there. She wasn't the least bit envious of my country. She pointed out, on several occasions, how grateful Americans ought to be for such a wonderful land of opportunity. She taught me how much we take things for granted in the United States. We assume that we'll always have loved ones nearby and time to spend with them, and often get rattled when we don't. We have grown accustomed to the belief that we'll always have physical comforts, an endless supply of food, transportation, good health care, and entertainment. How blessed we are. But are there any guarantees in life? Were there ever?

Catalina demonstrated her love for all living things on Earth. She had an intimate connection and profound respect for

Pachamama, as she called Her. She understood its transformative power and trusted that, if we care for Her, Mother Earth would always provide for us. She could make do with less material wealth than me, and she never complained about what she didn't have or couldn't do, not because she deserved less, but because her faith and trust lay in something greater. And, she knew the value of gratitude. A wise woman. There was a long silence. I tried to control my emotions enough to speak.

I said, "*Adios*. I will never forget you."

"*Sí, vas a olvidarnos*. Yes, you will forget us. We, however, will never forget you....but, yes, you will forget us," Cata said.

I thought about where I had been and where I was going. Perhaps Catalina was right. Her words made the parting more difficult, more poignant. Would I forget the Peruvians in Takana, in Chuqiyapu, once back in the United States of America? Tears flooded my eyes. I chose a seat on the bus and settled into what would be another long, bumpy bus ride back to the Southern coast. Aware that I would soon be on my way to my country and excited to see family and friends, I wasn't at all certain whether I would recognize the young woman who had left home almost four years earlier.

To my surprise, there was one more farewell: Sister Tricia had left a letter on the kitchen table the morning of my departure. I saved it to read when I arrived in Takana.

Dear Kara,

Many thanks for your visit and the work you did in Chuqiyapu. I thank God for you, your love for the least of our brothers and sisters,

241

your simplicity and the joy you find in living. I regret that at times our religious community was not able to see this quality in you.

Peace in your heart as you return to your dear mother, father, and brothers. The enclosed money is for a set of slides you may find helpful in sharing the Peruvian reality with others.

Take care. Be gentle and be you...you are a touch of beauty.

Gracias, Sister Tricia

Saying goodbye to *los lugareños*, the locals, was so difficult. Saying goodbye to the Flores family, especially adorable Saida, was excruciating. Then there was Eduarda Quispe, and other women from the knitting/sewing group from Chumpe. Pantaleón Campos and his sheep. The teens from my confirmation class. Díaz Quispe, his mother and little sisters. The Cabral Family from Yanajaja. *Doctora* Ana; and Eugenio, the sacristan at Santo Domingo Church.

None of my soft-spoken friends had said much when I announced I was leaving. No one was surprised; they knew the day would come when the American, *la gringa*, would depart. As "all of them do," I had overheard a local man say. And yet, they all showed up at the plaza for *la despedida*.

What did I leave behind? Had I accomplished what I set out to do in Chuqiyapu? It was hard to know how to measure that. It still is. Perhaps I received more than I gave. *Los lugareños* showed me the beauty of life, and death. I learned that no life or death is more important than another. Each moment shared with the people was unforgettable and meaningful for me; I hoped the feelings were reciprocal. We carried pieces of our existence in each other's hearts, this I knew. We all grew

love and prayers. Kara

inwardly in intangible ways rather than in outward expressions or precise calculations. We lived in the same place for a moment in time. We respected each other. I grew from their generosity, patience, and perseverance. I wondered if I would ever know whether I had impacted their lives, too.

love and prayers, Kara

244

Chapter 22
Two Worlds

When I moved Perú, the more I learned, the less I knew or understood. But, I knew more about the country than my friends and family in the United States. How was I to share what I had learned? How would it sit with them?

Back in the States I was a new version of myself. At first, it was difficult for my friends and family to interact with the person I had become—I had slipped out of the image they had of me. Within months of returning to the States, I found a teaching job in New York City. I taught high schoolers at Metro Academy, a small private co-ed school in Manhattan. Working in a school provided fertile ground for planting seeds about Perú, I thought. I landed the well-paying job quickly and was earning a good salary for the first time in my life, living comfortably in one of the most expensive cities in the United States.

The initial culture shock after returning from Perú eased over the months and years but my awareness of the stark contrasts between daily life in the States and in Perú gnawed at me each day. Living in the Big Apple didn't make it any easier.

I longed to return to South America and the Andes mountains. I missed my Peruvian friends, their kindness, humility, and love. I longed for the simpler, slower paced life in *el campo de Chuqiyapu.*

I taught humanities at Metro Academy, following in the footsteps of Mr. Monroe, my junior high teacher. It took considerable effort to articulate the distinctions between American and Peruvian cultures to my students. I found it tough to reconcile the wealth and opportunities my American students had while many Peruvian students struggled to acquire daily essentials. My students in New York were not much different than I had been at their age; even though I had attended public schools, I too had been oblivious to the truth of other people's suffering. Before Perú, my world revolved solely around my needs and my country. I didn't understand that all people are interconnected, that our joys and sorrows are one in the same, and we are all made of the same stuff. Volunteering in Takana and Chuqiyapu changed that. I strove to teach students from a new understanding.

I covered a wide range of topics in Humanities class. It felt like teaching about Latin America kept my mental health in check; staying connected to the place I loved so dearly was one way to integrate my experience. I told fresh, vivid, and potent stories that often made the students fidgety. I didn't care; I felt it necessary to be truthful. Some of the students at Metro Academy drove Porsches, Mercedes, and BMWs to school. They hadn't a clue how to live without their car, let alone all the abundance in their lives. For my students, a good education was guaranteed, as was food, clothing and medicine. My intention wasn't to make students feel badly about their wealth, but rather to open their minds, ask them to question their reality. I was honest about the poverty and exploitation I'd witnessed. The administration cautioned me, and some families accused me of having a communist agenda. What did it mean to teach if not to open minds to a world larger than what they could conceive? I jarred their perspective.

After several years, I organized a student trip to Latin America. Only seven kids signed on to my first trip to Costa Rica, the safest of the Latin American countries, according to the parents, and therefore the easiest for me to sell. One step at a time, I thought. If all went well, Perú would be the next student trip.

In June 1994, six years after returning from Perú, I read a review of an exhibit at the American Museum of Natural History in *The New York Times*. The exhibit of the Royal Tombs of Sipán from 350 A.D. featured artifacts from a present-day Peruvian excavation. I never could have imagined that within two years of my return to the States, in the late 1980s, some of the world's richest and most extraordinary tombs would be discovered on the northern coast of Perú in the town of Sipán. The finding from three tombs of the pre-Columbian Moche society nobles was on display at the museum. I bought a ticket. When I arrived at the main gallery of the exhibition, I saw a recreation of the tomb of the warrior-priest, the "Lord of Sipán." Displayed in a case to the side of the tomb was a large hammered gold headdress that had been found under the body of the Lord of Sipán and a gold and silver scepter found in his right hand.

Not long before these treasures were dug up, I had walked on the very site of the excavation of the Sipan tomb in 1985, unaware of the contents below. I stifled a scream, honoring the gallery etiquette. I walked into another room and found a life-sized mannequin of the Lord of Sipán dressed in replicas of ceremonial regalia. The curator's interpretation of the man, the warrior-priest, sent chills through my body. He had a scary presence; his harsh gaze had no mercy. As I confronted him, I came to a halt, frozen in awe.

"Tell me," I said aloud to the figure, "about the people you ruled." The security guard asked me to be quiet, but I wanted to talk to the dead. "Where are the common people buried? Were the graves of ordinary people dug up too, and put on display?"

I was searching for the assurance that all people, regardless of their birthplace, wealth, or status, had a proper burial and were remembered with dignity. The mannequin couldn't answer me.

Before I'd had any success convincing families at Metro Academy that their children ought to travel to Perú with me, in the summer of 2003, I booked a flight for myself. It had been fifteen years since I had returned, and it was long overdue. It was easy to lose track of time in the comfortable life I was living.

In part, my decision to return was triggered by a note I'd received from one of my former Metro Academy students. Bruce wrote that he had gone to Ecuador the summer after he graduated from college to help build latrines in poor communities. He shared in his letter that he was still in the country and worked with a non-profit. He continued, saying he planned to travel throughout South America and would make Perú a priority. He remembered stories about Perú from Humanities class, and said, "Ms. Kara, you would light up when you talked about your time there and the people you met." He added, "While living in Ecuador, I understood for myself the joy you felt while working in Latin America. It changed my life, as it did yours, forever. Thank you."

I was in desperate need of a change in my life. I had just broken up with a man I'd been casually seeing for several months, and I had worked myself to the bone at the Metro Academy. I was too busy, or too tired to reap the benefits of the great metropolis surrounding me. I'd become part of the cog in the wheel I preached against when I was a college student. Bruce's letter gave me the nudge I needed.

I left for Perú as soon as the school year ended. Many of my colleagues at Metro Academy assumed I was traveling to the well-known Sacred Valley or Machu Picchu like so many other tourists. The destination had found its way onto many folks' bucket lists since I had lived there. In the late 1980s, Machu Picchu had just under two hundred thousand visitors, a number that would more than triple in the next fifteen years. By 2000, the number was approaching half a million. But my trip wouldn't be a typical tourist trip; I would return to Takana and Chuqiyapu. I'd also learned of other hard truths about Perú since I had left. I learned from a friend in Takana that, between 1982 and 1986, more than 6,000 people were killed at the hands of the terrorist group *Sendero Luminoso* in the state of Ayacucho alone, most of them unarmed civilians. I hadn't had a clue of the immensity of the crimes against humanity committed when

249

I lived there. By 1997, there were "more than 70,000 deaths," she said.

I approached the Newark/New York airport, much as I had on my first trip to Perú fifteen years earlier, excited and nervous. I had packed an arsenal of questions along with my baggage. *What has changed in Perú in all these years? Have roads been paved in remote areas? Has electricity arrived in Chuqiyapu? Has the Catholic Church granted more privileges to women? Have women gained more respect? How have I changed?*

Chapter 23
El Retorno

I landed in Lima in late June 2003 with plans to stay the night in the city before traveling north to Piura in the morning. Other than my initial hopes of seeing Augusto Benicio Sánchez (my singing buddy from the days living in the monastery), there wasn't any reason to stay for more than a night. Unfortunately, I had fallen out of touch with Augusto, and I wasn't interested in opening a can of worms by contacting the monastery to enquire about his whereabouts.

I spent a few hours walking the streets before sunset. I left my B&B in Miramar, a suburb of Lima, and strolled along a busy avenue in search of an ice cream parlor. Lima was nearing the population of New York City in 2003; it was very congested. There, I found little respite from the fast-paced hustle and bustle of my American city. It took some self-talk to propel myself through the first leg of the trip. I traveled alone and that made me just as self-conscious as I had been fifteen years before. I was a tall, white woman with no wedding band on my left finger; this last detail would not be lost on some men and would invite flirtatious banter on every corner I passed. I had learned before that this was part of the territory in the streets of Perú. Some of the hissing was innocent fun, but mostly it was unwelcome. I was annoyed.

In the 2000s women were still living with heavy expectations and constraints placed upon us. The grip was loosening more rapidly in the United States, but traditional thinking still persisted and often shamed single, childless women. However, more and more women, including me, were postponing marriage and childbearing. In the States, we had the freedom to choose what to do with our pregnancies, unlike our sisters in other parts of the world. In Perú, as I had witnessed first-hand, there was still less freedom for women. Abortion under any circumstance was illegal. Catholicism also hindered their choices. The Church conjured the myth that it was a married woman's duty to birth children; women who chose not to would lose favor in God's eyes. In a country where many women marry and have children, perhaps it seemed strange to Peruvians that more women in the United States were postponing these family commitments and were making different choices altogether. I felt fortunate to have the freedom to choose for myself. I never placed my worth in whether I was married or how many children I had. There were many children in the world to love, I thought. I had never shaken the memory of *Soledad* who I lost in Takana; it influenced my outlook on whether to have my own children or not. There were many lives to attend to, I learned. Adoption was a viable option, too. I felt satisfied with my life and pleased that I hadn't joined the convent, after all. I returned to Perú unattached, no man, no children, no institution, and happy.

I stopped to buy a cone in a small corner establishment that looked nothing like the *Baskin Robbins* store back home. Here the seating was sparse and ice cream was flavored with local tropical fruits from the *la selva*. Among the flavor selections were *lucuma* and *chirimoya*—neither fruit was available in my country. I had a hard time deciding between the two flavors since I had craved both fruits for years. I ordered a large *chirimoya* cone, and a bottle of mineral water *sin gas* to take back to the hotel room. Two male Spanish-speaking customers seated near the counter immediately took note of me and, assuming the American wouldn't understand their language, tossed a few vulgar words in my direction. *Las palabrotas*, crude words, immediately landed in my ears as clear as my own tongue. I was proud of myself; I had maintained Spanish fluency by seeking out opportunities to keep using the language. Now approaching forty, I was comfortable in my own skin, I was able to let the comments roll off my shoulders without making a scene. But the remarks kept coming.

"*Oye mamacita... ven acá... que te quiero mostrar algo*" *I want to show you something.*

Another man slapped his hands on his lap and said, "*Siéntate acá mi niña.*" *Sit down here little girl.*

To some degree, the suggestive comment stroked my ego: I could still draw the attention of men. Or was it more likely the fact that I was so tall, or that an American woman stood out? Regardless, it was unnerving. I left the parlor with a sigh of relief. Shortly after exiting, I noticed that I was being followed. The man following me was one of the pesky men from the parlor speaking to me in Spanish and trying to please me with a bit of English.

"I will accompany you, take care of you, and make sure no one bothers you."

"No, *gracias, estoy bien.* I am fine, I don't need anyone to accompany me," I said.

He attached himself to me like a mosquito and followed me for several blocks.

"You…very pretty. What your name?"

I tried to ignore him, but he wouldn't detach from me.

"*Teléfono*, you …me…please, please."

"*Déjeme en paz, por favor!* Leave me alone, please. You are bothering me," I said.

Surely, I did nothing to invite this behavior. Was I still an anomaly on these streets? The incident reminded me of harassments that had made my life uncomfortable years before. I was disappointed, and my heart sank at the realization that some things had not changed.

After a night's sleep, I headed to the airport where I would wait for my flight to Piura. We boarded the plane on time but had to disembark soon after. We were told that the plane's engine had to be replaced, and we would be boarding another plane within the hour. I had been in Perú for less than twenty-four hours and already I showed signs of impatience. But newcomers to Perú were far more vocal about their displeasure. A young American woman took a seat beside me in the waiting area.

"What brought you to Perú " she asked.

It was a great question, but it was difficult to answer. I mean, *should I get into the whole story? How can I make this simple?* I thought.

"After graduating from college, I wanted to volunteer in another country and I came here," I said. "This is a return trip for me."

"Why Perú? Couldn't you volunteer anywhere?"

She had a point. *Had I chosen Perú or had Perú chosen me?* I didn't want to get into any real details about my life, the job offer, and motivations so I redirected the conversation to her. "What about you? Why Perú?"

"Oh, I am going to a yoga retreat in the Sacred Valley," she said. "I came with a group of women. I understand there is a high spiritual vibration in the Sacred Valley. We're staying in a beautiful retreat center in Urubamba. Six days and five nights, all the yoga classes you want...and the classes are in English," she said. "Oh, and a trip to Machu Picchu is included."

"Very nice. What do you hope to get out of the trip?" I said.

"I just need a getaway, and this yoga retreat was very cheap," she said.

"I hope you have a wonderful stay," I said.

The intercom announced that the next flight destined for *Cusco* would be delayed another few hours.

"Geez, this is crazy. Why didn't they tell us before that we were going to be delayed again? I can't believe it....this sucks," she said.

I thought to myself, *she may be in for a long, long wait, I hope she's up for it.* "There's nothing we can do about it," I said.

She didn't respond to my comment.

love and prayers, Kara

The eventual flight from Lima to the northern city of Piura took less than two hours. From the Piura airport, I paid a *taxista* one hundred and forty American dollars to drop me at the door of a spa on the coast. The town of Máncora itself was not very picturesque, but the locals were still exploiting tourists even years after Ernest Hemingway had vacationed there in the 1950s. I never went to the center of town; there was enough beauty on the beach to satisfy me. I stretched out on a lounge chair, ate fresh tuna tartar, ceviche, and mussels, and drank pisco sours. I tracked the rhythms of the ocean's waves and watched seagulls fly over crumbs left behind by foreigners. I closed my eyes and concentrated on the sound of the waves. Their ebb and flow quickly synchronized with my breath. I was exhausted from the school year. As best as I could, I tried to let go of the past and the future. I remained in a meditative place for a long time. No longer needing a church—I had let that devotion go years before—nature was my temple now. The silence was grand. I felt the breeze blow through my hair with great intensity; I smelled the salty air and felt my whole body blanketed with the warm sun. The repetition of waves crashing in and flowing out reminded me that change was a constant part of life. When I opened my eyes, my mind was clearer.

After relaxing for a few days in Máncora, I left for Lambayeque Valley. I could visit all the archaeological sites I so desired, and I would finally visit the Brüning Museum and surrounding burial sites. Most of what I would see had not yet been discovered when I first visited as a young twenty-something woman. Now at forty years old, I was still filled with the curiosity and enthusiasm of a child. What had been discovered since the site's first excavation? I had seen some of what was dug up in the museum in New York City and was intrigued. Since then, the excavations had continued and would continue. For years to come, new levels of the tomb would be unearthed. *How far down would the archaeologists dig before they came up empty-handed?* I wondered. Perú's past civilizations might shine some light on its culture and history, but would I get any clearer about the mystery of death? I asked the owner of the Máncora retreat if she had heard about the first discovery of the Royal Tombs of Sipán, and she said, "Everyone in the area has. The discovery rivals that of Carter and Carnarvon in Egypt."

When I arrived the next day at the Brüning Museum hoping to find the museum's director, Walter Alba, I was told he'd return soon. As I looked around the grounds of the museum, my first impulse was to snap several photographs of *las huacas* scattered on the landscape beyond the museum building. It didn't matter that they didn't make great photos — they were much more than mounds of dirt in the middle of nowhere. The Quechan word *huaca* referred to a place or ritual that was revered. It was sacred dirt I stood upon. If I was being honest, the ancient sacred site, at least from where I was standing, was underwhelming and disappointing. Did I think that photographing these large mounds of dry dirt would capture the fleeting life of the dead?

When I met with Walter Alba later that evening, my disappointment vanished. The Lambayeque Valley was full of rich, yet to be discovered, treasures, he told me. *Huaqueros,* gravediggers, roamed the area day and night in hopes of finding precious artifacts that could be cashed in for *soles*, maybe put some food on families' tables. I had heard all about the *huaqueros* on my first trip to Perú. I could only imagine the excitement of the locals uncovering the riches—gold in all shapes and sizes—from *la huaca*. Alba told me that just prior to the first major discovery of the royal Sipán Tombs, the looters had excavated non-stop for three days and nights at the site.

"They met an unanticipated fate as one man's human nature got the best of him: one *huaquero*, feeling he had not received his fair share of the treasure, turned informer to the police," he said. "The police raided the site, and soon after, bags of gold were laid out on a table in the police station."

"Where were you when all this happened?" I said.

"I was in bed when the police called me. I was very sick with bronchitis, and I didn't want to answer the phone. But thank God I did because that phone call changed my life," *Señor* Alba said.

While the police held several *huaqueros* in custody, he said, Alva was called upon to share his expertise about some looted items that were retrieved. Although he felt miserable and was barely able to get out of bed, he magnanimously agreed that he would go over to the station first thing the next morning. But the policeman insisted, "Tomorrow would be too late." They were right; when Alba got to the police station, he couldn't believe his eyes. Walter Alva continued to provide more details of that night, his face animated and his hands and arms flaring every which way with passion.

"When I arrived at the police station, I was presented with items roughly wrapped in paper: a pure-gold face, with wide unblinking turquoise eyes; two giant peanuts made of pure gold, three times normal size; a feline head also of gold, with jagged teeth of shell set in an angry snarl. At that moment, I completely forgot about my illness and no longer felt sick. I was astonished."

In decades of scientific research, such items had never been found before—yet all came from an unprepossessing pyramid site of Huaca Rajada, not far from the local village of Sipán. Alba shared the story of the discovery of the warrior's tomb with an enthusiasm I could relate to. What a privilege to hear a firsthand account of the discovery directly from him. The buried treasures—gold, silver, textiles, pottery, and a whole wealth of archaeological data about a lost civilization—were extraordinary, but the objects themselves weren't what mattered most to us, to me. I had come for answers about death.

Walter Alba spoke of death that evening. "No one will escape death but perhaps lessons of how people lived would ease our fears. The insights into how people lived and died is what we all crave. That we care enough to remember and learn from them is what matters most." Señor Alba said he had made a decision that night. "I will build a museum right here. It will be called *el Museo de las Tumbas Reales de Sipán* and will replicate one of the tombs found beneath the ground. All visitors will find meaning in their lives by studying our past."

Julie and I had never said goodbye. When we last spoke in the hospital before her death, how could I have known that it was our last time together? I hadn't gone to Julie's burial. Death and cemeteries scared me. I visited her tombstone months later, but I was still numb. I could have honored this important passage of life with more respect, I thought. As a young woman, I didn't understand the importance of bidding farewell or giving her a proper send-off. Now that I was older, I still wished I had.

The next day, as I stood above the ancient gravesites of Sipán, the sacred ground shook. I had lived through earthquakes before and this tremor might have registered a four or five, but it left no destruction in its path. Nothing around me fell and I was still standing. When I got my wits about me, I felt Julie's presence with me.

"Julie, are you there? I miss you," I said.

"I'm here. I miss you too," she said, "but it's time to say goodbye."

"I know," I said.

"It's time to move on from death's shroud, Kara. Go, enjoy life, love again, and again."

"Goodbye."

*

The anticipation of my arrival in Takana after fifteen years stirred emotions. Fifteen years is a long time. During the plane ride I tried to calm myself. I attempted to release all expectations about the trip, but my mind listed them anyway: see old friends; return to the hospital with Sister Sarah; return to Chuqiyapu. I considered a visit to *Colegio Ignatius Loyola*, then I discarded it from my list. When the pilot announced our descent, I gazed out the window to see the same endless extension of the desert I knew from the past. Looking down on Takana, I still saw more sand and scattered dwellings than trees and vegetation. My belly began to feel the effects of my nerves.

I thought I might get the runs. It occurred to me that I might not recognize my old friends and acquaintances; everyone had aged, including me. My quality of life maintained youthful skin and hair color, but would my friends show signs of aging? Wrinkles and white hair? Some had birthed children, and others had suffered loss and illness in the years since we'd seen one another.

As I disembarked and walked down the portable staircase, I began to perspire. Nerves. I had to loosen the collar of my blouse to allow some air in. The hot, humid air I had left on the east coast in the States was now damp and chilly.

But none of my concerns appeared to matter when my feet hit the pavement in Takana. I immediately recognized another version of myself. Someone more open, untethered, and trusting of life's mystery. It was as if I was having an out-of-body experience, and someone I hadn't seen in some time showed up. I watched this woman, myself, as if in a movie, walking toward the terminal. *Who was this woman?* Stripped of a country, a language, a job, a car, an apartment, and a family, what part of her was showing up after fifteen years? There were material objects in view that I hadn't seen in recent days. All that was in view — the forms, colors, sounds, and smells — were different from those I left behind the day before. Why do material objects carry so much weight if, within hours they no longer exist? New objects and people appeared. Who was I when stripped from all I know?

The reception at the airport was in typical Takaño style: before I even got into the terminal, several close friends were waving and shouting, "Kara, *mi amiga*, Kara." on the tarmac.

Mercedes, Rina and her children were at the greeting party. My girlfriends and I embraced and kissed. Some were thicker around the waist and others had toddlers at their hips. I was thrilled to see them. It felt as though the years between us hadn't created distance.

I asked, "And Father Ignatius?" The Jesuit and I had fallen out of touch. The man was responsible for my introduction to Perú, he who first greeted me some eighteen years earlier. On the one hand, I regretted not making any effort to stay in touch—I had the immaturity of an early twenty-something girl to blame for that. Now a little wiser, I was able to acknowledge the valuable role he had played in my life; if not for him, I never would have gone to Perú.

They would be the bearers of the news that he no longer lived in Takana. The Society of Jesus had called Father Ignatius to a mission in Iquitos, a city in the Peruvian jungle. Father had answered the call, and there he would serve in a Jesuit mission on the border of Perú and Brazil. In all likelihood, I wouldn't travel there any time soon.

While waiting for my luggage at the carousel, we all reminisced about our days at *Colegio Ignacio Loyola*. Before my friends could whisk me off to a nearby restaurant, where I would devour *Ají de Gallina*, one of my favorite Peruvian dishes, I heard a male voice calling my name out of nowhere.

"¿*Kara, Kara?* ¿*Es usted?* Is that you?"

I turned towards a Peruvian young man. He was tall, slender and handsome.

"You were my art teacher at *Colegio Ignacio Loyola*, right?"

With some difficulty, I tried to recall one of the over one hundred students I had taught seventeen years earlier. He spoke in Spanish with a few English words thrown in.

"*Me llamo Miguel Angel Jurado Jiménez*...you remember? I was in the class of 1987."

"Oh, *sí,sí* ...." I said. But I lied: I wasn't sure which young person he was from those days in my classroom at *Colegio Ignacio Loyola*. Perhaps it had been too many years, maybe too much had happened in my life over the past fifteen years, or possibly I had shoved down most memories from the Jesuit school. I instantly recalled a comment that Catalina had made when I left Chuqiyapu: "You will forget us, but we will never forget you." It held some truth. I didn't recognize the young man. When I had last seen him, he had been a seventeen-year-old boy. Now he was a grown man. For all I knew, he might have been one of the boys at *Colegio Ignacio Loyola* who had annoyed *la maestra* with his pranks. Maybe he was one I wanted to forget. Did he grope me on the bus on the way to the beach? Initially, I didn't know.

"How have you been?" I asked.

"*Pues, es una historia.* Well, it's a long story. Many things have happened. I studied in university, had a daughter, got married, and divorced."

"*Sí*,... lots has happened. How old is your daughter?"

"You haven't changed a bit," he said.

What did he mean? Had he noticed what I had? Who was the woman who had landed on Takaño soil?

"*Muchas gracias*," I said.

"*¿Está casada? Tiene hijos?* Are you married? Do you have children?"

"No, not married. I don't have kids," I said.

I noticed that he was using the formal "*usted*" and I was a bit disappointed. It made me feel older and distant, but it was probably out of respect. I wondered if he was surprised that I was still a single woman — after all, fifteen years was more than enough time to get married and have a few kids. But there was not enough time in our short encounter to share the details of our lives. As we spoke, I felt light and flirtatious — it had never occurred to me that I might find a former student from Ignacio Loyola physically attractive. *He is a delightful man,* I thought. I became more aware of my physical appearance in his presence. It was apparent that nothing about my outward appearance resembled the girl that stood before the boys in the classroom years before. Now, the woman from NYC had soft honey highlights in her brown, and fashionable, shortish haircut. One could see her knees above the dress hemline, her long shapely legs accentuated by the three-inch heeled boot she wore. Everyone could see where her cleavage began.

The arrival of the luggage interrupted and cut short our conversation. As I headed for the exit with my girlfriends, Miguel Angel re-engaged, asking how long I would be in Takana, then grabbing a piece of scrap paper from his pants pocket and scribbling his phone number before passing it to me.

"*Gracias, cuídate.* Take care of yourself," I said.

We parted with a cordial kiss on each cheek, a custom not commonly shared between Americans and one I had dreadfully missed. I didn't make arrangements to see him during my visit

love and prayers, Kara

as I had other priorities, places to visit, and people to catch up with. I didn't call him.

love and prayers. Kara

Chapter 24
Rodrigo Mamani Mamani

The many abandoned children I met at *Hospital de Santa Teresa* in Takana would affect me for the rest of my life. I couldn't shake Rodrigo Mamani Mamani from my memory. I had spent so much time with Soledad that at first I hadn't noticed Rodrigo. But the toddler had been there all along. He too had been abandoned, however, unlike Soledad, his mother had never returned for him. I had not inquired about him since I left Perú, but I remained curious about what might have become of him after all those years.

Sister Sarah would be able to give an update and information about his whereabouts and progress when we got together. I couldn't wait to see her. After twenty-seven years of service, she was still living in Takana with the Marian Sisters community. She had aged in those years; her deeply wrinkled skin was covered in age spots, her hair was white, and she had arthritic hands. She no longer had a skip in her step as she did before. However, she was still doing the same outreach, still sprinkling the same love to everyone in her path and still visiting *Hospital de Santa Teresa* weekly, just as she and I had once done.

"What ever happened to Rodrigo? Did a family adopt him? Is he still living in Takana? Did he get eye surgery?"

"Oh, my dear, didn't I tell you about that?" Sister Sarah said. "Do you want to see him?"

"Of course," I said.

I was forever grateful to Sister Sarah for her kindness and devotion. I always appreciated her openness—unlike many religious Sisters, she had adapted well to the Catholic Church's Vatican II changes—and how she had introduced me to the mission of visiting the sick by example, not by forcing it down my throat. Together Sister Sarah and I had visited hundreds of children in Takana during the mid-1980s. Most of the children we visited had sad stories and heartbreaking stories had continued to fill beds over the years. Even among these, Rodrigo Mamani Mamani's story was compelling.

Rodrigo was a plump one-year-old baby when Sister Sarah first introduced us. He had been abandoned by his mother who was presumably not fit to care for the child due to mental illness. It was said that she had been admitted to a mental institution, but the whole story and the truth behind her disappearance, was not known nor would it ever be fully explained. As Sister Sarah always got the details of the children's illness from the physicians, so too had she spoken with Rina Rossellini, a pediatrician and friend, about Rodrigo's general health and eye condition. Dr. Rossellini was particularly helpful to Sister Sarah because she spoke good English. Sister often sought her help to understand the children's medical conditions. The boy had glaucoma in both eyes, a problem often seen among elderly people in the United States but rarely to the same degree as seen in Perú. In the case of Rodrigo, childhood glaucoma might have developed when he was an infant. If not treated properly then, the result might be problematic. The child had lost sight in one eye.

Over the course of two years of hospital visits, Sister Sarah and I grew fond of Rodrigo. All the nurses and the physicians who cared for the boy adored him; he had an engaging personality, was a bit goofy and, despite his abandonment, was a very affectionate child. Sister Sarah worked long and hard to find a home for him and, several years after I returned to the States, thanks to her efforts, he landed with an extraordinary family in *La Casa de Esperanza*, the orphanage in La Joya, Perú.

"Rodrigo loves his home in La Joya. He's been there for almost thirteen years now. It's been such a wonderful place for him, Kara. The younger kids in the house love and look up to him!"

"I am so pleased to hear that news, Sister. All thanks to you."

"And…my answered prayers," she said.

Sister Sarah had visited the orphanage over the years, always keeping an eye out for an empty bed for an unfortunate child on the streets or in the hospital in Takana. My visit to the orphanage with Sister Sarah in the 1980s had changed my awareness and definition of family. Sister knew it would be a perfect home for Rodrigo should there be space for a new member. The orphanage had a wonderful reputation in Perú and abroad, run by the Sisters of Our Lady of the Angels, the order I had lived with in the mountains. Because of this, it was able to sustain itself with generous donations pouring in from all over the world for orphaned children. Since I had been to the home, *La Casa de Esperanza* had grown exponentially, both a testament to how successful it was run and a sobering reality that there were so many abandoned Peruvian children. In the 1980s, it housed approximately thirty-five children of all ages; by 2003, it was a large children's shelter, housing over one hundred and fifty infants, toddlers, teens, and young adults. It was an exceptional place. Over the years, more Sisters were assigned to work at the orphanage, but it was not enough, and so, the nuns solicited the help of local volunteers and provided room and board to those who joined the mission from other countries.

Sister Sarah said she had "placed Rodrigo's name on a waiting list as soon as he was able to walk." Just after he turned four years old, a bed became available and Sister Sarah jumped at the opportunity. I was struck by the home's mission and its success. As Sister Sarah spoke about how Rodrigo had found a bed and ultimately a family in *La Joya*, I felt some regret for my lack of correspondence with the Sisters of Our Lady of the Angels over more than a decade. *La Casa de Esperanza* was a testament to the good works done by the religious order, their Christian mission firmly planted. I carried a bit of resentment since I'd detached myself from the *Santo Domingo* mission in the 1980s, but in time I had been able to forgive any harm the institution had caused. As for my faith, I no longer followed or practiced Catholicism. I had undergone my own inner transformation, a shift from fear to love. I no longer needed or trusted a church to console me; nature did that. I found security within myself and in the goodness of people.

A reunion with Rodrigo would be spectacular if Sister Sarah could make it happen. *Would I recognize him? Would Rodrigo remember me?* Rodrigo Mamani was almost nineteen years old, still living at *La Casa de Esperanza,* and excelling in his last year in *la secundaria* with high honors in his coursework. Like all his brothers and sisters living under the same roof, he had household chores and shared in the care of the younger children. A good example was set by his older brothers and sisters when he had first arrived there as a toddler. He was raised well. He now occupied the respected position of the oldest brother in the family.

Sister Sarah contacted Rodrigo and invited him to meet with us. We met on a Tuesday afternoon, in front of *Hospital de Santa Teresa,* as was customary for us in the earlier days. The visit would mark Rodrigo's first return to the hospital since he left. It was his first home, the place where he had been abandoned and where he had learned to walk. Sister and I met at the Marian house for lunch and then traveled on the local bus to meet the boy. We had a lot to catch up on.

"How were your travels to Perú, Kara?"

"No glitches, thanks for asking," I said. "Don't let me forget to tell you what happened at Takana airport when I arrived," I said.

"Oh, do tell," she said.

The bus made many stops along the way and each time Sister and I stood and moved to new seats to accommodate mothers and infants. Our conversation got sidetracked.

"I imagine you're happy to be back?" Sister Sarah said.

"You know, Sister, I feel like I am a different person here in Perú."

"What do you mean?"

"I am not sure. I can't put my finger on it. But I like it. I am still a bit wishy-washy about being back in the States. Even after all these years," I said.

"You'd consider moving back to Peru?" Sister Sarah said.

"Possibly. But when I arrived a few days ago, I felt some culture shock, too."

"What about it is challenging?"

"The disorganization, lack of sanitation, the lack of toilet paper in bathrooms, the *piropos* from men."

"Are those annoyances really important?" she said. "Give it time, dear."

"It will be interesting to see how my visit goes," I said.

Since Sister knew everyone in town, I was certain she would be able to tell me something about the family of the student I had met in the airport. "Does the name Miguel Angel Jurado Jimenez ring a bell?"

Sister Sarah said, "I remember the family. I think Miguel Angel is their eldest son. A very bright boy...I believe he had a full scholarship to the Jesuit school."

"I vaguely remember. Did they live near the school?"

"Yes, you must remember the family....such a wonderful family," Sister Sarah said.

As Catalina had predicted, I had forgotten a lot. The truth was that there were few former students or *Colegio Ignacio Loyola* families that I remembered.

"Why do you ask," Sister Sarah said.

"I ran into Miguel Angel in the airport when I arrived."

"Is that so? That's what was so interesting at the airport," Sister Sarah said. "I believe Miguel Angel went to Lima after graduating from *la secundaria* to study medicine, if I remember correctly. Rumor has it that shortly after graduating from Colegio Ignacio Loyola, he had a daughter. I think Miguel Angel was eighteen and the girl was sixteen."

"Did Miguel Angel finish medical school?"

"I think so. The baby's mother was young, you know…it couldn't have been easy. I don't know what happened to her, but she's no longer in the picture."

"I know," I said. "He told me."

"Hmmm. So, will you see him again?"

"I don't know," I said. "He gave me his phone number."

"How long will you be staying with us in Takana, Kara?"

"At least until the end of July," I said.

"That's not a lot of time, is it?" Sister Sarah said.

"We'll see. My school begins in late August."

We arrived at the hospital to find Rodrigo waiting on a bench at the entrance. The teenager still had the same pleasant disposition and the same big bulging eyes. Despite having had several surgeries to correct his eye condition, he was blind in the left one and wore dark large, rimmed glasses to correct the vision in the other. The glasses seemed too big for his face. He was short in part due to having been in a cast multiple times for so many months when he was a baby.

"*Hola, Rodrigoo. ¿Me recuerdas?* Do you remember me?" I said.

273

"*Sí, Madrecita,*" he said.

There it was again, *madrecita*. Even after so many years, I was never going to shed the name *Madrecita*, especially when hanging out with Sister Sarah and visiting strangers. Rodrigo was courteous. Although he said he remembered me, it was not clear if he did—I might have been just one of many *madrecitas* who had entered and exited his life. We all agreed we'd visit pediatrics patients on the third floor where Rodrigo had lived for just shy of five years.

I was shocked to see that, after fifteen years, the ward hadn't changed, and infants and toddlers were still laying in dirty sheets. Rodrigo became quiet and pensive as he accompanied us from crib to crib to see the children. I couldn't help but wonder what was going through the teen's mind. What memories stirred in Rodrigo? Were they happy ones? Were they painful? I soon realized that I was projecting my own uneasiness onto the situation. I had mixed emotions about visiting the children; a tightness in my chest signaled distress. Soledad came to my mind. My desire and inquiry about adopting her resurfaced. And her tragic death. *Beautiful solitude haunts me.*

We didn't stay long in the ward, just enough time to deliver some food, share a few smiles, and offer prayers and blessings. Several of the women who had nursed the children back in the day recognized Rodrigo. And he recognized his surrogate mothers, too. *Doctora* Rossellini was doing rounds on the floor; she remembered him as well. *Doctora* and the nurses were excited to learn of the boy's progress.

"Look at you…how are you?" *Doctora* said.

"*Bien, me siento tan agradecido.* I am forever grateful to all of you and everyone at the hospital for all they have done for me. You all saved my life," he said.

"And, it's thanks to you, *Madrecita* Sarah, that Rodrigo found a home in *La Joya,* and has received a great education," one nurse said.

"No, not just me," Sarah said. "So many people contributed to his success…"

"*Sí, Madrecita tiene razón. Hay que dar gracias a todos. Bendito sea el señor.* Sister is right, I must thank everyone. Blessed be God," Rodrigo said.

Before departing, all the hospital staff got their turn at embracing Rodrigo. Success stories were worth noting and celebrating.

While leaving the main entrance to the hospital, a tall, slender man in a white medical jacket leaned against the reception desk with his back to us. When he turned around, I recognized that it was Miguel Angel Jurado Jimenez.

"¡*Hola!*..what a surprise," Miguel Angel said.

"Well, hello! It's great to see you again," I said.

"¿*Cómo te va?* What brings you here to the hospital? Is everything okay?"

"Sí, todo bien. It's a long story. I am here with Sister Sarah. You remember her? y un amigo, Rodrigo. We were visiting some patients," I said.

I introduced Miguel Angel to Sister Sarah and Rodrigo. It took no time for Miguel Angel and Sister Sarah to remember that they had been neighbors for years when he was a kid. Greetings were exchanged in haste as it appeared that Miguel

love and prayers. Kara

Angel needed to be somewhere else. He turned to me, he said, "Pleasure to see you again. *Espero su llamada* — call me."

"*Muy bien, adiós,*" I said.

During our brief encounter, I felt a strong energetic pull toward him. *He wants me to call him.* I began rationalizing my way through what I was feeling: *he's no longer my student, he is now a man, he's divorced. It is completely natural to have a physical attraction.* I calculated that I would only be four to seven years older than my former student. While the age difference mattered then, it no longer did. Now we were peers. And I was curious.

Chapter 25
Chuqiyapu, again

I called Miguel Angel soon after we collided at the hospital. We met over coffee at Esperanza Cafe in town. I was certain after our first encounter that our friendship had the potential for something great. What were the chances that I would connect with a former student from Colegio Ignacio Loyola fifteen years later? Especially when I hadn't wanted any part of that past. After seeing him in the hospital, I figured maybe there was something to the concept of fate. I wondered if I chose my destiny or if it was chosen for us.

It's always joyful for a teacher to see how their students have grown, the people they have become. With Miguel Angel our conversation was effortless. There was a deep connection. We talked about politics, religion, friendship, love, children, science, space, the moon, and the stars. You name it, we discussed it.

I remembered that he had been the art student who had dared to leave his page blank, the one who had made me see differently.

We continued to meet, for *el almuerzo*, later in the week, then for walks that started at three o'clock in the afternoon and extended into the evening. Our meetings went on for days. Our conversations were filled with energy, curiosity, and wonder. They were unlike any I had had in recent years; there was no trying to impress or control. Just pure delight. Being from different backgrounds and cultures wasn't an impediment, but instead an allure, a seduction. We spoke mostly in Spanish, although there were opportunities for me to take the role of English teacher, and it was all lots of fun. I told him I still taught, but no longer art. He told me that he wrote poetry.

"Wonderful. Perhaps I will read one of your poems, someday?"

"I hope so," he said. "You know that Takana is a wonderful place to see the stars."

"Why is that?"

"We are just miles from the Atacama Desert; the conditions are great to see into space."

"How so?"

"The sky is so clear. I am told that in Chile there is a plateau in the desert that is one of the highest and driest places on Earth — a perfect place to see the cosmos. There is so much light from the stars that Indigenous people name the dark spaces in the sky instead of the stars."

"Wow, *vámonos*," I said.

"*Perfecto*. I don't think we can go to Chile, but we'll go stargazing one night before you leave."

I had never learned that when I lived in Takana in the 1980s. What else had I missed? The new relationship between

Miguel Angel and me stretched me in new ways and broadened my life perspective. We also talked about life in New York City; how congestion and noise filled the streets, and how lights dampened the brightness of the stars at night and made me feel less connected to nature. We talked about how Takana had changed — its population had tripled in size since I lived there, and traffic, the noise from the honking of horns, and the smog had changed the landscape of the place.

"What else would you like to do while in Perú, Kara?" Miguel Angel said.

"I'd like to go to *la sierra*. I would like to return to Chuqiyapu," I said.

"*Vamos*," he said.

"You'll come with me?"

"Sure, I've never been."

After meeting Miguel Angel, I began to feel as though I would need more time in Perú. I hadn't anticipated I would get sidetracked by an unexpected connection with a former student, and it was worth my time and attention. Time is precious, I thought, I must enjoy every minute of it. The more time I spent with him meant less time spent with former colleagues and girlfriends.

The women who nursed me back to health when I was sick, both physically and mentally, and boosted my confidence when I struggled in the early days in the country, deserved some time too. If not for the wisdom and love of those strong women, I probably wouldn't have stayed in Perú for as long as I had. We enjoyed cooking and hours of conversation chatting about life, my country, and life in NYC. It was marvelous to be in their company once again.

"*Oye*, what's going on with you and the former student?" Mercedes asked.

"*Nada*," I said.

"*Como que nada*. It is not nothing if you spend more time with him than us," Rina said with a laugh.

"We have a connection worth exploring. That's all I can say," I said.

"Life is short, but be careful," Mercedes said. She was a dear lady, perhaps a bit overprotective, but I appreciated her. I understood why she warned me—she knew of my past experiences with men in Perú—and I listened to her, but I knew in my gut that Miguel Angel was different. *He is a good man.* I trusted my instincts, called the travel agency and moved my departure date to the end of August.

*

Three weeks into my visit in Perú, I was on a bus to Chuqiyapu. *La sierra* held important personal significance to me; I found confidence and peace of mind in the mountains. When I had first gone to Chuqiyapu, I was considering becoming a bride of God. I now understood that loving a man didn't mean I loved God any less. Could I be the bride of a man? Of nature? I had a great capacity to love, and it grew as I learned to love and trust myself. I couldn't believe how lucky I was to have Miguel Angel along for the ride to this beloved town.

We arrived at the Takana bus terminal at five o'clock in the morning. There was already a line of people waiting for a seat on the daily bus. We got the last two seats in the back row. I knew what the ride would entail and that sitting at the back of the bus made it worse. Little had changed in Perú since I had last ventured into the Andes Mountains. The call for the bathroom came too soon and made the ride uncomfortable; each time we hit a bump I squeezed my leg together to prevent myself from urinating in my pants. I had matured a lot since the '80s — physical discomforts would never cease to challenge me but they no longer carried the same weight they had when I first made the trip to the mountains.

Not long after our midday stop, the worn-out bus had difficulty making its way up the hills and it gave out. There was something strange and inevitable about this road I had traveled before; it prevented any vehicle on its path from smooth sailing to its destination. All the passengers were asked to leave the bus with no explanation for the cause of the delay. We would spend hours on the side of the road waiting under the hot sun until the bus was repaired.

I started to get impatient and complained about the heat. Should we start walking? Should we wait? How far was it to Chuqiyapu on foot? Would we arrive sooner on foot or by waiting for the bus to be repaired? Miguel Angel, one hundred times more patient than me, convinced me it was better to wait. So we waited.

To the rest of the passengers, my impatience and complaints regarding the whole fiasco were comical. *For real*? I thought. Hadn't I learned my lesson years ago when I was in a similar situation? Had I forgotten my mantra — expect the unexpected. It still lurked somewhere in my psyche from previous experiences, but it would take a bit of effort to access it on this journey. After more than a decade, most roads leading to *la sierra* were only partially paved, buses still carried far more passengers than regulations required, and buses broke down on a regular basis. This trip required patience, calm and acceptance. I had to remind myself of the lessons I had learned in the mountains. I was better at going with the flow of life. Or so I thought.

Suddenly I spotted a woman who looked familiar in the clusters of people gathered around the bus. I said to Miguel Angel, "I think I know that woman over there from years ago. She lived in Chumpe and Chuqiyapu."

"Excellent. Why don't you approach her and ask her?"

It seemed simple and logical to him, but I hesitated for several hours. In the last hour of our long wait—not knowing why it had taken me so long—I found enough courage to approach the woman.

¿Eres Eduarda?"

"Sí, soy Eduarda."

She was the woman I knew from years ago. I helped her recall who I was, the volunteer who had lived in Chuqiyapu and worked with the *Madres* in *la Parroquia Santo Domingo*. I reminded her, "I taught knitting and sewing to a small group of women in Chumpe."

Her face lit up with delight when she recognized me. Then her arms encircled me in a firm embrace. The glorious encounter made the four hours of waiting worth it. With no effort, wind blew in the memories we had shared: her family's temporary stay at the church residence, our commemorative visit to the cemetery to see her deceased children, and the art classes with Hilda and Fidela.

"*Madrecita, todavía tengo el sombrero,*" she said, reaching for the brim of her hat. She still wore the hat I had given her, although it was now weathered, soiled and beaten by time.

I asked her about the parish and the Sisters. With a wave of a hand in the air, she said they had departed long ago.

Then, the passengers were called and told to board the bus. Everyone rushed to the door hoping to be the first to sit down; it had been long half-day waiting in the hot sun. It was evening by the time we approached the main town plaza of Chuqiyapu. I hardly recognized the town entrance—I was astounded to see lights leading the way. A small sidewalk lined with lamps and decorated with statues welcomed us to the main plaza, while a huge sign saying "Bienvenidos a Chuqiyapu" blocked the view of the picturesque landscape. The sign seemed misplaced, too big and the letters painted on it like a billboard I'd see in the city. Once we disembarked from the bus, Eduarda and others indicated where a new hotel had recently been built, and there, Miguel Angel and I would find a room for the night.

Eduarda and I said goodbye with a brief hug. So much time had passed since we were neighbors. I felt a degree of detachment and restraint in our parting—years, cultural differences, and economic circumstances created distance. We had little in common, now. A chasm had grown between us; respect for one another would remain, but a deep and lasting friendship most likely would not. I wondered what it would take to bridge the gap.

Miguel Angel and I were exhausted after a long day of travel. The lodging was only so-so; all that was available was a room with one queen bed, *una habitación matrimonial*, the clerk told us. We booked it. It was the only foreseeable place to rest our heads for the night. We hadn't talked about whether our friendship had romantic potential. There certainly was admiration, affection, and even chemistry, but neither of us initiated conversation about sex that evening. I felt more than friendship between us, but I was hesitant. He hesitated too. Our friendship felt too important to have just a casual fling.

Electricity was now accessible in Chuqiyapu, but not enough to blast significant light which made it harder to fight the drowsiness that had already crept in. We were fast to get under the covers for warmth. Both of us were respectful of each other and did our best to maintain physical distance in bed. I pulled out my journal to record notes of the day. Miguel Angel turned to me and said, "Aren't you glad you had the courage to speak to that woman?" He was asleep before I could answer him. But I thought about the question. Yes, I was glad. I had hesitated many times in my life and if it hadn't been for Miguel Angel's encouragement, I might not have spoken to Eduarda. *How many times had I resisted life's surprises out of fear? How many times had I robbed myself of fully experiencing joy?* I wondered.

Miguel Angel and I started the next day with a walk on the road behind *la Parroquia* to see *las chacras,* the farmland, the gorgeous countryside, and the majestic volcanos. The *Yanajaja* volcano had been sleeping for one hundred years. When would it awaken? *Yanajaja.* The joke's on us. Miguel Angel and I chuckled, just as Ryan and I had, when we said its name aloud.

Unlike *la Parroquia de Santo Domingo* and the church's steeple in the main plaza, nature's changes were less obvious. The landscape appeared unchanged since I had left. That offered me some consolation.

The white paint of the church steeple was now worn away from the effects of weather, exposing the brownish-gray adobe bricks beneath that made up its height. The church grounds around the residence had not been attended to in some time; overgrown grass, weeds, and plants covered the front door of what had been the convent, impeding entry. I heard a radio playing inside the residence, a possible sign that someone still lived there. A small handwritten note hanging in the window just to the left of the door confirmed an occasional Catholic Church presence. It read: Call Padre Wilbur, 920834025. I knocked on the door and waited a few minutes. No one answered.

My thoughts about the Church and my stay with the Sisters were muted now, and they no longer had power over me. I shivered at memories of me at the pulpit giving sermons. Thoughts of Ryan were pleasant, his love and kindness washed over me, bringing a smile to my face. He had passed away several years before and I hoped to document his remembrance by returning to the church. He would have been pleased that I had returned to Chuqiyapu and the parish with Miguel Angel. I thought about the fling I had had with David in the guest room and felt relieved that I hadn't taken religious vows.

I reminisced about the long days I had spent with Catalina, Saida, and their cattle in the fields. Nature's harmony produced music that was again playing in my head. Those long work days on foot, walking from one valley to another, never seemed long with the protection of *la Cordillera de los Andes* always in sight. The smell of eucalyptus trees and the distant crackling and smell of burning wood were comforting. All the days spent in nature filled my heart; it was where my true spirituality grew. It was there that I found inner peace for the first time since I had lost my best friend. I was filled with gratitude; Miguel Angel walked beside me, shared memories, and the view. His companionship added another layer of happiness.

After wandering down several dirt paths, we headed back to the main town plaza for lunch. There was only one restaurant in town. There we ate a potato stew and slices of bread with *el manjar blanco* as we looked towards the plaza lined with trees and benches. The bench in front of the church, where Ryan had kissed me, still sat there. After our meal, we walked over to the Town Hall. The medium-sized colonial-style building had been freshly painted a bright teal and royal blue while the doors and windows were trimmed in burgundy. The second-floor windows had iron bars in front of them; the small balconies were decorated with ceramic pots of flowers. The wall facing the plaza was marked *Municipalidad Provincial de Chuqiyapu*. We found a door ajar and entered. I decided to inquire about Catalina Flores and her family. I asked a man in the office if he knew of the family's whereabouts and if so, how I might reach her. The man pointed toward the plaza and said, "Her son is right over there, why don't you ask him yourself."

In front of the town hall, walking in our direction, was Edgar Flores. He didn't look like the Edgar I remembered from fifteen years earlier — this man had a plump face and a few gray

286

hairs peeking out from under his cowboy hat. From the waist up, he wore a more formal attire than in prior years, a crisp, clean white shirt and a blue tie safely secured under his belt. The Edgar I knew from before was *un campesino.*

"*Buenas. ¿Eres Kara George Grey?*" he said. His mannerisms and voice were recognizable. And so, apparently, were mine.

"*¿Cómo me recuerdas?* How is it that you remember me? It's been years."

"*Por supuesto, te recuerdo* …. how are we not going to remember our dear friend, Kara?"

Edgar filled us in a bit about his mother and sisters as the three of us headed down the street toward their house. I recalled how streets were nameless, their twists and turns had to be memorized, and only the details of found objects on a family's front door distinguished one from another. We needed Edgar's guidance. The Flores home had an orange cowbell hanging from its entrance. When Catalina opened the door, she let out a squeal of delight.

"*Para mi…es como un sueño.* It's like a dream come true," she said.

Her arms stretched out to hug me and her warm smile welcomed Miguel Angel and I into her home's courtyard. The family was utterly flabbergasted that I had returned to Chuqiyapu and visited them. Catalina kept repeating that it was a dream come true. When I presented Miguel Angel to her, she let out her large contagious smile.

"Who is this *hombrecito?*"

"Ahh, Cata, this is Miguel Angel," I said.

"A pleasure, *señora,*" Miguel Angel said.

"Oye, Kara, you have yourself a man? I thought you were going to be a nun."

Miguel Angel's big brown eyes caught mine and he chuckled. But it hadn't been a laughing matter, then. The truth was that I had lived like a nun long enough for the lines to be blurred, even for me.

Edgar was quick to chime in. "I knew that Kara was never going to be a nun," he said. "Do you remember dancing the *Huayno* and *Carnaval* with me?"

"Of course, it didn't happen all that often," I said.

We all laughed.

"Cata, I'm not sure I was ever cut out to be a nun. But it was when I gave my first homily from the pulpit that I knew I wasn't."

"I remember that day. It was a lovely homily," she said.

"Yeah. Something clicked when I looked down at the parishioners. I knew I couldn't go through with it."

Once the reaction to my big reveal subsided, we spoke about the year I had lived in the convent with the Sisters. According to Catalina, all the Sisters had left *la Parroquia* and the town of Chuqiyapu with little warning two years after me. They had never said anything about their leaving to the parishioners or the town. She told us that, as we had seen, the parish was practically abandoned, the building no longer well maintained, and the garden neglected and growing weeds. One month before the Sisters departed, she said, they had confided in her and Eugenio, the gardener and handyman at the parish, about their relocation, and asked them not to tell anyone else.

"*Bueno, las madrecitas* gave little explanation for why they were leaving," Cata said.

"Maybe that they didn't have a choice," I said. "Nuns have to go where the Order sends them."

I could see from the expression on her face that the lack of explanation left a bad taste in Catalina's mouth. After years of being a loyal and trustworthy confidant and servant to the Sisters and the Catholic Church, she told us she didn't want anything to do with the Church ever again.

"I don't want to suffer anymore. It is very difficult when missionaries leave. I was very close to the Sisters, I did a lot for them…and then, they left. They just left us."

I had never seen Cata raise her voice before. Part of me wasn't surprised that the Sisters hadn't explained their situation to the locals. I didn't want to make anyone, especially Cata, feel worse by adding fuel to the fire — plus, I didn't know the details — so I kept silent. In a way, I had done the same thing, leaving for no apparent reason. I felt badly and wasn't sure how to respond to Cata's comments.

There was a long pause before we changed the subject and continued to reminisce. We laughed and joked about the times I had followed her to *el campo*, how I had looked so out of place at first, but how eventually the people greeted me in *la plaza* as one of their own. She thanked me for the attention I had paid to her daughter Saida during my stay.

Catalina was probably in her mid-fifties now but looked much older from working in *la chacra* every day in the bitter cold and intense sun. Her brown skin had deeper wrinkles than when I had last seen her. As had always been the case, there was no mention of a husband or father to her children in her home. Her only son, Edgar, continued in the role of man of the household. Despite the temptation to move to the coast—for he was one of the brighter young men in town—he remained in his beloved Chuqiyapu. I knew he would never abandon his mother and he told me that many years earlier. He was a very loyal son and became *el alcalde*, the mayor of Chuqiyapu. The oldest daughter, Maruja, was still living with her mother as well. During our visit, she was tending to the cooking in the room adjacent to the large outdoor patio. She poked her head out to say hello. When I asked about Saida, the youngest of the siblings, a deep sadness came over all their faces.

Speaking on behalf of the family, Catalina said, "*Saida murió en Takana de tuberculosis hace años.*" The beautiful girl had died in Takana of tuberculosis years before.

"Oh, my dear, I am so sorry to hear that," I said, fighting back tears. "How old was she when she died?"

"*Tenía solo catorce años,*" Edgar said. Fourteen years old. *Too young to die.*

After a long uncomfortable silence, Miguel Angel kindly offered to take a photo of the family and me, *como un recuerdo,* he said. I had written, in Spanish, a few times to Catalina after I returned to the United States. I was aware that it would be her son who would read the letters, for she was not literate. I included several photos taken of us during my stay. I would send this one to her as well.

"Have you any news of Fidela or Hilda?" I asked.

"*No mucho.* Last I heard they were still living in Puno but we lost touch years ago."

She asked if I had ever heard from the tall, white priest who lived with us for a time. We giggled. Cata was very intuitive. She indicated she knew all along that Ryan and I had special feelings for one another. I told her that I had corresponded with him and that the last I had heard from him he told me that he had stage four pancreatic cancer and had been undergoing treatment. He assured me that he had lived a full life and was ready to face his death.

"When he didn't respond to my last letter," I said, "it confirmed that he had died."

When I left Chuqiyapu in late 1988, Cata's parting words had been: "Soon you will forget us here in Chuqiyapu." To some degree she had been right. My stay had given me so much: a broader vision of the world, a fluency in Spanish, and lessons on life and death and the power of nature. Peace of mind. How had I not kept in touch with her family? I could have made excuses, but the truth was, I left them behind. But, while I didn't communicate with the Flores family much in those years, it was also true that they were never far from my mind and heart. I assured the family that those parting words had never left me. "My return is proof of that," I said.

Cata was also good to her word. She pointed to a far wall in the main sitting room. Hanging there was the photo of us — Catalina, and I — standing beside the bus I boarded the morning of my departure from Chuqiyapu in 1988. Saida, the youngest daughter, had taken the photo with my camera. Next to it was another photo: Saida sitting on a pile of freeze-dried potatoes with a lamb in her lap. I remembered the day I took the photo. Catalina said, "You sent these photos to us from Takana, you

291

remember?" I was surprised to see the two photos hanging on the wall. "They have been there for fifteen years," Catalina said. I was speechless. Moved to tears, all I could do was embrace her.

Catalina invited us to stay for a midday meal, but we decided it might be best to fend for ourselves, and graciously declined. After we left, I realized I had forgotten to ask Cata about whoever appeared to be living in the parish house. I meant to. Catalina and I left many things unsaid.

*

The visit to Chuqiyaqpu stirred an interest in finding out more about the Aymaran girls who had been my roommates in the parish residence. My desire to locate Fidela and Hilda was strong and when Catalina and Edgar confirmed with a neighbor in Chuqiyapu that the girls, now grown women, were still living in Puno, I asked Miguel Angel if he would go to Puno with me. "Absolutely," he said and he called the hospital in Takana and made plans to get coverage for a few days.

I had a return address from the envelope Hilda last sent me more than ten years before but I was hopeful that we might find her. Early that evening, Miguel Angel and I hitched a ride with some strangers on a truck heading to the city on the shores of Lake Titicaca.

Miguel Angel was the best travel companion in the world, so easygoing, patient, encouraging, and kind. We were getting to know one another better. The truck driver suggested a charming and comfortable hotel on Lambayeque Avenue not far from his home. The man dropped us off at the curb, and we entered and booked several nights at the three-star Hotel el

Buho. We decided to take advantage of our stay in Puno and visit an island in Lake Titicaca. After checking into the hotel, the front desk clerk assisted us in scheduling a trip to the Islands of Amantani for the next day. Then we headed out for a bite to eat and in search of Hilda and Fidela. It turned out the only address I had to work with wasn't much help. Once again I learned that many postmarked addresses in Perú only indicated postal boxes, not domiciles. All we knew was that she lived somewhere in Puno, an area spread out over a region of fifteen provinces! A needle in a haystack. But we were in Puno District so we started there, kept an open mind, and asked around. I had Hilda's surname — Mamani — although it was one she shared with about forty-five percent of the population of Puno. *If it is meant to be, we will find her,* I thought. I was learning to believe in destiny.

I had been to Puno with Sister Sarah in the '80s, but Miguel Angel had never been. The day after we arrived, we took a launch to Amantani, the biggest of the islands on Lake Titicaca. The lake was spectacular; its hillsides were lined with terraces that were planted with wheat, quinoa, and potatoes. Neither of us had been to the island before and we decided to stay for a night. The island is about forty-five kilometers offshore and has a population of about two thousand people. The people were kind, hospitable and eager to share their homes and culture with visitors — they reminded me of my friends in Chuqiyapu. We spent the evening at one local family's home. They had a small room detached from the main house for visitors. There was an outhouse a few yards walk away from our quarters, but the bedding was uncomfortable and insufficient for the cold night. We slept in the same bed because of the bitter cold but it wasn't romantic in the least — we kept on our winter coats, hats, and even gloves to stay warm. The food served was scarce and hard to digest, but nonetheless, it was a beautiful night lit by the light of the moon, and stars closer than I had experienced in quite some time.

The next day we returned to Hotel de Buho and booked a room with twin beds. I was overjoyed to return to the hotel — I needed a hot shower and a decent bed.

"Oh my God, it'll be great to finally have a hot shower and sleep in a decent bed," I said.

"Haven't you ever gone without a hot shower, Kara?" he said in Spanish.

"Of course, I have," I said.

"The way you are going on and on, I would think differently," he said.

"I am sorry about the complaining....it's just that, you know, I am not so used to living without a bathroom, a comfortable bed, a hot shower," I said.

"Hmmmm," he said. "Many people live without these things."

I didn't respond and we went to sleep in our separate beds. The conversation wasn't picked up in the morning. He made a good point, and I got it. Miguel Angel wasn't immune to discomforts, just used to them.

It was the first disconnect in our friendship, and it created a gorge we would have to cross if there were a chance of us being a couple. When we went to the reception desk to check out, they told us that the truck driver who had dropped us in

Puno had been looking for us. He had left a note saying he might have a lead on where Hilda Ancota Mamani lived. The note said the house was on "a corner lot at the intersection of Calle Bolognesi and Avenida Piura in an area on the outskirts of the city called Barrio Mañaco." It was all we had to go on. It seemed a lot, so we trusted it.

We traveled to Barrio Mañaco per his instructions and located a small two-room adobe house in the spot described in the note. Might Hilda Mamani live there? I knocked on the door twice. When a woman appeared I told her, in Spanish, that I was looking for Hilda Ancota Mamani.

"Do you know where I might find her?"

"*Soy* Hilda Ancota Mamani," she said, recognizing me immediately.

I tried not to look too surprised. Did Hilda's grandmother have the same name as her granddaughter? The woman standing before me could not have been Hilda, a thirty-something-year-old woman, I thought. Her skin was so creased and deeply folded, and her body was bent over at a thirty-five-degree angle so that she looked well into her sixties or seventies.

"Kara, the Americana, from Chuqiyapu, ¿*no?*" she said.

"*Sí*, Hilda. You remember me?" I said.

"How would I ever forget you, my dear. What a surprise. Please, sit down."

She addressed me with the formal *usted* and invited us to take a seat on two stools beside the door. It was then that I noticed she had a large stomach beneath her skirt. We spoke briefly, long enough for me to learn that she had a thirteen-year-old son, a toddler, and a baby on the way. She was no longer

295

living with the young children's father and had no idea where the oldest child's dad had moved. She hadn't worked for the Catholic Church in years, and she was selling vegetables and homemade *chicha* at the local market. As we spoke, she moved to a gas stove in the corner of the room. She was cooking and stirring the corn for the fermented corn drink she would later sell. While I was thrilled to find Hilda, to introduce her to Miguel Angel and to reminisce about our shared life *at la Parroquia de Santo Domingo*, it quickly became obvious, in a similar fashion as it did with my encounter with Eduarda, that we had less in common. We quickly ran out of things to talk about. This awareness left a pit in my stomach, an empty disappointment. The long silent pause made me uncomfortable. I asked about Fidela. Hilda said she hadn't seen Fidela in years and had heard "through the grapevine" that she had died. She said, "Fidela's death might have been due to tuberculosis or hepatitis, it was hard to say." It was clear that Hilda was not as devastated about the news of Fidela's death as I was. It was common in Perú to hear of people dying of these diseases, another indication of the distance between our worlds. With little else to chat about—I had no children to gloat over— we parted ways in the congenial spirit as I had with Eduarda. So many women bond over the experience of motherhood, I thought. It was an experience I did not have.

The next day, Miguel Angel and I departed Puno on a bus headed toward Takana.

"You know, it's hard for me to relate to women whose whole life revolves around children, especially since I don't have any," I said.

"You have lived a very different life, Kara," he said. "Have you thought about having children?"

"Of course I have but I have always been more interested in adopting than having my own. And I'm not getting any younger."

"Would you seriously consider adoption?"

"I would."

"Me too," he said.

We dropped into silence and soon into the long bus ride, we fell asleep. My body leaned in Miguel Angel's direction and landed there. When I woke up, and felt my body against his, I straightened up. During sleep all was at ease and peaceful in his presence, but as soon as I opened my eyes, my mind did its best at inventing all kinds of obstacles and planting fear. Our relationship was growing—reading more into it might jinx everything. *Could we be a couple? Time will tell,* I thought.

When we arrived in Takana, we shared a taxi to the other side of town where Miguel Angel would leave me at my hotel. He continued on to his home—he had his teenage daughter to tend to and work in the morning. Before I exited the car, he handed me an envelope.

"Thank you for a wonderful trip...I wrote you a poem," Miguel Angel said.

"*¿Un poema*? For me?" I said. "When did you write me a poem?"

"Yesterday, *en la mañana.* before you woke up," he said, "You can read it later."

"Thank you for coming with me to Chuqiyapu," I said.

"*De nada.* It was a pleasure."

297

Back at the hotel, I read the poem he had written in Spanish for me.

Para Kara

long before you were born
before your clear, brown, sad eyes were formed
you were destined to come here.
destined to leave your family
your hometown
your hopes, and dreams
and even your understanding of yourself.

And, in letting go of everything you knew, you were born anew.
Filled with love and wisdom,
traveling freely through this world.
May you always be free to proclaim the lessons of my country.
Don't fear,
tear away hate, break down walls,
and build new dreams.

Leave this family,
if you must,
your country needs you too
and awaits your return.
Know that you will always
be welcome here, in your new home.

love and prayers, Kara

Thank you for showing me
that a broken heart can expand, and grow,
for that is what is happening to mine
as you carry a large part of it with you.

love and prayers, Kara

Chapter 26
Under The Same Sky

Miguel Angel's poem beautifully captured my long-lasting relationship with Perú—one that spanned almost twenty years. He was able to articulate my experience and its effect on my life, perhaps better than I could myself. To my delight, the poem also confirmed that the love and admiration I felt for him was mutual.

The next evening Miguel Angel and I got together for my last day in Takana before I returned to the United States. We had a nice dinner at a local restaurant. I thanked him for the poem, although I didn't directly address its content. After the meal, Miguel Angel invited me to go for a ride to the beach, about twenty miles outside of Takana.

He said, "There it is quiet, and we can gaze up at a clearer sky."

Takana was not the city that Lima was, but nonetheless, it was necessary to go outside of the city to capture the darker sky full of constellations. On the ride, we chatted about chance meetings, our visit to Chuqiyapu, and how, within days, I would be back in the States and starting a new school year in Metro Academy.

"How has your time in Perú been over all?" he asked.

"Wonderful. It was great to see old friends," I said, "I got to write and think about life."

"What about your life?" he said.

"This trip was a time to reminisce about the years I lived in Perú."

"They were good memories, I hope?"

"Yes, good years, important years," I said.

"Are you glad you came back, Kara?"

"Of course," I said.

"*Déjame preguntarte,* Was the trip what you expected? You got the answers you looked for, Kara? About Perú, your life, etc?"

I took a moment to consider Miguel Angel's question. I suppose I had been looking for some closure with Julie's death ever since she died. My trip to the northern coast had been meaningful.

"*Sabes,* when I came to Perú for the first time in the 80s, I was grieving the loss of a best friend. I needed to revisit those years in order to move forward," I said.

"And, did you find what you were looking for?"

"Yes, I did. The trip has been wonderful. And, meeting you has made it more extraordinary."

"Yes, I am glad," he said.

"Me too," I said.

I had traveled 3,500 miles from the United States to Perú to gaze upon the same sky. Looking into the stars, it felt as though there was no distance between our two worlds. I felt at home. In a short span of time Miguel Angel and I had connected on a deep level that I had never experienced before. It didn't matter the language we used; as we endeavored to express our feelings, words were insufficient as we tried to wrap our minds and hearts around something larger than ourselves. Our relationship had just been discovered — it was new and exciting. It was also scary. Only time would tell how deep it would grow and what would come of it in the future.

I still had questions I wanted to ask him. "What do you think, Miguel Angel, *¿A dónde vamos cuando morimos*? Where do we go when we die?"

"Hmm, *no sé*. I think that people want to believe that life continues. But does it? *Creo que la vida se acaba*. I think it ends," he said.

"But it also carries on. I believe life also goes on — just not as we knew it," I said, "The body dissolves, but I think life takes a new form when we die."

"What form is that?" he asked.

I thought of Julie's last words to me. "Love," I said.

*

The natural life cycle of birth and death kept churning. June, July and August had flown by. Within weeks, September would arrive, marking the end of the summer in my country, bringing cooler days, and the start of a new school year. In Takana, *la primavera*, Spring, was about to erupt. I could feel relief coming in the warm breezes that signaled the end to long, damp, cold nights. I was leaving Takana just as Spring's color, fragrance and warmth surfaced, flowers blossomed and rebirth exposed its face.

What a wonderful return to Perú it had been: visiting with the *Takaños,* many with newborns and toddlers; reconnecting with Sister Sarah and seeing the young man Rodrigo had become; traveling to Chuqiyapu and Puno on new paved roads; seeing Eduarda, Catalina and Hilda, no longer devout Catholics, but still holding up their families; learning about the passing of others; and bumping into and befriending a former *Colegio Ignacio Loyola* student.

The return visit had begun while meeting with Walter Alba who told me the story of the excavation in Sipán. I understood that visiting that burial site had set me up well for the whole trip and my future. After chatting with Julie, I could let go of the pain of the past and open my heart, again. I thanked my beloved Perú for the many gifts she had given me. Despite all her chaos and despair, Perú had offered me a home when I was most in need. Her people had welcomed me, challenged me, and embraced me. My faith in life and love was restored there. For that, I will be forever indebted to Perú. The country's vast desert bathed me with warmth and light as we approached the Takana airport. I don't know if my best friend, Julie, had to die in order for me to land in Perú, but I know that after her passing, I was led there. It was there that I learned to rejoice in the goodness of others.

I climbed the staircase and turned to see Miguel Angel smiling and waving to me from the gate. I was sad to leave but I didn't cry. I boarded the plane, located my row, and crawled over an elderly woman assigned to the aisle seat to take mine by the window. Miguel Angel was still smiling and waving when I looked through the pane of glass.

"*Hola, buenos días*," the woman said.

"*Hola, buenos días. Cómo está usted?*" I said.

"*Bien, gracias*," she said. "*Pero…un poco nerviosa*, it's my first time flying."

"*Tranquila, señora*, it will all be fine," I said.

The airline attendants came onto the intercom and said the crew was waiting for several remaining passengers. "As soon as they arrive, the door will be secured, and we will be on our way," she said. "In the meantime, be certain to stow away all personal belongings, and fasten your seatbelts."

I helped the woman next to me fasten her seat belt. Once my seat belt was fastened, I felt a pang in my chest. It felt as if I was having a heart attack. Then I heard my inner voice say: *a woman of substance can make a life anywhere. A woman of substance is confident, able to handle anything life throws at her and do it with grace and love. She trusts herself.*

I was no longer the twenty-one-year-old woman who had just graduated from college. I had had a change of heart. *Love again.* I listened and trusted it. I was being called to a new home. *It's time to dance with a larger family. There's no time to spare.*

I leaned in towards the older woman in the seat next to me and said "It was a pleasure meeting you. I know you'll have a great trip." Then I stood up and walked to the front of the main cabin. Seconds before the door closed, I stepped forward without hesitation and got off the plane.

The End

love and prayers, Kara

love and prayers, Kara

Acknowledgements

I started writing in a journal when I was seven years old. There was, and still is, a comfort there. When I lived in Perú in the '80s, I kept a journal, too. During the COVID pandemic lockdown in 2020, I dug my Peruvian journals out of boxes I'd stored in a closet. After almost forty years, I am thankful I never threw them away; they gave me some of the memories and descriptions I used for this book.

I want to keep this simple.

A big thank you to my editor, Susan Fish, who I met virtually after attending a writer's workshop. She took my first attempts at putting words from journals and letters on paper and taught me how to make them into a story.

Thank you to any and all friends who knew of this project and had some role in keeping me moving forward with it. The same to my family: my deceased father, who passed the writing bug onto his children; my mother, a strong, intelligent woman and voracious reader; and my three loyal brothers, each unique and wonderful men. Thank you.

Thank you to Juan Carlos, my dear friend and muse.